P9-DNQ-608

QUILLER IS

"BETTER THAN BOND, MORE INTERESTING, MORE REAL." —*Minneapolis Tribune*

Praise for Adam Hall's Previous Thrillers:

"Quiller is the spy's spy." —*Phoenix Gazette*

"Fast-paced, hard-hitting and surprising."
—*Chattanooga Free Press*

"White-hot intensity!" —*Washington Post*

"Hall is indeed a master of the contemporary espionage novel." —*Denver Post*

"Skillful as ever at stretching suspense to the screaming point." —*Publishers Weekly*

"Very much in the James Bond tradition . . . It's all good fun. Not clean fun, but good fun."
—*New York Times*

"Quiller's the classic man of honor in a dishonorable world." —*Espionage* Magazine

"Breathless entertainment!" —*Associated Press*

QUILLER KGB

ADAM HALL

CHARTER BOOKS, NEW YORK

QUILLER KGB

A Charter Book/published by arrangement with
the author

PRINTING HISTORY
Charter edition/July 1989

ISBN: 1-55773-217-5

Charter Books are published by The Berkley Publishing Group,
200 Madison Avenue, New York, New York 10016.
The name "CHARTER" and the "C" logo are trademarks
belonging to Charter Communications, Inc.

To
ROLF *and* **RAYMA**

CONTENTS

1

BERLIN

My arm was getting numb but I didn't move. I wanted her to go on sleeping for as long as she could, dreaming of God knew what. The worst wasn't over yet, I knew that.

The next time she woke up she began shaking all over and I held her more tightly, telling her it was all right, though of course it wasn't. Then the sobbing came and she tried to stop it, burying her face against me while her whole body shook and the tears began falling onto my hand.

"Let it come," I said, "don't hold it in."

It helped, I think; she was making more noise now. A stewardess came over with a box of Kleenex and I pulled out a handful.

"Is there anything she needs?"

I shook my head, and held the tissues against Corrine's hand so she could feel them.

"Oh, *Christ*," she kept moaning.

We'd reached our ceiling and levelled off; the jets were quieter now. One of the people across the aisle was looking back, glancing across us with his eyes deliberately blank, wasn't even seeing us, just looking at the view. No one else was taking any notice; London had booked us first class for the sake of more privacy; decent of someone, or perhaps it had to do with guilt.

"All I want to know . . ." Corrine was saying now, a lot of it muffled, ". . . all I want to *know* is whether he'd been sleeping with her . . ."

I tried to understand why it mattered.

"No," I told her at once, lying, or probably lying. "She was just someone in his courier line, that was all."

That was all, but sex too, probably; he'd been moving in to the end-phase and it was going to be dangerous. "He didn't," Holmes had told me over the phone yesterday, "fancy his chances." And when we don't fancy our chances, my friend, we look for the good graces of a woman, any woman, to help take the edge off and allow us to go in relaxed, less tense, less vulnerable. But no, that's a lie too—lies come easily to us in this trade. The truth is that we want it on the principle of just-one-more-time, if that's all there's going to be.

"I suppose it doesn't make any sense," Corrine was saying, her head off my shoulder now as she messed about with the tissues. I moved my arm at last and felt the circulation tingling. "I mean he won't be able to—" But that thought broke her up again, expectedly. When she'd calmed down I said:

"It doesn't matter why it's important to you. The thing is, she was just a courier, and that was all."

We're trained to lie through our teeth but this time it

wasn't to get me out of a death trap or anything; it was for personal reasons. I'd got the idea now: she couldn't let herself go, couldn't cry over the coffin and things like that, if she thought he'd gone out doing it with someone else. I suppose there was a certain raw logic in that.

"How do you know?" she asked me.

"Because I knew him." A bit of false anger—"Do you think we ever have *time*, for Christ's sake, when we're pushing a mission at that pace?"

After a while she said, so softly that I only just caught it, "I so much want to believe you."

"Then you can."

I had to protect him, too.

They were sending him back on a freight plane in the morning, the coffin, anyway, though God knew what they could have found to put in it: the opposition had set up an ambush and blown the car apart, both of them in it, the girl too, the courier, bits of her in the same coffin with him, unavoidably, and if that wasn't the ultimate act of intimacy what was it, what did the sex thing matter?

But Corrine was his wife—widow, yes, not just a girl friend, so she'd expected some kind of fidelity from him, not knowing much about the job we do, the kind of stress we work under. The shadow executives don't often marry; there are no promises we stand much chance of keeping.

One of the flight crew, three rings, put his head through the doorway and spoke to a stewardess and went back onto the deck.

"He was good," Corrine said, "wasn't he?"

"One of the best."

"They told me he helped someone get through, once."

"Yes." But there hadn't been much point because Thompson had spent the rest of his life—three weeks—in a hospital linked up with tubes and monitors until he'd got someone to smuggle a capsule into his room.

"Not many people do that," Corrine said.

Save lives. "Very few."

I suppose this was the way her grief was taking her: she had to create the idol she would later venerate, a hero, faithful to the last.

She uncrossed her legs and half-turned to look at me, her eyes puffy from crying. "If you knew him like you say, this isn't much of a fun trip for you either, is it?"

"Not really."

"Excuse me, sir." The stewardess was leaning over me. "You're Mr Stephen Ash?"

"Yes." Cover-name for the assignment.

"They've got a call for you on the radio. May I show the captain some kind of identification?"

I gave her my Barclay card and she went forward and tapped on the flight-deck door, three long, three short. Someone in London was panicking: we were due in at Rome in twenty minutes and they could have paged me there.

"Is something up?" Corrine asked. Her tone was like a robot's, with no feeling in it; the world was going on for everyone else and she was forcing herself to take an interest.

"Could be," I said. They wouldn't call me in flight just to get my debriefing on Hubbard. They'd sent me to Bombay to see if we needed any smoke out after they'd got him, and to bring Corrine back, look after her. I couldn't see there was any rush to debrief me: I'd sent them a clear-field signal from Santa Cruz Airport.

"Is everything all right?" Corrine had turned to look at me again.

"Perfectly. He left a clear field. Don't worry." She

worked in Codes and Ciphers and knew some of the routine when an agent blew it. She wanted to feel sure Hubbard hadn't messed things up. "Feel like another drink?"

She thought about it and then said, "No. I've got no excuse to get smashed." I'd given her two brandies, one before take-off and one an hour ago.

"Mr Ash?"

The stewardess gave me back my card and led me to the flight deck and the skipper introduced himself.

"This phone here. George, can you shift over a bit?"

The flight engineer twisted out of his seat and passed me the phone.

"Ash."

"Parole and countersign." Tinsley's voice, from the signals room: I could hear the background.

"Fanfare."

"North 5. We want you to change flights in Rome for West Berlin. There's a Lufthansa leaving at 19:07 hours for Tegel Airport direct, which gives you twenty-two minutes to switch. That's ample. Have you got any baggage?"

"No." But I didn't understand. "Is this for debriefing?"

Just the slightest hesitation—I only just caught it. "Yes."

"In *Berlin*?"

"What we want you to do," Tinsley said carefully, "is to put down at Tegel and go to the Hertz counter and wait there. You'll be met by two of our people and the parole is for October. Have you got that?"

"Yes."

All I could think of was that Hubbard's ambush had started making waves and either there was a West German connection or my debriefer was going to fly with me to London and go through it on the way. It was no good asking Tinsley anything: he'd just told me to shut up. I looked past the battery of circuit-breakers on the engineer's panel at the lights of Rome glowing in the windscreen. Maybe he hadn't left a clear field after all, Hubbard, and in London they were waiting for some kind of shit to hit the fan.

"What about his wife?" I asked Tinsley.

"We've sent someone to meet your flight in Rome and take over the escort. A woman, name of Baker, October parole. How's Corrine doing?"

"All right. Look," I said, "I've told her he didn't mess anything up. If he has, don't let anyone tell her."

"I am not," Tinsley said evenly, "a total idiot. And how are *you* feeling?"

"I'm used to it, and I'm not his wife." The floor of the deck shuddered slightly as the undercarriage went down and locked in.

"How are you feeling in *general*?"

This time I didn't let him get away with it. "I've no information for you if you've none for me."

"Over a telephone?"

With Tinsley you can't win. "I'm feeling normal," I told him, "whatever that means." I waited for another question, one that might give me a clue. I was picking up some nasty vibrations in the background and they were reaching the nerves, because they'd been left exposed by the Hubbard thing: I'd known him for five years and worked with him twice and when someone gets blown apart there's always the thought in our minds: *it could have been me*.

"The two people," Tinsley said, "who are going to meet you at Tegel Airport are rather high in the echelon, and they'll handle you extremely well. Total reliance. Is that understood?"

"Roger." I knew one thing now: Hubbard *couldn't*

have left a clear field, and if high-echelon people were moving in to debrief me I didn't want to think what kind of mess he'd made out there. I also knew another thing: they weren't going to send me back there to clear it up.

When I got back to my seat I found Corrine staring up at me with her eyes haunted. "What went wrong?" she asked me.

"Nothing went wrong." She was shivering, and I rubbed her hands. "They want me to switch flights, that's all."

She almost flinched. "You're going back to Bombay?"

"I am *not* going back to Bombay. I'm wanted in Berlin."

We began lowering into the approach path.

She wouldn't let it go at that. "What are you going to tell them, when you're debriefed?"

"I'm going to tell them he left no traces, nobody involved, nothing that's ever going to blow up in anyone's face." I could have bitten my tongue because there were better ways of putting it than that. "Look," I told her, "he was doing his best and he bought it. Did you love him?"

"Yes."

"Then settle for that. What else matters, for God's sake?"

They were standing near the Hertz desk in West Berlin, hands tucked behind their backs. I'd never seen them before; they could have been twins, both a bit overweight, pink-faced and recently-shaved, formal blue suits and bright polished shoes—I thought of Loman—and with an air of being totally in charge, not a thing for me to worry about, just leave it all to them, so forth.

Parole and countersign for October but they also asked for my card, the heavy one with the Queen's coat-of-arms embossed on it, kept in the lining, not in my wallet.

"Splendid," one of them said, "then we'll be on our way. No baggage, is that correct?"

They could almost be Foreign Office, not Bureau; except for one or two people like Loman we look like down-at-the-heel Fleet Street stringers out of a job, part of the cover—but then Tinsley had said these two were "very high in the echelon," and that explained it: they spent their days in the rarefied atmosphere of Administration high under the roof of the building in Whitehall, with nothing much more to worry about than how to get the pigeon-shit off the windowsills, though that's not actually true; it's just that we don't like the bastards—at any given hour they can hit their computers and bring up a man's name and put him down for a mission and send him headlong into God knows what kind of mayhem, ours not to reason why, so forth.

"I'm Chandler, and this is Elliott," one of them said— the shorter one with the trimmed military moustache—and pushed open a swing door and got us into the Customs and Immigration hall. "We shan't be delayed very long, just a formality."

They guided me right past the end booth and told me to wait on the cleared side while Elliott spoke to a plain-clothes immigration officer and flashed his identification and signed something and came back and joined us.

"Terribly cooperative chaps," he said briskly, by which I suppose he meant we were sailing through the formalities under the NATO flag.

Just to debrief me on Hubbard?

"Car outside," Chandler said. He spoke like a very quiet machine-gun. "Shan't be long now."

"You're wasting your time," I told him.

They both gave me a half-glance and Chandler coughed discreetly and no one spoke again until we'd got into the black 420 SEL outside and driven to the corner of the east car park and stopped and waited with the engine off but the side-lights still burning.

A cold drizzle blew around the overhead lamps and frosted the bonnet of the car.

"Wasting our time?"

Chandler.

"Whatever kind of mess Hubbard left out there in Bombay, you'll have to get someone else to wipe it up."

They've done that too often—pushed me into one red sector or another with a checkpoint blown apart or a body in the street with dangerous papers on it or a courier line scattered and one of them sitting under a bright light with his brains being picked. Not this time. Not again.

"We've got a few minutes," Elliott said, and pulled out a mini Sanyo and slipped a cassette into it and snapped the cover shut. "Let's just do a little debriefing on that one, shall we?" Smoother than Chandler, not a machine-gun at all, more like a soft-shoe shuffle, almost apologetic.

He pressed the record button and held the thing closer to me and I gave it to them again: they obviously hadn't recorded my signal earlier from Bombay. "From what I could get out of the local sleepers, Hubbard got in the way of the security people at the Soviet consulate without knowing it and one of their station staff put a man on him and reached a contact and took him inside and grilled him—a Pakistani, not one of ours. When they'd got enough on Hubbard they must have thought it was safer to push him right out of the picture and warn us off, so they did that."

"You don't feel he could have told them anything useful first?" Elliott.

"Whether I do or not, *they* didn't, which is what matters. I don't know enough about his operation to give a valid opinion."

Chandler, sitting at the wheel, kept his head turned to watch the nearest entrance to the car park.

"What about the woman?" Elliott asked me.

"She was the final link in the courier line and the instructions from the director in the field were for her to go with Hubbard as far as the rendezvous with the Afghan contact and then leave him and stand by in case she was needed."

Elliott leaned with his arm on the back of the seat, holding the Sanyo at an angle between us. "As regards timing, how long were Hubbard and the woman in the car before he started off and met with the ambush?"

"Three hours. They had to wait for the Afghans to make a signal."

"Three hours." Elliott pressed the pause button while he did some thinking.

All I want to know is whether he'd been sleeping with her. Corinne, her eyes puffy with crying, brandy on her breath. How the hell did I know, but what are you going to do to pass the time for three hours closed up in a car with a young woman when you don't have the slightest idea whether or not the rendezvous could have been compromised and you could be lying on the floor of a detention cell by this time tomorrow with nothing ahead of you but ten or twenty years in a forced-labour camp in the Gulag without a woman in sight?

No, she was just someone in his courier line, that was all. With one of her blackened finger-bones or the charred remnant of an ear lying inside the coffin by mistake, to be prayed over in ignorance by his grieving widow—how complicated life can be, my friend, how very poetic.

"What traces might he have left?" Elliott was asking me.

"None at his safe-house: I went in there. All his signals were verbal, the last three to London by phone at a courier's flat. His code book would have been on him in the car."

The beam of some headlights swung across the windscreen as a BMW came into the car park and went past us, accelerating. Chandler started the engine.

"What about the courier?" Elliott asked me. "The woman?"

"You mean traces?"

"Yes."

"I don't know. The whole line went to ground the minute the news got out. You'd have to check through their base."

We started moving, following the BMW.

Elliott switched off the Sanyo and put it away, leaning forward and saying something to Chandler; all I caught was "till they signal," or it sounded like that. Then he sat back again.

"Is that it?" I asked him.

"Oh—" he turned to me quickly—"yes, many thanks. We just needed it on the record, confirming your report from Bombay."

"So what am I doing in Berlin?"

"We did the debriefing—" he looked at his nails— "because it was convenient. We want you here to meet someone." A quick smile. "Won't take long."

He was being too bloody reassuring, and I had the sudden feeling I was sitting here on my way to an execution.

"Who?"

I shouldn't have asked, but it was too late. Showing my nerves. It was six weeks since I'd got back from Singapore and I'd been standing by for a month and no one had remembered my existence until the phone call to the plane. The thing is we come off the last time out with the blood still up and the nerves at the pitch where we've stopped being scared any more, and at that point they could send us straight out again and we wouldn't miss a beat; but then there's the debriefing and the medic exam and two weeks' paid leave with an air ticket to wherever we want to go or a stint at the spa in Norfolk with breakfast in bed and Swedish massage and saunas and the whole treatment; and then we're put on the list for standing by and the rot sets in—the nerves have come down and the blood's cooled off and we've had time to remember that it was only a bit of luck that got us back the last time, or at least a calculated risk that worked out according to the book. We shouldn't be here; we should have stayed stuck under that boat with the air-line still snarled or been pushed into a cell with the light still boring a hole in our head or found by the garbage men in the first grey light of the dawn with half the skull gone and the grin lopsided. So what do we want to go out again for, why push our luck?

The answer's another question. What else is there?

Elliott's voice came into my thoughts.

"Do you remember Yasolev? Viktor Yasolev?"

Looking at his nails again.

"Yes."

"Got on well with him, I believe."

"As well as could be expected."

He smiled indulgently. As well as could be expected, considering that Viktor Yasolev had been a colonel in the KGB and had come extremely close to throwing me into Lubyanka.

"I mean," Elliott said carefully, "you found him, as an adversary, an honourable man?"

We turned left onto the Saaltwinkle Damm alongside the canal, with the windscreen wipers clearing the way through the drizzle and the rear lamps of the BMW still ahead of us.

"Yes." Viktor Yasolev, tough, dangerous, deadly in a corner, but yes, honourable. "Why?"

"It is our hope," Elliott said carefully, "that you might agree to work with him."

I swung my head and he gazed back at me steadily, his eyes expressionless.

In a moment I asked him: "When did he defect?"

"He didn't. He's still in the KGB."

2

ECHOES

"We'll get out here," Chandler said, and turned off the engine, prodding his seat-belt release.

The BMW had parked in the next aisle and there were three other cars farther away among the concrete pillars. Two men were standing farther away still, near the entrance, where the ramp sloped down from the street. Pilot lamps burned in here above the parking-bay numbers, throwing a bleak light through the gloom.

We got out and stood doing nothing for a minute, breathing in the exhaust gas.

"Not Yasolev," Elliott said quietly. "We're not meeting Yasolev here, of course. It'll be Mr Shepley."

I looked at him but he didn't turn his head. He was watching the BMW. I'd heard of Shepley but never met him before; not many of us had. He was the head of the Bureau. His status was approximately that of God.

Shepley *in Berlin*.

According to legend he never left London, never, some
said, left the building in Whitehall with the false door
behind the lift shaft and the mole's citadel of rooms above
the street with no numbers to them, no names. Legend also
had it that Shepley was a former colonel in the SAS and
had taken a leading part in the raid on the Iranian Embassy
in Princes' Gate; but then legends, with or without substance, are to be expected in a place like the Bureau,
where we bury ourselves in deep cover as a matter of
principle.

"Chilly," I heard Elliott say, "for this time of year."
He gave me a faint smile, and it occurred to me that
underneath his air of calm his own nerves were running
close to the edge. It could have been because it doesn't
give me the giggles to be in the presence of people very
high in the echelon. They get my back up, and I suppose
he didn't want it to happen now, with God here.

A police car went past the entrance like a bat out of hell
with its siren waking the night; then it was quiet again
down here until a door of the BMW came open and Elliott
touched my arm. "It would be quite a good thing," he
told me in an undertone, "to listen, and not say much. The
final decision must be yours, remember, so you've nothing
to worry about."

Nerves on his sleeve. It didn't help.

Two men were getting out of the BMW and came round
to this side and then someone else got out of the back and
stood with his hands buried in the pockets of his raincoat,
and for a moment looked at no one as we walked over and
stopped near him, the soft echoes of our footsteps dying
away.

I could actually hear Elliott's breathing, it was so quiet
here. Chandler hadn't said anything since we'd got out of

the car; he was on my other side, opposite Elliott, and they were both standing a little way back from me.

"Who are they?"

The man in the raincoat had his head turned towards the entrance to the garage. His voice was so soft that I'd barely heard him.

"NATO guard, sir, major's rank." It was one of the men who'd just got out of the BMW.

Shepley's head moved again. "What about those?"

He was looking at a dark grey Mercedes in the far corner, with two faces only just visible behind the windscreen.

"Police, sir. In case anyone tries disturbing us."

Shepley turned his head again and looked at me. He was nondescript, in some ways: average height, average weight, coarse, untidy hair, a bank clerk or an insurance man— nondescript except for his eyes, a washed-out blue but with a steadiness that made me feel he was quietly taking every nerve synapse in my brain apart and checking it for wear. Nondescript, too, except for his voice, which was so soft that you had to focus in on it and ignore all other sounds, if you wanted to hear what he was saying.

"You're the executive?"

Chandler spoke from slightly behind me. "Quiller, sir."

The pale eyes went on looking at me without any reaction; then, when he was ready, he brought his right hand out of his pocket and offered it to me. "Good of you to come. I'm Shepley."

A cold hand, hardened by holding things that might have blown up if he hadn't been careful—this was how I thought of it.

"My privilege, sir." To put poor old Elliott out of his misery.

Shepley put his hand back into his raincoat and leaned

against the car, his head turned a little to the right but his eyes watching me. "You've been told we'd like you to work with the KGB on a certain assignment?"

"Yes."

"How does it appeal?"

"I'll need more information."

He looked away, at the guards by the entrance or beyond them: I think he'd stopped actually seeing the environment, and had slipped into alpha waves. I noticed pock marks below his left ear, some kind of scarring left by an explosion, perhaps, a grenade. It would explain why he always turned his head to listen with the other one.

"More information," he said softly, "of course." He looked back at me again. "This man Yasolev. Would you trust him?"

"What with?"

"Your life."

I thought about it, then said, "I'd trust him to keep his word to me. If he said, for instance, that whatever the orders from Moscow he wouldn't cut me down, I'd accept that."

"Would you."

It wasn't a question. I didn't add anything; he was giving me the information I needed by asking me things and listening, so that he'd know what his next question should be. That sounds complicated but it isn't really; it's the classic technique for limiting the information to what the other man needs to know, so that the least amount of information possible is given. I wished him a lot of luck in this case because I was going to want a *lot* of data before I'd consider working with the KGB, and he knew that.

"Would you be prepared to work inside the German Democratic Republic?"

"Under what kind of cover?"

"Whatever you felt comfortable with, plus the option of going clandestine at any given time."

He meant I could bolt for a burrow if things got hot.

"I'd want a guarantee," I told him, "that you'd pull me out of there if I made the request."

It didn't sound a lot to ask but he knew what I was saying. It could mean having to send a chopper across the frontier under the radar and locate me and get me out of whatever hole I was in, and do it in a rainstorm or in the dark with not much time left before the opposition closed right in on me or I lost too much blood or couldn't signal or give my position or lift a finger for that matter. Or it could mean calling a whole covey of sleeper agents and contacts and couriers out of the ground and sending them in to find me if they could, and that meant that Shepley could reach the point where he'd have to balance the value of this single shadow executive against the risk of exposing half the resident moles and sleepers and agents-in-place in the whole of East Berlin or the whole of East Germany, and if the scales didn't tip in my direction he'd *have* to go back on whatever guarantee he'd given me and throw me to the dogs.

He was watching me steadily.

"We can't do that," he said, "as you know."

I'd just been trying to find out if he was ready to promise me the impossible in order to tempt me into the mission. So far he was playing straight.

"All right." I shifted my stance, feeling the need for movement. Standing as close as this to Shepley was like standing under a high-voltage powerline. Maybe he didn't always pack this amount of tension but he was doing it now. He hadn't, after all, come to Berlin to try the *apfelstrudel*. "All right, then I'd want your guarantee that you wouldn't cut me down, whatever the pressure on you."

He looked at his shoes.

I think someone made a movement beside me, Elliott, on my left, a more vulnerable man than Chandler, more easily embarrassed; or he knew—where perhaps Chandler didn't—that two missions ago London had put a bomb under me because I'd become suddenly and critically expendable, and I'd only got back because I'd found it and pulled out the flint. I didn't want them to do it again.

"That would be difficult," Shepley said, and looked up at me with his pale mother-of-pearl eyes and began sorting out my synapses again to see what I was thinking.

"Yes, but that's what I'd need from you. From you personally."

"That would be an irrevocable condition, if you agreed to work on this assignment?"

"Yes."

It was warm in here, in this waste of cold concrete on an October night in latitude 52, the sweat creeping on my face, on my hands. I hadn't been ready for this when they'd told me to land in Berlin. With the head of the Bureau out here and with the timing so tight that they'd had to switch my flights without warning and shove me into an underground garage face to face with the stark proposal that I should work in liaison with the KGB, I was feeling the heat. God knew what the background was to this thing but it was obviously ultra-high-level and I suppose there was a degree of paranoia creeping in—I felt these people were pulling me into a vortex before I had a chance of getting clear; otherwise I'd never try making conditions like this without even knowing what they wanted me to do.

"By 'cut you down,' " Shepley's soft voice came, "you mean order your death. Is that correct?"

I liked him for that. We're all so fond of euphemisms like eliminate, terminate, cut down, so forth, but this man said what he meant.

"Yes," I told him.

He didn't look away. "You mean you'd put your life higher than the success of the mission? Of a mission as important as you must realise this one is?"

I turned and took a step, looking at the oil-stained concrete, kicking a broken chip of it with the toe of my shoe, watching it skitter and come to a stop against a pillar.

"No," I told him. It was the only answer. It's what we settle for when we sign up, and when we sign again at yearly intervals to confirm our commitment. It's on this one that most of the new recruits back out, and I don't blame them. I'd signed because this was the life I wanted, and I was ready to accept the death they might one day want of me. At the Bureau we don't have a licence to kill; we have a licence to die. "No, I wouldn't put my life higher than the success of the mission. But look—" I turned back and met his eyes again—"all I'm asking is that you'll let me do it for myself, that's all. If—"

"There might not be time to ask you."

"But you wouldn't have to. I'd know if—"

"Not necessarily."

"Look, I'm seasoned, you know that. I've—"

"You're being impractical."

"With my life on the line, surely I—"

"We can't let you tie our hands."

"Oh for Christ's sake, I'd have a capsule on me, so what are we talking about? I just don't want to be stabbed in the—" but I stopped right there because I could hear the tone in my voice, pitching a degree higher, showing my nerves, no better than bloody Elliott.

The sound of an engine came suddenly and headlights swung into the entrance, dipping as the car reached the ramp, and by this time we'd all turned and were standing with our backs to the light, our faces hidden, our shadows standing against the wall like a group photograph in silhouette, none of us moving as we stood listening to the whimper of tyres as the brakes came on, a man's voice— one of the NATO guards—then another voice, fainter from inside the car, the engine idling and then speeding up, the sound of the transmission in reverse, the group of silhouettes against the wall shifting to one side as the headlights swung away and the gloom came down again and we turned like puppets, taking up our positions again.

"You have a reputation," Shepley's soft voice came, "of showing resistance when offered a new mission. I'll suffer you not to waste my time."

"This thing," I said at once, "was thrown at me cold."

"I take your point. But time is of the essence. We need to hurry."

"All right, but *I* need to know more, a lot more."

"Of course. You'll be fully briefed. For the moment—" he began pacing suddenly and I joined him, glad of the chance of movement—"for the moment I simply want you to agree to a meeting with Yasolev. It would take place in East Berlin; he wouldn't come to you, but you would go to him. This was a concession on my part during the initial approach. For your protection—or for the protection, shall I say, of the executive undertaking the assignment—I pushed the KGB very hard for a hostage for us to hold in London, and they finally agreed to sending a major-general of the Red Army.'' We reached a wall and turned back, our footsteps raising small echoes. ''I also demanded four of our agents—SIS, not Bureau—to be freed from captivity in Moscow and returned to London, together with three Americans. I therefore offered the token concession of our meeting Yasolev on his home ground.''

''Alone?''

''Yes. Again, you'll be fully briefed. You should also know at this point that the mission is to be strictly confined to the intelligence community in London, with no slightest involvement with the Foreign Office or overseas embassies—unless the circumstances of the mission call for it. But if you accepted the assignment you would have the exclusive energies of the Bureau at your command, under my personal and constant supervision.''

He stopped short of where the other men stood waiting, and faced me with his head turned slightly to the right, his eyes trapping light from a pilot lamp overhead. ''This, I think, is as much as you need to know at this stage, but I'm prepared to answer any question, providing it's of the most vital consequence.''

He wouldn't give me long. He'd told me all he was going to tell me, because if I refused the mission he didn't want a critical mass of information loose in my head: any agent at any time can be got at and picked clean, even between assignments, if someone suspects he's loaded with some kind of product. Until I accepted this one I'd be told nothing more.

There was only one question I could ask Shepley that would give me an idea how big this assignment was, and whether I should even look at it.

"It wasn't Yasolev," I said, "who made the approach off his own bat. He's not big enough. So who was it?"

"General-Secretary Mikhail Gorbachev."

3
PICNIC

We inched forward again, the lamps sliding past the tinted windows of the Mercedes and throwing shadows across the driver's head. He hadn't spoken until a few minutes before, when we'd reached the checkpoint. ''We could go through the official-traffic lane, but we'd call more attention. Is that all right with you, sir?''

I'd said yes. Shepley had told me there'd be no delay getting through—no one would check us—but I wanted to attract as little notice as I could.

The driver had fallen silent again. The figures outside looked almost faceless through the smoked windows and my dark glasses; their voices were faint. It was four in the morning, a dead hour, with only half a dozen vehicles ahead of us.

We moved again, the engine's note soft, muted, the lights on the dashboard glowing.

Are they going to interrogate us?

She was shivering, curled against me, her woollen coat soaked from melted snow. One of the guards outside the hut was coughing again, the cold air freezing his lungs.

Not you, no. You don't know enough.

Margaret. Margaret Someone. Jennings? Fenning? Something with *ing* at the end. In three years you can forget your own name, in this trade.

"Which road are we taking?"

The driver turned his head slightly, his eyes in the mirror. "Through Bernau. Be an hour, maybe. A bit more."

Car doors slammed ahead of us. Peaked caps, the angular roofs of low buildings, the silhouette of an alarm siren against the haze beyond.

She can go, the guard said, coming in, his face muffled in wool against the cold. *Come on—move!* Kicked her foot.

She turned her head to look at me, but I said in English, *Don't question it. Get going.*

The Mercedes was new, smelling of leather, not the kind of transport you normally get from the Bureau. And a uniformed driver. Perhaps not the Bureau, then, perhaps by courtesy of the General-Secretary. I didn't think this was going to be my kind of thing, too political, too distinguished, not the job for a ferret. But I'd nothing to lose.

We inched forward again, and the peaked caps gathered immediately outside, turned towards a civilian with papers in his gloved hand, orders.

But what about you?

I knew she'd say that.

I can look after myself. Get going, for Christ's sake, before they change their minds.

She struggled to her feet, giving me a last look, her eyes frightened, but for me now, not for herself. *It makes me feel awful.*

I jerked a hand. *Just get going.*

The voices outside the car had stopped, and we moved on again, this time accelerating through barriers.

"Is that it?"

"Yes, sir."

I looked at the clock on the dashboard. An hour, maybe a bit more, would bring us to the rendezvous just before dawn.

She lurched to the door of the hut, her legs cramped from the long night, the long waiting, and when she'd gone I asked the guard in Russian: *On whose orders?*

Comrade Colonel Yasolev's.

I put away the sunglasses, and the environment took on brightness, colour: a steady 3,500 rpm on the revolution-counter, the star mascot outlined against the wash of the headlights, a signpost sliding by— *Bernau 22 km, Ebers-walde 47 km.*

He'd known of course, Comrade Colonel Yasolev, that it wouldn't have been worth putting her under the light, wearing her down; she knew almost nothing; she'd been a contact for the frontier line pulled in at the last minute to cover a gap in communications; she hadn't even been briefed, just told to get there and wait for instructions. She'd only made contact with me as a matter of routine to establish liaison, and that was when they'd caught us, holed up under the floorboards of a rotting wharf with our hands and faces darkened with some soot I'd scraped from a boiler and one of her feet shoeless, which was how they'd got on to us: the other shoe had come off when she'd run headlong for cover.

And what would have been the point, anyway, for them

to put her on trial and send her to a penal settlement? Another mouth to feed, however many mailbags she sewed, however much wood she hauled. But that wasn't why he'd let her go. It had been a gesture. I'd got to know Comrade Colonel Yasolev quite well during the three weeks of the mission and I'd picked up a few things about him from the KGB lieutenant I'd pinned down and grilled in a cellar in Klimovsk: Yasolev was the son of a Soviet Army general, and a graduate of the Moscow State University with a degree in Japanese and some post-graduate work put in at the Institute of Oriental Studies. In 1985 he'd served undercover for the KGB as Bureau Chief of the Soviet magazine *New Times* in Tokyo; then he'd been brought back to his homeland to run clandestine operations from Moscow, trapping Western spooks for the counterespionage division and pulling in Price-Baker, Johnson of the Company, Foxwell and Grant and Bellows from the SIS, all of them senior people, most of them now in the Gulag, Foxwell dead and Johnson exchanged for Pitovsky a year ago.

But the most interesting thing I'd picked up from the lieutenant in Klimovsk was that Yasolev was a chivalrous man, enlightened, though not soft: *He bullied the prosecutors for the maximum term in every case, and got it*. He also had a daughter, Ludmila, who was now studying at the Academy of Science in Moscow. All right, for Margaret, read Ludmila; they'd be about the same age or at least the same generation. And reading a little closer, between the lines, yes, his casual act of clemency had been subjective, self-indulgent; but the fact remained that I'd been there personally in that freezing hut and I'd seen her small huddled figure go lurching through the doorway to freedom and when the guard had told me whose the orders were I'd felt a moment of warmth in that bitter cold and had been astonished by it, because in this trade the smallest act of charity can have the force of revelation.

There'd been a postcard, a month ago, from East Grinstead just signed "Margaret"; she still kept in touch.

"About another ten minutes," the driver said.

It was still dark.

"Are you armed?"

His eyes flicked to look at me in the mirror. "No, sir. Those were my instructions. You're not expecting any kind of trouble?"

"No." If he'd had anything on him I'd have told him to throw it away. *The rendezvous is to be made,* Shepley had said, *according to the strict protocol of a diplomatic exchange of courtesies, and both sides understand that.* Otherwise I'd never have agreed to go through the Wall in the wrong direction, not on your bloody life.

I still can't believe you managed it, she'd said in her postcard. *It means so much to me.* Because when she'd gone through that doorway she was certain I was up for a life term in Siberia and so was I. But on the way to the railhead at Vaznesenkoe one of the guards had wrenched his ankle in a hole under the snow and there'd been a chance and I'd taken it and the best they could do was a bullet in the shoulder and a bit of scalp ripped off before I'd got some trees behind me and found a refuge and lain on my back for three days under a snowdrift until they gave it up and left me for dead.

"My instructions," the driver said, "are to wait for you, within sight. Is that right?"

"Yes. How far is it now?"

"We're nearly there."

"I could be quite a time. Did you bring anything to eat?"

"Got some sandwiches and a flask. They told me."

I didn't know who he was. Certainly not Embassy; he'd been in the field; it was written all over him. I'd been told to ask no questions on this trip, give no answers, except at the rendezvous itself.

A crack of light had come into the sky ahead of us, above a mass of dark trees that rose on one side of the road. The driver pulled onto a patch of rough ground and cut the engine.

"It's here?"

"Yes, sir." He hit his seat-buckle release and got a folded sheet of paper from his pocket and opened it out and showed it to me. "Just up there, in the trees."

I looked through the tinted window. He'd switched off his lights and I couldn't see a thing so I pressed the button and got the window down as far as I needed. Cold air came in against my eyes. I still couldn't see more than a dark mass of rising ground, heavily wooded, with no light, no signal from anywhere. It was very quiet.

"Is he coming down here?" *He'll be at the rendezvous alone,* Shepley had said.

"No, sir. You're to walk into the trees." He folded the little map and put it away.

"We're seven minutes early."

"Yes, sir."

I suppose he meant yes, we were seven minutes early but that didn't have to stop me getting out and walking up there into the woods, better early than late, but then it wasn't his bloody neck. Shepley had spelt it all out, the strict protocol of a diplomatic exchange of courtesies, so forth, and they'd got a Red Army general under house arrest in London and the head of the Bureau—the *head* of the Bureau—wasn't likely to send one of his top executives straight into a trap, but the paperwork was over now and this was where the action was and I was sitting in a car at dawn on the wrong side of the Iron Curtain and I was expected to get out and walk into those trees and not question anything, doubt anything, but listen, I don't like trees, standing as these were, deep as black water, with somewhere inside them a KGB officer waiting for me.

Alone?

What could I do if they were setting me up again, the Bureau, just as they'd set me up before, that time with a bomb, this time with something much more subtle? What if they were using me as bait in some kind of diabolical trap that Shepley had rigged, throwing me to the dogs in the sacred cause of expedience?

Nothing.

I could do *nothing.*

I'd want your guarantee, I'd told him, *that you wouldn't cut me down, whatever the pressure on you.* He'd looked at his shoes. *That would be difficult,* he'd said.

I watched the clock on the facia glowing, digital, marking off the last minutes of the night. *Listen, suppose they'd set up this rendezvous to send me straight into a—*

But this was nonsense because Shepley wouldn't have come out here personally just to kill off a bloody ferret; it was paranoia, that was all, so I got out of the car six minutes early and slammed the door and stumbled through the low scattered bushes and then climbed, moving into the trees with my hands dug into my coat pockets and my breath clouding on the cold air and my eyes on the trees, on the gaps in the trees, my feet tripping sometimes in the undergrowth because it was still too dark to see much, my mind confident on a conscious level that all was well, that Shepley was playing it straight this time, while in the subconscious my shadow creature came with me, shaking like a leaf.

Rough ground, difficult ground and the smell of damp earth after rain, the crack of dawn in the east casting yellow light among the trees and giving them substance, defining them, beginning to throw shadows as fine as grey gossamer and sending ghost figures moving through them, one of them halting and standing perfectly still.

"Good morning."

Yasolev.

I stopped dead and he came towards me, a short man in a black overcoat and hat, his face pale, jaundiced with the creeping yellow light of the morning, his small eyes resting on mine with a steadiness that I believed was costing him an effort.

He was offering his hand; it was cold, dry, impersonal: he took it away too soon. He'd spoken in English; I spoke in Russian; from his thick accent I decided we were going to speak in his tongue, not mine, because I was fluent and I didn't want any misunderstandings.

"How are you, Yasolev?"

He inclined his head; it was rounded, balanced on his thick neck like a boulder; it looked heavy, like his body. But this was deceptive—I knew that his brain was capable of cool, incisive thought, accurate and assertive and un-cluttered by emotion. He'd come up from the ranks and survived in an organisation that didn't suffer fools gladly.

"I am—" in English, then a shrug as he slipped into the comfort of his own language—"I am well. And pleased you have come. I was not, as you can imagine, at all certain of it."

He turned and led me to a clearing, and on our way I looked back down the hill and saw the two cars, the one that had brought me here and his own, half-hidden among the bushes and with two men standing by it. The light was brighter now, pouring below a ceiling of mist that hid the treetops, making it seem that we'd wandered into a petri-fied forest.

"Not quite a banquet," he said with a shrug, "but—" he left it. He'd draped a rough linen cloth across a tree stump and set out a couple of cardboard picnic plates and some canned caviar and what looked like a bowl of stuffed *pirozhki*. Two thick tumblers and a bottle of vodka—not a banquet, no, but a good enough effort, an acceptable gesture.

"Rather grand," I said.

A deprecating tilt of his head. "I chose this place for our meeting because I wanted you to be sure there weren't any little beetles around."

He meant bugs, a joke, I supposed. There was a faint smell of tobacco smoke on the air, but I couldn't see any butt he might have thrown down. The trees were thick here; you couldn't see more than thirty yards.

"Civil of you," I said.

"Of course—" one of his little shrugs—"I could be wired. Do you wish to search me?"

This was major, a *major* point in our relationship, if there was going to be one, in the whole mission, if there was going to be a mission. I didn't answer right away because I wanted him to think I needed time. Then I said: "I believe we're here on terms of mutual trust."

He nodded gravely. "Yes."

"Then I don't want to search you."

He opened his hands—he was busy with small gestures, Yasolev, and this one meant, I think, that I could indeed trust him, his hands being open, empty, with nothing to hide.

We ate some caviar on strips of thin dark bread, and he offered me some vodka but I said it was too early in the day; he drank some, almost half-filling a tumbler. The mist was slowly lightening above our heads, and somewhere a bird had started piping.

"And how is Margaret?" he asked.

The girl in the hut.

"She's well."

He'd done his homework, got her name out of the files, and was reminding me that he'd been chivalrous. Trust again: he wanted my trust.

He'd have to work for it. "How many men did you bring here?"

His eyes flicked away. "Six. There are two waiting by the car, and four are dispersed at a distance." But not at a great distance, because of the tobacco smoke. "And you?"

"One." He knew perfectly well how many I'd brought: he would have monitored my passage through the checkpoint by radio-phone. "Unarmed," I said, to make my point.

He looked down. "There are hunters in these woods. We don't want to be disturbed."

Then we both fell silent, each waiting for the other to take things further. I wasn't in any hurry, but it wasn't long before he half-filled his tumbler again and took a swig and said:

"Let me tell you that we need someone from London who is willing to work with us for a time. My department said there was no one, but I told them that I believed there was such a man. We need someone still active in the field, a man who knows how to take care of himself, because this will not be easy, you understand. It will not be—" gesturing towards the remains of our meal—"a picnic."

I didn't say anything. He offered me the last *pirozhki* but I shook my head.

"There is some tea." He brought a huge thermos flask

from behind the tree stump and filled two plastic cups, his
hand shaking a little. For the first time it struck me that at
this precise moment his nerves weren't any better than
mine.

"No," he said, "it will not be a picnic." The tea
steamed thickly, giving off a sharp earthy scent. "My
assignment has been handed to me indirectly from Comrade General-Secretary Gorbachev, as you have been told.
If I make any mistakes, I shall be cut down in the middle
of my career. My career means a great deal to me. It
means everything."

He had small nicotine-brown eyes sunk under a deep
brow, and at this moment I had the impression they were
looking out at me from shelter. The risk, I could see now,
wasn't going to be all mine.

"Gorbachev called you in?"

"Yes, but—"

"I mean personally? You met with him about this?"

"No." He looked quietly appalled. "And I have to be
very careful to keep his name out of it. After the most
careful deliberations I decided to trust your Mr Shepley—"
he pronounced it as Shepili—"and to trust you. But if I
am wrong, I am finished."

I could see what he meant. They're not terribly chari-
table in Moscow towards people who screw up. I waited
for a bit and then said: "I can't speak for Shepley, but on
my own account you can trust me as far as your first
wrong move, and then God help you."

He opened his hands again, bringing his head an inch
lower in a perfectly clear gesture of submission. "That is
perhaps more than I could hope for. We shall be working
under a great deal of stress, you see, a great deal of
pressure, and it might sometimes be easy to suspect each
other of duplicity. We must avoid that. Above *all* we must

avoid that.'' Turning away, turning back, ''My superiors have been understandably reticent on the matter of Comrade Gorbachev's personal involvement in this, but it is not precluded that an exchange has taken place between him and your Prime Minister Thatcher. Unofficially, of course. Has Mr Shepley mentioned this?''

''No.''

''It is my opinion. We are dealing with—'' his eyes held steadily on mine at last—''a matter of extremely high security, not only within the intelligence community but on the highest levels of government.''

Shot.

''Then you might have to find someone else.''

A slight chill along the spine. It had only been faint, but I suppose it was the suddenness, and the image of a man going down.

''Someone else?''

''To work with you instead of me.''

''Why is that?''

''It sounds too political. Too big.''

It came again and he took out a miniature walkie-talkie and pulled the antenna up and switched it on and spoke into it. ''Keep them away.''

Not man, rabbit, that was all. I took a sip of tea and burned my lips but the flavour was good, rich and raw and leaving a bitter after-taste.

''I would not have asked for you,'' Yasolev said, ''if I didn't think it was something that suited your talents. Later I shall reassure you.''

''What's it to do with? Give me the gist.''

He hesitated and then pulled himself upright in his black coat, as if suddenly called upon to account for himself. ''There is a British mole buried in Berlin, on this side. He is a grave danger.''

"So what's the HUA doing?" East German Counterintelligence is very efficient, normally.

"They cannot reach him."

"What about you people?"

"If we could reach him, we wouldn't have asked for your help."

"Quite a mole."

"He is more than that."

"More than a mole?"

"Yes. From what we have learned, he is here in order to fulfill a specific assignment."

"For the British government?"

"No. For whoever is paying him." He took out a rumpled handkerchief and unfolded it.

"You don't know who's paying him?"

"We believe it is someone in the Kremlin." He blew his nose, making much of it, giving his nerves some action.

"Jesus Christ," I said and started walking about. "I'm surprised you didn't ask *me* if I was wired."

He folded his handkerchief carefully, his eyes watering in the cold air. "We made the approach. We have to trust you. And your Mr Shepili."

I took a minute to think and then said, "You've got the wrong word." He'd used *krot*. "You don't mean he's a mole, Yasolev; you mean he's an operator." *Rabotnik*. "So let me straighten it out a bit: you're talking about a British operator buried in East Berlin and preparing some kind of a strike, and he's being paid to do it possibly by someone inside the Kremlin. Is that right?"

"Yes."

"Who's his target, then?"

"Comrade General-Secretary Gorbachev."

Oh my God.

British.

Of course. They couldn't risk using a Soviet.

"Are you sure?"

"Yes." He was watching me steadily now, with the eyes of a man who had just thrown down four aces. "So you see, we felt that your department might agree that it would be in the best interests of the British government for you to help us."

I didn't show anything. In a moment I said: "No wonder you're nervous, Yasolev."

"No more than you."

"I haven't accepted the mission."

He shrugged, kicking up the fibrous earth with the toe of his creased black shoe. "I hope you will."

Hope on, then, comrade. Two heads on the block, Thatcher's and Gorbachev's, if that operator pulled off his assignment: Gorbachev's because he was the target and Thatcher's because if a British national hit the Chairman of the Presidium of the Supreme Soviet her government wouldn't last the night.

Not quite my cup of tea, but I suppose it was a compliment that Shepley had called me in and I'd been sent to this rendezvous to listen to Yasolev and check out the job, so I'd better do that.

"What makes you think I can do what the HUA and the KGB combined can't do?"

"This man is British, and you have resources in London that we can't tap. You might—" shrugging—"how shall I say? You might pick up his trail from there."

"How much time have we got?"

"Think of it as a short fuse, already burning."

"All right, so I could make a start over there and with a bit of luck pick up his trail and then move into Berlin for the kill, but what about you, Yasolev? Where would you be?"

"In close support."

"You mean you'd be running me?"

"We would be supporting you, as a free agent under our protection."

"We? The whole of the KGB?"

"No." He took a step closer. "Just my immediate cell, inside the department."

"Your *immediate* cell?"

Quietly he said, "You must understand that inside the Kremlin there are factions opposed to the Comrade General-Secretary's policy of *perestroika*. That is why he dismissed Yeltsin, the head of the Party. Inside the KGB there are certain factions similarly opposed." Drily— "Internecine warfare along the corridors of power is not the exclusive prerogative of democratic governments."

"Jesus Christ, Yasolev, I wonder you can ever sleep at night. Is there any more tea in that thing?"

He got the thermos flask and poured me some. My feet were frozen and the chill was creeping all the way up my spine because the more I heard about this thing the more it looked like a massive iceberg somewhere out there on the night-black sea, drifting towards us.

"I will give you some time to think," Yasolev said. "Excuse me."

He went across to pee against a tree while I stood there doing a lot of very fast thinking, holding the plastic cup of tea and taking small sips at it, burning my mouth, taking in its raw black essences with a certain relish now because there was absolutely no *question* of letting myself get sucked into this kind of operation—it was strictly a five-star spectacular and I wasn't qualified to take it on and if

Shepley wanted that operator blown out of his basement he'd have to come over here and do it himself.

"It's not on," I told Yasolev when he came back. "But I've left some tea for you."

He stood very still with his small brown eyes watching me from the shadows of his brow as if he'd suddenly found me holding a gun on him.

"Tea?"

"There's some left. But I can't take this thing on. It's not my style."

"Style?"

It was only then that I knew he'd thought I was a certainty; that Shepley had told him I wouldn't refuse. Or maybe he was just thinking like a KGB man and believed I had to obey orders, as he did.

"Look," I told him, "it's far too political, far too important. There's so much in the running: if you don't manage to put the skids under this operator, you're going to lose your General-Secretary and we're going to lose Thatcher and let those snivelling socialists back in to screw up the economy again. Listen, do you mean they're planning an actual *kill*? Are we talking about attempted assassination?"

In a moment: "We don't know."

"All right, even if his operation is aimed simply at getting Gorbachev out of office, then you've not only lost him as a leader but in my opinion we've *all* lost the biggest chance of genuine world peace we've had for the last fifty years, if the Americans can find a president like Nixon who can really get down to brass tacks at a summit meeting. So this is something I'm not even qualified to touch. Sorry."

I thought he'd never answer.

"It frightens you."

"How did you guess?"

"Your Mr Shepili believes you are the best agent for this."

"He's not infallible."

"You'd say that, to his face?"

KGB thinking, yes.

"Of course. But it's not only the size of this thing, Yasolev. You want me to work with your people in close support. I couldn't do that."

"Why not?"

"It'd hamper my movements. It'd mean tagging, and not always in good light. I wouldn't necessarily know who the tags were—yours or the opposition's. That's dangerous, could be fatal."

I finished my tea and put the cup down onto the rough linen cloth and looked at my watch.

"But of *course* we would have to put tags on you—" suddenly animated, his thick square hands coming out of his coat pockets and chopping at the air—"how else could we possibly work? We—"

"I work alone, unless I call people in. You're—"

"Mr Shepili would allow that?"

"Of course. He—"

"But you would be working with *us*, the KGB."

"I know that."

"Perhaps—" on a sudden thought—"it's this that frightens you?"

"Perhaps."

"Without *reason*." Hands chopping the air.

"Possibly."

"Then I do not *understand* you."

"And that's the problem," I said. "We can't even agree on basic principles, so what d'you think would

happen if we tried to get through an entire mission together? Christ, it'd be like a dog fight.''

He didn't leave it at that; I didn't expect him to. We
started walking, to keep our feet warm, in and out of the
trees and down the slope and up again while Yasolev made
his pitch and I countered when I had to, not wanting to
leave him with *nothing* in his hands, because they'd made
the approach, the KGB, or his department of the KGB,
and we didn't have any reason to turn them down without
grace, without respect.

The normal trappings of a mission on foreign soil weren't
applicable: there'd be no need for courier lines or contacts
or drops or a safe-house because Yasolev's network would
contain all those things; I'd be noted by the East German
police and secret services as an agent to be left alone but
given assistance if I asked for it, and that would be totally
acceptable; but it would mean working the mission under
the concerted scrutiny of those same organisations, a fly in
a spotlight, and that was enough to chill the nerves of any
agent even before the action got under way.

If I took this thing on I'd be one small alien cog
enmeshed in the machinery of the most powerful and most
ruthless intelligence organisation in the world, and it could
reverse its direction at any given stage of the mission and
grind me into pulp if it suited its purposes. Let's face it:
that shot we'd heard earlier, deep in the trees, had triggered the image of a man going down because the last time
I'd been fired on it had been by *this* man's agents, less
than a year ago.

It was two hours before he saw I meant it, and then he
walked off along the top of the slope to isolate himself and
do some thinking, and when he came back his face was
expressionless and he just said:

"Very well."

Not quite that, exactly—the words he'd used were *Horocho . . .Tak e buit,* with a more fatalistic tone: So be it.

"Sorry," I said. "It could've been a whole lot of fun."

I screwed the top back on the thermos flask and he pulled out his radio and told them he was escorting me to the checkpoint and we left the remains of our little picnic on the tree stump and went down the slope to the road, and in the car I said, "But listen, Yasolev, you'll *have* to find someone to do this for you. No one in their senses wants anything to happen to your man Gorbachev. It's just that I can't work like that, you understand?"

He ignored that, and sank into a brooding silence all the way to the checkpoint. His car had followed us up and he got out of mine and told the border guards the score and then leaned in to look at me with his eyes sunk deep under his brows and his hands still in his coat pockets and said with a tight mouth:

"You under-value your talent, you know, and that is very disappointing for us. For all of us."

He slammed the door shut and stood away and we got rolling and when we were back in the West I leaned forward.

"British Embassy, on Unter den Linden."

By the time we got there I was starting to sweat and I showed my identification in the hall and took the stairs two at a time and went into the signals room without knocking and asked the man at the desk to put me on the scrambler to London through the Government Communications HQ in Cheltenham. Time hadn't meant anything when I'd been talking to Yasolev in the woods but I was in a hurry now because I'd had a chance to do some thinking on the drive to the checkpoint and the whole thing had come spinning round full-circle in my mind and I knew what I had to do.

"Anyone specific, sir?"

"What? No, main signals board. No, cancel that. Ask for Bureau One. Are you already on the scrambler?"

"Yes. I'm trying them now."

He pressed three more keys and I stood waiting with a cold skin and the heart-rate elevated: I could feel it under the rib cage. The thing was, the *whole* thing was that I'd been looking at this project as if it were just another mission and it wasn't, it was *not,* and I suppose it had taken a bit of time to sink in. Either that or the subconscious had already made up its mind that we should keep well clear, and it had steered my conscious decision-making. Put it in English: I'd been shit-scared. All right, it was indeed the size of the thing that had rocked me back and it was certainly the idea of working with the KGB that had sent the nerves running for cover but I'd overlooked the obvious, the absolute.

I didn't have any choice.

"Main board, sir."

"Can't you get Bureau One?"

"I'll ask them. Just telling you we've got through."

Photos all over the wall of hang-gliders, I suppose that was his thing, picture of Diane, sign of the times, she was nudging the crown for wall-space in all the government offices I'd been in lately, you couldn't wonder. *For Christ's sake hurry.*

"You're on, sir. Bureau One."

I took the phone from him.

"Ash."

"Oh, yes."

His voice was just as quiet at the console.

"I've just left him. I told him I couldn't take it on, but I've changed my mind."

"Why?"

"Because I want this one. I want it badly."

"Anyone would."

"Yes."

Everything closing in.

"How long ago did you leave him?"

"Say fifteen minutes."

"Did he have a phone in his car?"

"I don't know. He came as far as Charlie in mine."

I heard him turn away to speak to someone else, something about fully urgent. He'd have to contact Yasolev now, see if we still had a chance. The KGB wouldn't necessarily want to work with someone who'd shown cold feet. I'd left Yasolev in a rage.

Everything closing in, the walls crowding me. I still didn't know whether the Bureau was setting me up, using me for what I was worth, selling me the pitch that even a top shadow executive could go into a mission this big and bring it home. And I didn't know whether the KGB was trying to use me too, Yasolev for the furtherance of his own career or the whole of his organisation for their own cryptic purposes.

All I knew was that the temptation for me to go into this, the challenge, was enough to bring me in here and have me lay my neck on the block in the name of blind ambition.

But the blood was running cold.

"What reason—" Shepley came back—"did you give him?"

"Too big, too political. And having to work by their rules."

"That's understandable."

"He didn't think so. I left him furious."

"That's understandable too. But I need this from you.

Are you prepared to undertake the mission on their terms, if we can't talk them down?''

Now is the chance, my friend, the last chance, if you want to say no and save yourself.

"Yes. On whatever terms."

Blood running cold.

"Very well. I want you here on the first plane. There isn't too much time."

I gave the phone back to the man and stood doing nothing for a moment, letting the psyche centre if it could, while at the brink of consciousness I caught glimpses of the pretty coloured hang-gliders and the man watching me and then another face, Yasolev's, and the faceless, nameless people in London who were prodding the new mission into life on their computers, getting the facts in order, *November 3, 09:54 hours, signal from the Embassy, Berlin: the executive accepts the mission.*

Running cold.

4

DAISY

I can't do that.

"Why not?"

They know where I am.

Slater glanced up, looking for Croder, but couldn't see him. He looked down again, leaning forward over the desk of the console, thinking. Slater was new at the signals boards. We always feel vulnerable, with someone new.

"You mean you can't get clear?"

No way.

The voice on the radio was steady enough, but I caught a tone of false nonchalance; probably the others did. I'd spoken like that myself in the earlier missions; when you're certain you can't get clear and all you can do is let them come for you or pop the capsule your voice sounds like this at the signals board in London, because your greatest fear of them all is of sounding scared.

"Look," Slater said, "if we can do anything, we will. But—hold it a minute."

Croder had come in and Slater told him the problem. Croder took over the microphone, his mechanical hand resting on the desk like a steel skeleton. "Stay precisely where you are and wait for dark. At some time before midnight you'll get a signal from the Embassy. If they can reach you, they will. If they can't—" he broke off and there was dead silence in the signals room and I noticed Holmes swallowing—"then I shall trust in your own discretion."

The Bureau can't actually tell you to use the capsule; all they can do is to issue you one in Clearance when you go out. But if you've really got your back to the wall and there's any major information inside your head the opposition could get out of you, then your "discretion" is expected.

We didn't find the contact. Instructions?

Different voice, different board. There were three in here. Slater's had *Pineapple* chalked at the top of the black Formica console; this one had *Quarry*. No one had told me what the code name for my own mission would be, but at this stage they were going from P to Q.

"Get hold of your director in the field. It's his job. Ask for a new rendezvous. Weston's ETA is 11:06 hours and you'll have to be at the airport by then."

Roger.

There was some Morse beeping somewhere; we wouldn't have anyone using it; it was just part of the slush. I saw Holmes turning away and pouring himself some more coffee, worried sick about the executive for *Pineapple*. He always worries, being more human, I suppose, than the rest of us.

Not that I was all that cool. I'd got on the first plane according to instructions and they'd shoved me into a

police car at Heathrow and dumped me outside the building ten minutes ago and if I never hear another siren again
I won't complain: it's not the most reassuring of noises.

She's just a bloody whore.

Malone's voice, you couldn't mistake it. Costain, sitting
at *Peashooter*, said briefly: "Explain."

That word from a signaller means a bit more than what
it says. It means shut up and mind your language and give
exact details, because one of the top Controls is in the
room.

*C-Charlie told me the silly bitch was a Venus trap for
the militia but he was dead wrong. She's just a tart. One
thousand pesos and not even a good fuck.*

It was no use telling Malone what the word "explain"
meant. He was furious; he hates wasting time in the field.

"Tell C-Charlie to report. Where is he now?"

At field base. Now listen, I want new instructions.

The lights dimmed, flickered and came back on, less
bright now.

"Power cut," someone said. "It's the storm."

Most of the room was almost dark: the high ceiling and
the spaces between the consoles; they stood out like ships
in harbour at night, lit overall. There were no windows
here; this was the basement.

Two people were talking on the other side of *Quarry*,
one of them Stapely, back from Sri Lanka with no injuries
and *mission completed* in the record books. I didn't know
the other one. The auxiliary generators had started hum-
ming and Costain was talking to his ferret and Holmes was
standing near *Pineapple*, brooding, when the door opened
and Shepley came in and the atmosphere changed at once.
Even Croder hadn't got this kind of presence in the signals
room. I'd never seen him here before, never known him
control a mission personally.

"When did you get in?" His voice quiet, no expression.

"Ten minutes ago."

He watched me in the wash of light from the boards, looking for any signs in me that I was nervy. I didn't show anything. He'd thrown an ultra-grade operation into my lap and put me into a rendezvous with a KGB colonel east of the Curtain and I'd turned the whole thing down because of cold feet—*he knew that*—and changed my mind and put my neck under the sword and he was looking for any sign that it had built up my stress level to a point where I couldn't be sent out. He didn't know me personally, had never seen me before the meeting in the underground garage in Berlin, and all he'd got to go on was my track record and he wasn't a man to make a major decision without checking me out at close quarters and with a *lot* of eye contact. The interrogation cells—the really effective ones—had people like this in them and I knew their style.

Softly: "What made you change your mind?"

Anyone else, even Croder, would have taken me somewhere else and asked things like that in private. There was no traffic on the boards at this precise moment and you could hear even this man's voice quite clearly. The others in the room were listening hard because this was Bureau One they'd got in here and it amounted to a priority-alert phase at the end of a grinding mission.

"Personal pride."

His head turned a degree more to the left, favouring his right ear. "Oh really?"

"Yes."

He went on watching me obliquely with his washed-out blue eyes while I spent the time trying to guess what his next question would be, but it was difficult because it wasn't just a stare he was giving me; I had that feeling again that he was thought-reading, tinkering with the cerebral energies.

"Very well."

No more questions, then. I felt a palpable break between us, between our personae, when he turned away and stood with his hands in his side pockets, the glow from the signals boards highlighting his coarse, untidy hair.

"Mr Croder, what's your position?"

"The executive's in a tight red sector, sir, and I've asked the Embassy to see if they can get him clear."

"Do you believe they can?"

Beat.

"No."

Shepley turned his head a little. "Is he a married man?"

"Yes, sir. Three years."

Shepley looked across at Slater. "What about your operation?"

"Malone's gone in, sir, and he's well placed. We're looking for a winner."

"Malone. He was in *Keyhole*?"

The signaller glanced across at Croder, who nodded. "Yes."

Shepley looked at the man running *Quarry*. "What about you?"

"We went into the end-phase early this morning, sir. I'm waiting for completion."

"What are the chances?"

"First rate, sir. I won't be handing over at this stage."

Shepley took a step closer to *Pineapple*, and Croder moved with him. "Mr Croder, where is Fosdick?"

"Milan, sir. He's on standby, with contact through one of our sleepers."

"And Stoner?"

"I'll need to ask." Croder went across to the central

phone console. Shepley took another step nearer *Pineapple,* scanning the chalked lines of information on the board: running-time, status, phase, target, with map references and a quickscan chart of the executive's environment: backups, contacts, communications, travel patterns.

Quarry.

"Yes-yes?"

Shepley's head turned and Croder looked across at the board from the phone console.

I've put him in a car for them.

"You've *got* him?"

That's right. He's a bit dopey but he'll be back to normal by the time they reach the border.

I was watching the black plastic speaker-grille on the console. We all were.

"His papers are good?"

They're perfect. Calthrop did them for us.

Holmes glanced across at me and back to the board. Croder wasn't talking on the phone, just holding it with the contact down. I'd never been here in this room when a mission was running clear through the end-phase to the objective with the voice of the executive himself on the speaker. We're usually in the Caff, hanging around on standby between missions, when we get this kind of news at second hand: *Winthrop's moving in but Control says he's taking too much risk. Someone told me* Fanfare's *coming apart but they're sending Kennedy in to see if he can patch it up. And Donavon's bought it in Beirut, only last night.* But it's never reliable.

"Can you pull out okay?"

No problem. Clean up the base, send a little smoke out, then I'm leaving. All right with you?

"Yes, but keep in contact."

The signaller flipped a switch and Shepley asked: "Who is the executive?"

"Roberts, sir. Sending a dissident across."

Slumped in a car with false papers, a couple of our people with him, their faces calm but their stomachs cold as they neared the frontier and the checkpoint and the end of their mission—the end of *Quarry,* whether or not they got the man through. I didn't know who he was, but he wouldn't be small fry if the Bureau were bringing him across.

A Soviet dissident, whose name is being withheld for the sake of his family and friends, reached London last night from West Germany, after successfully crossing the frontier from the East. His application for asylum is being considered by the Foreign Office, and is expected to be approved.

And tomorrow, and the days, the weeks after tomorrow, the debriefers would be sitting around the table, going through the wads of paper the man had brought with him, their hands shuffling them with the avarice of men seeking gold, while somewhere else, in the stuffy little offices of Her Majesty's government, other men would be clearing their desks with their hands shaking, the quiet and industrious little moles blown out of their skins and with only a dog's chance of getting across the Channel and running for home.

"Tell him to report here," I heard Croder saying at the phone console, "as soon as he can. This is fully urgent." He came back to the signals board where Shepley was waiting. "Stoner's in London, sir. They're calling him in right away."

Shepley nodded slightly. "Very well. Meanwhile, get Fosdick into Prague, very quickly indeed." He took another pace and put a hand on the signaller's shoulder, dropping onto the stool and opening the transmission.

"This is Bureau One. Please acknowledge."

Hear you, sir.

"I am obliged to shut down on your mission, and this is the last signal you'll receive. But I'm sending two agents to your sector with all possible despatch. They are highly experienced in these situations, and it's vital you remain where you are. Be of good cheer."

He touched the switch and got off the stool and went over to Croder at the central console. Croder had a phone in his hand but cupped the mouthpiece. "Get those two people into the sector," Shepley said, "and tell them to gun him clear if they have to. Who's chief in here?"

"Myers, sir."

"Tell him I want that board cleared and reset for my own operation. What's the next code-name available?"

"Quickstep."

"Very well. I want it operational as soon as Myers can do it." He turned his head. "Quiller, we'll go in there."

One of the crew rooms, the bed made under an army blanket and the signaller's things scattered around: windcheater, track shoes, a pair of five-pound weights, copy of *Omni,* couple of paperbacks, one of them by P. D. James. He'd be the man running *Quarry* through the end-phase: *First rate, sir. I won't be handing over at this stage.*

"All right," Shepley said, and pushed the door shut. "Personal pride. I suppose that's the only reason we ever do anything, anything worth doing. But why did you turn Yasolev down in the first place?"

He pulled the small upright chair away from the desk and put a foot on the seat, resting one arm across his knee. I didn't want to sit on the bed, the only place left; in the short time I'd known this man I'd learned to stay on my feet in his company: you can't sit down and relax when he's busy fine-tuning your reflexes.

"Yasolev's a career man," I said. "He'll sacrifice me without even thinking about it, if it suits him."

"I don't doubt he'd try. But you'll be given very considerable protection. I'm at present hand-picking your support in the field."

"I expected that too, sir. The thing is, I don't like a lot of people around when I'm working. Ours or theirs."

"Then you'll have to adjust, at least on our side. There's no other way, if you want the mission. We also have the hostage. He took a lot of getting." I felt that snapping of tension again as he took his eyes off me for the first time, looking down at his hands. "I'm assuming your change of mind was final, or we wouldn't be in here."

"Whatever the terms."

"Very well. As a matter of fact they've improved. When I talked to Yasolev on the phone while you were airborne, he believed he'd lost you. He was therefore ready to listen when I made a few demands on your behalf." His head swung up. "What would they have been, if you'd made them yourself?"

"Contact with Yasolev alone, with no KGB people in the field."

"I've got that for you."

A lot of weight came off and I took a breath. "I'm impressed."

"I thought you would be. What else?"

"Signals direct from me to London, not through his field posts."

"I've got that too. So you're beginning to see how keen he is to have you. What else?"

"My option to drop the whole operation and get out, given your own sanction."

"Yes, he wasn't terribly keen on that one, but I managed to get it for you. What else?"

"That's all. That's first class."

"Thank you. Now there's a man called Hood. That's his real name, but we believe he's using the cover name of Horst Volper in East Berlin, where he may be using very deep cover as a German national. Don't you want to sit down?"

I shifted the paperbacks and dropped onto the bed. "He's my objective?"

"Yours and Yasolev's. We know very little about him. He's a lone operator, linked by underground rumour to the Aquino assassination and that of the Swedish Prime Minister in 1986, also with various high-level wet affairs in Paris, Rome and the Orient. He is known to have been in London until three years ago, a socialite moving mainly in government circles as an international financier, under a different name." He'd begun reflectively massaging the pock-marked skin below his left ear; I'd seen him do it in Berlin. "We know he left London at that time en route for Geneva, where he sank without trace. We'd been keeping a record on him simply because he's a major figure in clandestine operations, even though he covers his tracks with the greatest efficiency. The next we heard of him was a week ago when the KGB got in touch with the Foreign Office through the Soviet Embassy. A request was made to me personally to find, fix and strike, by whatever means." He'd said that last bit slowly. "Questions?"

"Is there a dossier?"

"For what it's worth. They'll give it to you when you go through Clearance."

"When I find him, whose responsibility is it to cut him down?"

Shepley looked away. "That will depend on the circumstances. You might have the option of handing him over to the KGB or taking care of it yourself. Again, you might not have any choice at all. You know better than I do that we can't foresee the situation.''

I didn't take him up on it, though he probably expected me to. The only time I'd killed except in self-defence had been for personal reasons, to avenge a dead woman, and it had happened between missions. Shepley knew that, but there was no point in talking about it now. I'd make my own decision at the far end of *Quickstep,* and God knew where that would be or how it would come, or whether I'd still be alive.

"Can I have Ferris?" I asked him.

"No. He's been over there too often. I'm giving you a new man for your director in the field, cover-name Cone. I'm sure you don't need his credentials, since I picked him myself.''

"Where do I meet him?"

"In Berlin. He's there now, finding you a base.''

"And a safe-house?"

"Your safe-house at any given time will be the nearest KGB Headquarters.''

I didn't take him up on that either. I'd find my own safe-house when I got over there. There are times when you've got to *vanish,* if you can.

"This hostage,'' I said. "He's a major-general?''

"In the Red Army.''

"Where is he now?''

"In Belgrave Square, technically under house arrest.''

"I'd like him released and sent back.''

Shepley tilted his head an inch. "Why?''

"A major-general isn't very big, with a mission this size on the board. And I want to get Yasolev's trust.''

In a moment, "Well, now.'' He got off the chair and pushed his hands into his side pockets and looked everywhere but at me, absorbing the idea and testing it out. His head lifting, eyes on the ceiling—"You like sailing close to the wind, don't you?"

"I'm not suggesting it for a dare."

He looked down at me. "I realise that. So you believe Yasolev is a man of honour?"

"I don't think that matters. It's a question of pride."

His pale eyes resting on me—"And you know all about pride, don't you . . . The problem is, do I let you risk the mission. If—"

"It'd give us a big advantage, if I'm right. We'd be able to trust him, in turn."

"And if you're wrong?"

"I don't think we'd lose anything. They'd sacrifice one little major-general if it'd pay them."

He turned away. "I'll let you have my decision before you're sent out. Have you any more questions?"

"Is there a dossier on Yasolev?"

"Yes. You'll be given that, too, when you go through Clearance. Anything else?"

"Not for now."

He moved to the door. "Please know that I shall be controlling *Quickstep* personally, from my office and from the signals room. I'll be available to you at all times. At *all* times." He opened the door. "Phone me before you leave if you need to."

Doubts.

"Weapons?"

"No weapons."

She turned a paper on the desk. "Initial there, will you?"

She gave me a pen and sat worrying her nose with a small rumpled handkerchief.

"Here?"

"No. This box. Would you like an immunisation shot?"

"What for?"

"So you don't catch this," her watery blue eyes concerned.

"I eat too much garlic to catch a cold."

"Does that help?"

"Never fails. Lose all your friends, that's the only thing."

"Who needs friends like that? Beneficiary or beneficiaries, any change?"

"No. Home Safe."

"I checked on that. They've gone out of business."

"Any other battered wives' home, then.. I don't care which."

"There's the Shoreditch Refuge."

"That'll do."

She wrote it down. "Everything you possess?"

"For what it's worth."

"Sign here, will you?"

Doubts, following me through the building as I left her and checked in at Codes and Ciphers, certain now that they were setting me up, both of them, Yasolev and Shepley, not necessarily in collusion but each in his own way and for his own ends.

"Give me a plain substitution crypt."

"One of the alphas?"

"No. A ten-character limit. An aristocrat."

He flipped through the clear plastic sheets, going from blue to red printing, the light from the window passing through one of his thick lenses and casting a pool across the file. "What about Little Mary?"

I started to feel trapped, forced into using a code that could blow me if it'd been filched. This room had a steel

door and a security man outside and you had to draw a
special pass to get in here, but suppose this clerk had been
got at by—oh Jesus *Christ*, is there an immunisation shot
for paranoia?

"Look, give me Beta-3, the short version for the field."

"Fair enough." He swung round and pulled a drawer
open and gave me the pad. "Have you got the Cheltenham
scrambler prefix?"

"If I haven't now, I never will."

"Sorry, I'm new."

"We've all got to start somewhere."

Walking through the corridors like a rat in a maze, the
subject of an experiment, not a rat, a guinea-pig. It had
been too easy; Yasolev had given in too fast—I did *not*
believe a seasoned KGB colonel would partner an operation on East German soil with an agent from the West
unless he'd got the entire field staked out with his own
little army. Well there was *this:* the instant I got one whiff
of his people anywhere near me I'd use my option to pull
out and ditch the mission.

"When?"

"Three weeks ago, at Norfolk."

Medical room.

"Phyllis, no blood to draw. Where's his chart?"

A small room, too small, too confining, to paranoia you
can add claustrophobia, but listen, this wasn't normal at
this stage; a show of nerves on the way through the access
phase, yes, but this was too soon, too severe.

"Heart-rate's up a little. Is that usual when you're going
out?"

"Yes."

Say yes to anything.

"Diastolic's a little high, eighty-nine. Is that normal
too?"

"Yes."

And why *not* Ferris for my director in the field?

He was too valuable to lose.

"Are you drawing a capsule?"

"Yes."

He got his keys and unlocked a cabinet on the wall and took down a phial, pressing hard to undo the safety cap and shaking out one of the small grey cylinders with the red band. "You need a container too?"

"Yes."

Another cylinder, bigger, heavy steel, uncrushable.

"All right, sign this, would you?"

Signed.

Travel Section.

"Do you need maps?"

"No. I'll get them locally."

She gave me the passport. They never give you one with a number that was never issued.

"Whose was this?"

She looked surprised. "I don't know."

He didn't need it any more—but of course he could've retired, could've *retired*.

They weren't ready for me in Final Briefing so I went down the circular staircase with the worn plum-red carpet and the mahogany banisters and the scuffs on the wall where people had come down in a hurry, bouncing off the curve. The only man in the Caff was Decker, a new recruit to this echelon from ten months' training in Norfolk; he was sitting at the counter chatting with Daisy, and when he laughed it sounded hollow, so I suppose he was going out on his first assignment and sweating ice.

Puddle of tea on the first table I came to—there is *always* a puddle of tea on the table in this bloody place, though God knows why because Daisy's always got a dish-rag in her hand, I've never seen her without it.

"Hello, love."

Blue eye shadow, caked rouge and bright brass hair, body like a barrel, I *do* wish they'd get a girl in here you could actually *look* at while your nerves are running a temperature; it'd help bring it down.

"Tea, Daisy."

"You want a bun?"

"God, one of *those*?"

"I keep tellin' them, but it's all they seem to order." She mopped up the puddle and rolled away, lopsided, rheumatism, poor old baggage.

Very well, then, we have to work something out, don't we? Into the breach, dear friends, let nothing us dismay, so forth, a matter of life and death—actually, yes, quite possibly, my life and my death, if I get it wrong.

And a matter of conscience. Shepley and the Bureau and Yasolev might well be setting me up for extinction as a means to an end, but did that justify my accepting the mission and letting them think I was going through with it on *their* terms and not mine? Because if I were going out there for them I'd have to work solo and find my own safe-house and go to ground at whatever stage of the mission if I needed to, without consulting them. They were—

"Sugar, love?"

"No."

She slopped some tea into the saucer, par for the course.

"Thank you."

They were going to put the whole energy of the Bureau behind me and the whole of Yasolev's department of the KGB but I couldn't work like that *and they knew it*, or

Shepley did, the Bureau did. So why did they choose me for this one?

Why did they choose *me*, Daisy old dear? With four boards running in the signals room it meant there were five other shadow executives hanging around between missions, five others with my ranking and experience and capability, and three of them—Fletcher, Wainright, Piers—*preferred* to work with a whole back-up system of supports and contacts in the field. So why didn't Shepley choose one of them?

Scalding-hot tea, just how I wanted it—there's a degree of eroticism in wanting to burn your lips, a nice bit of titillation for the mucous membrane, soothes the nerves. Good old Daisy, it's always piping hot, but listen, what am I going to do?

I could assume they thought I was the best man for the job but even if it were true, Shepley knew the way I liked to work, solo, and he must have given it some thought and he wasn't your common or garden moron. *Did he realise that if I took on this one I'd work my way through it alone, deceiving them, and was he prepared for that?* It'd salve my conscience, wouldn't it, Daisy old love, but a bit too easily.

The alternatives, then: I could go into *Quickstep* and work solo without their knowing it and risk blowing up the mission by leaving myself exposed, vulnerable, isolated, or I could go across to the phone over there and call Shepley and tell him no, it still wouldn't work, he'd have to get someone else.

Got a laugh like a barmaid, shaking with it over there by the tea urn, enough to bring her wig off; we secretly believe, you know, that it's really a wig.

And let this be known, my friend: if I walked out of here without going near that phone it would mean that in the name of pride and vanity this shadow executive was ready to go behind the Curtain and try to work through a mission within a mission, already cut off from the people who were running him and already cut off from his Soviet collaborator. And *still* bring it off, *still* reach the objective.

The word for this, I truly believe, is megalomania.

Sitting in my sweat, hunched over the table, hands round my cup of tea, torn this way, torn that, a solitary spook goaded by ambition and pricked by conscience and frightened, *oh my God if you knew how frightened*.

I don't remember how long it was, how long it took, but the dregs of the tea were cold in the cup and I felt old before my time.

"That's all right, love. On me. I don't see you in here very often."

A woman who knew how to love.

I kissed her dry rouged cheek and walked out past the telephone and into the mission, alone.

5

CAT

Steel everywhere, everywhere you looked, steel and concrete and blank walls and the stink of latrines and Lysol, the jingle of keys and the plodding of boots and the creaking of leather belts, echoing, every sound echoing along the corridors and the metal galleries under the high shadowed roof.

"Wait here, sir, please."

The sound of keys again, a huge bunch of them hanging from his belt, the trappings of power, of one man's dominion over another. Let me tell you something: I wouldn't last more than a couple of weeks in this kind of place without going mad or getting out, one way or another, with a hacksaw blade or a filched key or a bedsheet, one end round the bars and the other round my neck. That's why I can't stand zoos.

"Right-o, sir, just follow me."

A tone of cheerfulness, business as usual, we don't like it any more than you do, so forth.

Another door clanging shut behind us, and I wanted to turn and look back.

Cell Block D. 26–50.

"Here we are, sir."

We stopped. The guard went in first, then I followed.

"Scarsdale, here's Mr Ash to see you. Now I'll be waiting outside. You need me for anything, sir, you just give a call," his voice lowering to give a semblance of confidence, though the man in the cell could still hear him.

"He's not violent," they'd told me in Final Briefing.

That was only an hour ago; I'd come here straight from the Bureau and the car was waiting for me outside.

Shepley had given me Pauling, a dry, thin, former executive who'd been taken off the active list because he'd got too close to the edge a couple of times and it had fried his nerves.

"In fact he's rather mild, though you may find him obstinate. His name's John Bryant Scarsdale and he'd been with M.I.5 nearly six years before he was caught at Victoria Station with a brown paper shopping bag full of photocopies one night when someone tipped them off." He was reading from a file. "Tried at the Old Bailey in November last year, convicted on all nine charges. Lord Lansworth said, and I quote, 'It is quite plain to me that you are a dangerous man. You have disclosed the identities of certain British agents working in Moscow, and it has quite probably led to their death or imprisonment. That, of course, is quite apart from the irreparable damage you have done to your country's safety.' Unquote. Some of the stuff found at his flat in Croydon was so sensitive that even the Attorney General, who prosecuted the case, didn't have the security clearance to see it."

He tugged a drawer open and shook a pill from a box and palmed it into his mouth. "You know what happened, of course, with M.I.5 a while ago—people complained that they were an upper-class club, and the PM told them to draw recruits from all walks of life. It didn't work with Scarsdale. His father was a factory worker and he didn't feel at ease in the company of what he called 'toffs'—now isn't that a lovely old-fashioned word? That's what turned him Bolshy, it seems. He told his interrogators that the Soviet system appreciated people like him, with 'an honest, working-class background.' Do you want to take notes?"

"No. What did they think of him in Moscow?"

"It's rather interesting. He did a specific job for them, which I think was quite valuable. He gave them a list of the known Soviet agents in Britain, so that they'd know who their unknown agents were. But he fumbled the ball on other assignments, and unintentionally got one of their Embassy contacts arrested when he was taking a brush pass from Scarsdale in the Piccadilly Hotel. They finally got fed up and tipped us off about him. I—"

"The Bureau?"

"No, the Secret Service. Scarsdale had asked to meet a Soviet agent in Zurich when he was on a cheap tourist trip, and they thought we were trying to plant him on them as a double. That's how he was picked up at Victoria Station with a bag full of photocopies: the KGB made a fake rendezvous and never turned up. Now that's about all we've got on him, but—" the phone rang and he reached for it—"but you can check with Records if you like. Excuse me. Hello? Yes, sir." He passed me the phone. "Mr Shepley."

"Quiller." I said.

"Yes, I've given some thought to your idea of releasing Major-General Solsky. It's a big risk, but I like your thinking and I'm going to agree to it. You're still of the same mind?"

"Yes. It's going to make our credit good, if we need to cash in." I didn't tell him that a hostage was even less useful now, because if they got me into a corner I'd be better off vanishing into a safe-house than relying on mutual trust.

"Very well. I'll talk to him personally and tell him why he's being released. Is your clearance going well?"

"Perfectly."

"Do you want to see me again before you leave?"

"Not really."

"Then I wish you Godspeed."

When I put the phone down Pauling handed me a briefing wallet. "Colonel Viktor Yasolev's personal dossier. About your cover—it'll be watertight, as long as the KGB play straight. They've got a lot of influence, of course, with the East German secret police, but they're still alien overlords and they can't trust the HUA. However, there's a reliable captain in Berlin whose name is Karl Bruger. Your own cover is that of an HUA captain on leave of duty, and you'll pick up your identity papers over there from Cone, who's directing you in the field. If at any time your cover is questioned, Captain Bruger will support you."

"Fair enough." Bruger, not Yasolev. That was my own doing: I'd said I didn't want any overt connection with the KGB while I was working the mission.

"Any other business?"

"No." I'd got all I needed from Clearance.

"Good luck with Scarsdale."

Short, round-shouldered, his body sunk into prison denims a size too big, standing in a kind of crouch as if he'd just been hit, didn't expect me to shake hands, already seemed to have forgotten the customs of polite society, was waiting for me to speak, his eyes wary.

"How long have you been in?"

He didn't seem to have heard, or perhaps he'd lost track of time and didn't remember. He looked pinched, cold, abandoned.

"Month."

A *month*. And it had done this to him.

"How long are you in for?"

His face flinched.

"Thirty years."

Never make it.

"It's good of you to see me," I said.

"What?"

He didn't seem to realise he could have refused, that he had any rights at all, any claim even to his own soul. In the middle of life he'd had what amounted to a terrible accident, and it had flung him into this place and left him here, forsaken, while the world went on its way. *A dangerous man,* the lord chief justice had called him. And most dangerous of all to himself.

"I believe you had some dealings with Hood."

His breath came out with a jerk as if I'd hit him, and he turned away but left his eyes on me obliquely, watching me from cover. It was so difficult to talk to him that I'd decided to get down to basics, but it'd been too fast.

"I brought you some Mars bars." I held out the bag. "They said you're partial, like me."

He watched the bag as if it had a snake in it. A man had

started singing in one of the cells along the gallery, "My Wild Irish Rose," I believe it was. Others began shouting at him, and a guard blew a whistle and the man stopped. I wondered why they didn't like it; he had quite a good voice. Perhaps it was too much for them, the thought of a rose, a woman, in a place like this; it could break their hearts.

"Hood?"

Scarsdale had turned his head back to look at me full in the face again, a tension in him that I could feel in my nerves.

Very gently I said, "We want to know where he is."

In a moment his eyes moved downwards, aware of the paper bag.

"Mars bars?"

"That's right."

"You brought them for me?"

"Yes."

"Why?"

"They said you liked them."

He took the bag and dropped it onto the bed. "Are you from the Foreign Office?"

"Yes."

He turned away suddenly and put his stubby white hands into the pockets of the denims. "I wouldn't meddle with *him* if I were you."

"We just want to know where he is."

"He's in—" and he stopped, watching me. "Why should I tell you that?"

"We might be able to do something in return."

In a moment: "Well it'll cost you more than a few Mars bars."

There was life coming back into him, a sense of the

outside world. I'd given him back his personhood; I wanted
something he had.

"If you feel like telling me all you know about Hood,
I'll find out what we can do for you."

"No, it's the other way round. You tell me what you
can do for me, then I might give you the information. And
I've got a lot."

"I can't take your word for that. Not with your record."

It broke him up and he buried his face in his hands and
swung to and fro and I thought *shit* I'm going too fast
again. He'd started to get tough and it had looked as if we
could talk business.

"Christ's sake go easy on me," he said, or something
like that, his face still buried. "I don't know how much
longer I can stand it in this place."

He'd never grown up; he'd just thought it was a game,
playing at spies, getting his own back on those bloody
toffs. *Thirty years*. He must have gone white in the dock
when he heard that.

"We could knock something off your sentence," I
said. "It depends how valuable the information is to the
country."

He straightened up and took his hands away but couldn't
look at me. "I know a lot about him."

"Then try this. *We* know where he is. Do you?"

His head turned slowly until he was looking at me, his
eyes red. "East Germany."

"What part of East Germany?"

"Berlin."

I got out the mini Sanyo. "Put it all on tape and I'll play
it to my superiors. They'll see what they can do for you."

He watched me for a while, his body shivering the
whole time, his mouth slack, half open. "Tell them

they've got to spring me first. Or they won't get another word.''

"You'll have to be practical, Scarsdale. You're too dangerous to the country.''

It sounded almost like a laugh. "What, *now*? You think I'd risk being put back in *here*?''

Probably not. But if Shepley could get him out, it'd only be for as long as it took him to give us all he'd got on Hood; then they'd start hounding him and pick him up on a trumped-up charge and slam him back inside. That had been the end of his life, that night on Victoria Station.

"I don't think you'd risk being put back in here, no, but it's not up to me. Let's try one more question. Why has Hood gone to East Berlin?''

He went on staring at me and finally shook his head. "That's the main thing, though, isn't it? That's what you're dying to know. But you'll have to spring me first.'' Still shivering, couldn't stop. "And tell them they'll have to be quick, because I don't know how long I'm going to last in this place, I really don't.''

Three street lamps, darkened windows, shadowed doorways, and the bleak perspective of the road. In the last hour we'd seen a couple of taxis, half a dozen private cars and a police patrol.

"Fill you up?''

"No. You finish it.''

The sweet smell of cocoa inside the Vauxhall. Pauling had run the engine for a few minutes to bring some more heat in, but now we'd had to open a window.

"It was extremely difficult,'' Shepley had told me. "No one can be 'sprung' from prison without a retrial or the Queen's pardon, and we haven't enough time. I need hardly warn you that this is ultra classified.''

They'd had to brief the warden and two guards. It was
to look like a carefully-planned job, with another inmate
helping Scarsdale and a getaway car cruising past a side
gate.

Pauling reached for the phone and dialled. "What's the
hold-up, do you know?"

A starved grey cat was coming down the pavement,
going into a crouch when it picked up the sound of Pauling's voice from inside the car, moving at a half-run
now, ears flattened, amber eyes burning; then it was
gone.

"The warden got cold feet," Pauling said and put the
phone down. "They've got the Home Secretary out of bed
and Mr Shepley's gone to see him."

"Christ, we're going to be found frozen to death in the
morning."

"There's another flask."

Bloody cocoa. All I wanted was Scarsdale at a table
with a tape-recorder going, spilling it all out for me so that
I could go into Berlin and get a fix on Hood and throw him
to the KGB and come back home with a whole skin.
Quickstep wasn't precisely my idea of a shadow executive's favourite mission; I'd be more like a rat out there
running for its life.

At 02:34 the phone rang and Pauling took it and said
Roger and put it down again.

"The warden's satisfied. Anytime now."

But it was almost another hour before the Austin came
round the corner and flashed its lights off and on again and
pulled up and a door swung open and a man got out and
began walking towards us, pale-faced and hunched in a
dark coat, crossing the road, walking right into the middle
of the road as another car came blinding along from behind

us and froze Scarsdale in its headlights and kept straight on and sent him spinning off the front end with his arms flung out and a scream coming and then cutting off as he curved through the air and dropped as the car reached the crossroads and turned with its tyres shrilling and left an echo in the night as the grey cat leapt for the top of a wall and vanished.

I heard Pauling say, ''You're going to have trouble with Hood. He's a professional.''

6

CONE

They've got concrete flower-boxes strung across Friedrich-strasse on the north side of Checkpoint Charlie because a couple of years ago Hans-Joachim Pofahl rammed his fifteen-ton Skoda dump-truck through the three red-and-white barriers and the six-foot-high steel doors in front of fifty armed guards and made it to the West. That had been on a summer night with a clear sky but tonight it was October and close to freezing as a cold-air front came drifting through from the north.

There were only two guards on the West side and they checked me through and the third barrier swung up under the floodlights and I was into East Berlin, no one there to meet me, just the directions: *turn right into Leipzig-strasse and go three short blocks. The hotel is on the left.*

He was waiting for me in the car park, Cone, standing

there with his feet together and his hands in his raincoat pockets and his collar turned up, didn't signal, just waited for me to get out of the BMW and go across to him.

"Maypole."

"Faerie Fey."

Hand freezing cold, just touched, just a gesture and back in his pocket while he studied me through a pair of dark glasses, couldn't see his eyes.

"Any trouble coming through?"

"No."

A narrow head and narrow shoulders, a face with a mortuary pallor and a raw-skinned nose and a mouth like a recently-healed wound. His thin body was hunched, as if he'd been born in a bitter wind and never found shelter from it, never even looked for any, knowing there was none.

The director in the field for *Quickstep*.

His hand came out again. "Give me the keys of the car. Here's your new set. It's over there, the black Lancia." East Berlin number plates.

"I'll have yours sent back. When did you last eat?"

"I don't need anything."

"But when was it?"

"A couple of hours ago."

Well on the ball—if he heard I was in some kind of trouble at any stage of the mission—snatched, missing, gone to ground—he'd want to know how fit I was, what strength I had, how long I could last out. In Final Briefing they'd told me he'd worked on *Nightlight* and mounted his own personal manhunt for his executive after he'd been signalled as missing for two weeks, and pulled him out of a cave in the mountains still alive and covered in batshit. "Cone's like Brighton rock," Pauling had told me, "lasts all the way through."

"All right," he said, "this is your base."

I went with him into the hotel and he waited while I registered. In the lift he pressed for the third floor and took his dark glasses off but didn't look at me; he had a slight squint or a glass eye, something not quite right.

"Have you met Yasolev?" I asked him.

"Oh yes. We're knocking on his door first. Protocol —he wants to show you into your room. The KGB are paying, so technically he's your host. He's in 308, you're in 357, I'm two floors up in 525. Best we could do—the place is crowded." He gave me a key. "This is for my room, a spare one, if for any reason you want to duck in there instead of your own. I'll be available most of the time but if I've got to go out I'll let you know." He spoke in a monotone as if he were reading aloud, and there was a dry harshness in his voice, maybe an echo of the wind he couldn't escape.

Yasolev opened the door in his shirt-sleeves, hurrying.

"Come in—you're earlier than I expected." He looked at me hard with his nicotine-brown eyes, assessing me. A lot had happened since we'd last met: I'd turned the mission down and then changed my mind, and he'd have got the news about Scarsdale. "Have a drink, gentlemen." He gestured towards a side table and got a jacket out of the closet, shrugging into it. "Or a chocolate."

Personal traits, it said in the dossier they'd given me in Clearance. *He's prone to sinusitis in the winter, hates homosexuals, is allergic to cats, has a collection of Samurai swords from his stint in Tokyo. Fond of sushi, oysters, chocolates.*

"I'll show you your room." On our way out he stopped to give me another straight look. "My department appreciates your instructions that Major-General Solsky was to be released, and so of course do I. That was a bold move."

"It's the only way we can play."

"I agree. But still a bold move." He took us along the corridor, leading the way, energetic, rebuttoning his black jacket because in his haste he'd done it up the wrong way. "You have the key?"

I gave it to him and he unlocked the door and pushed it open and stood aside. "I hope you will be comfortable."

Not really. It was a modern hotel and this was the third floor with a sheer drop to the street, no fire-escape, guttering, drainpipes, creeper, no ledges below the window, just a view of the Wall with its floodlit wire and watchtowers and gunposts—they wouldn't have *that* on the postcards they sold in the lobby.

Cone went straight over to the phone while I was looking round. "Binns, will you come up?"

Yasolev stood with his hands behind him for a moment, then went across to the bathroom and looked in, I suppose to see if the towels and things were there as they should be. Cone didn't introduce Binns when the man came in; there wasn't really time before he opened his black zippered bag and got out a transmitter detector and started sweeping the walls with it while Cone opened the closet and showed me the clothes he'd got for me; they would have been bought locally.

"I'm not sure of the shoes—you've got a narrow foot. Better try them. When you've got out of the clothes you're wearing, put them in that bag and I'll deal with them."

There was a tray with some beer and glasses on it, but no opener.

"We're out of vodka," I told Yasolev. "What about a beer?"

"No. I have had enough vodka." He gestured with the flat of his hand up to his neck. "I was anxious, I might tell you. I might tell you, I was anxious."

"You didn't think I'd come?"

"Not after what happened."

To Scarsdale. "It was a set-back," I said, "that was all."

"But quite a big one. I understand he was in possession of valuable information on Horst Volper."

"So we'll now have to get it ourselves."

Binns was taking the lamps to pieces.

"Then you have other leads?"

"No," I said.

Nothing showed in Yasolev's eyes but he tilted his head an inch, and I was beginning to read him. In this case it meant Jesus *Christ*. "You have *no* other leads?"

"Not really. We've got to find a different way in."

It was eerie. Yasolev was in effect my host, but we were having the guest room swept for bugs. He was a KGB officer but I was talking to him about the mission I was working, and he wasn't sitting on the other side of a two-hundred-watt lamp with its shade cut in half, forcing the information out of me. Pauling had warned me about this in Final Briefing. "I'm sure you've considered it, but you'll find things a bit odd over there. This is the first time London has ever liaised with the KGB and you're the guinea-pig. But Yasolev's going to find it odd, too. We're running you in a field where the KGB connection's going to give you a window on their system, and you'll be bringing back information it'd take an entire infiltration job to get hold of. And if anything goes wrong it'll be his fault because it was his idea."

The phone rang and Cone took it. Yasolev wasn't interested. He was watching me with his head still on one side, waiting for me to tell him how I was going to find access to Volper. There was only one way but I couldn't tell him that.

"Everything is very nice," Cone said and put the phone down. His German accent was a shade off, but I'd been briefed that his Russian was good enough to follow what Yasolev and I were saying.

"That's it," Binns said. It was the first time he'd spoken. "We're all clear." He shoved the transmitter detector in the black bag and went to the door. Cone thanked him and Yasolev gave an energetic nod.

"I insisted," he told me. "I insisted. We wish you to be comfortable here."

"Civil of you."

But no one was taken in, Binns included. He could sweep this room forever and pull the wallpaper off but he couldn't tell if anyone was aiming microwave beams at the windows to catch voice vibrations on the glass, and without X rays he wouldn't know if some of the bricks had bugs or crystalline mikes put into them when the hotel was built, and he'd have to dismantle the walls to find non-metallic optic fibres hooked up to amplifiers in another room. Yasolev was simply making a diplomatic gesture to show his trust and we were meant to accept it.

"Now I shall leave you to settle in. We'll talk when you gentlemen are ready. My room number is by the telephone."

He inclined his head and left us.

"He's nervous," Cone said, "but you don't need me to tell you that."

"He's not the only one."

"You'll be all right. You've got massive support."

And the thing I couldn't tell him was that he was wrong. I would keep him as my director and go through the gestures but I was going to run *Quickstep* on my own. I'd never manage it with a horde of Bureau people and a horde of KGB agents tagging me through the streets wherever I went.

"A few numbers for you," Cone said and gave me a memo pad. "Karl Bruger is the HUA captain who'll support your cover if needs be, and this is his office number. This one's the direct-line number of the military attaché at the Soviet Embassy. You can call him if Yasolev isn't available and you need official assistance, urgent or otherwise. If the military attaché isn't available this is the direct-line number of the Soviet Ambassador. The code-intro in both cases is *Liaison*. And this one's the direct-line number of the cultural attaché at the British Embassy, Dickie Pollock. He's been here for three years and he knows his way around, so he'll be your most useful contact. And here are some mug shots of Horst Volper."

"When were they taken?"

"During the last two years."

I put them away.

"All right," Cone said, "I'll let you try some of these clothes on. Let me know about the shoes especially. Might need to break into a trot here or there." He said it deadpan. At the door he turned and levelled his squint at me and said, "Yasolev's going to ask you how you'll be planning your access to Volper. Will you tell him?"

"No."

"Do you know?"

"Yes."

He took his hand off the door-knob and came back into the room a little. "Are you prepared to tell me?"

"You wouldn't like it."

He watched me steadily. "How much protection are you going to need?"

"None."

"My job," he said in his dry monotone, "is to get you through *Quickstep* with a whole skin. I'd rather you didn't make it difficult for me."

"Look, it's out of our hands. Put it this way: they went for Scarsdale and they got him. They thought it'd warn me off, but it didn't, so now they'll go for me. And that's the *only* access we've got, and I'm going to use it. Don't worry, they won't be long."

7

AMNESIA

"Are they tarts over there?"

A man in a black leather coat rocked our table as he squeezed through.

"Verzeihen Sie."

"Macht nichts."

Place blue with smoke.

"Tarts?" Pollock said. "I don't think so. I've never been propositioned, anyway." A clean white smile, his glasses reflecting the coloured lights over the miniature dance-floor. "I think they're just here for a good time."

"Any swallows?"

"What? I suppose they might be, some of them anyway. We get a few KGB chaps in here from their embassy, though of course they call themselves attachés of some sort or another. In fact a lot of the people who come here are from the embassies—American, British, French, Soviet. It's in walking distance, for most of them. Are you sure you won't have anything stronger?''

''I'm too thirsty.''

''This is my favourite haunt, actually. I mean apart from the embassy connection it's close to the Wall—that's why it's called *Charlie's*. There's always some kind of intrigue going on.'' Another clean smile. ''People talking about getting across, especially now that the guards have stopped shooting to kill.'' He waved for the waiter. ''But most of the talk's political, and of course very pro-Gorbachev at the moment. They're hoping he's going to do something big for Germany.''

''For the GDR.''

''For both, actually. *Dasselbe nochmals, Willi*. Everybody's seized on the idea of seeing *one* Germany again. You know something? A couple of months ago I had the chance of Rome—second cultural attaché—think of all that gorgeous art! But I turned it down. I've got a feeling something rather interesting's going to happen here before long, and I don't want to miss it. I mean, later I can always say *I was there*.'' Quick smile.

One of the girls was watching me from a corner table, under the amber lamp.

''You think he *is* going to do something big?''

''Our Miki? Absolutely.'' The waiter banged another pitcher of Heineker onto the table and altered the tab. ''*Danke schön*. Of course he's taking a huge risk with his *glastnost* policy. I mean it's all very nice to hear him talk about 'more flexible' relations between Moscow and the satellites but it's going to stir up the people in the streets. Once they get a whiff of freedom they're liable to want the whole thing, and we could easily see an outbreak of rebellions like the one here in '53 and the ones later in

Hungary and Czechoslovakia and Poland. That'd put Gorbachev straight out of office and bring the tanks in again. But you probably know all this.''

''Not all.''

''Does it interest you, or would you rather—''

''It interests me very much.''

Not actually watching me, just passing her glance across me now and then. Blond hair, blue eyes, the archetypal Aryan, bare-shouldered in a slip of a dress, smoking the whole time. She'd come in soon after we had.

''Well obviously,'' Pollock said, ''the East Germans are fervently hoping for some kind of reunification, because so many of them have got relatives in the West and they've been cut off from them all this time by the Wall. On the other hand, some people are scared to death, because if Europe becomes denuclearised—which is the way things are heading—the US is going to withdraw most of its forces and that'll leave West Germany without a security umbrella—and she's liable to look for a new one in Moscow.'' He spread his hands flat on the table and looked at me steadily. ''Can you imagine what the rest of Europe would feel like with a *reunited* Germany as an *ally*—not a slave state, but an *ally* of Soviet Russia? *That's* why lots of people are scared stiff.'' No quick smile this time.

''Jesus.''

''Didn't mean to spoil your evening.'' He drank half his beer in one go and then looked at his watch. ''But anyway I think they're wrong. I see a united capitalist Germany.''

''And anyway it'd take time.''

''Unless Gorbachev decides on a grand gesture. A symbolic gesture that would make its own statement and cut out half a dozen summit conferences.''

''You're thinking of something specific.''

''I am, actually. I believe it's in the cards, and that's

why I'm staying on here, in case our Mikhail takes a sledge-hammer to the top of that wall and knocks the first brick off.''

"You're serious, are you?"

"Absolutely. It'd be typical of him: he's a brilliant public relations man and a gesture like *that* would rate more live coverage world-wide than the Olympic Games. Go down in history, wouldn't he?" He finished his beer. "Well I've got to get some shut-eye. The Old Man wants me up early for a meeting tomorrow. But I'd really like to leave you with something more interesting to drink."

"I'm fine. I shan't be long myself."

It was 11:13 when he paid the bill and told me to phone him if I needed anything and left me, pushing his way between the crowded tables and dodging a waiter's tray.

She came over within a minute.

"I didn't want you to be lonely."

"I'm touched."

"This is the first time I've seen you in here."

"Yes?"

"My name's Hedda." Pulling another cigarette out of the pack. "What's yours?"

"Kurt."

There was a lot of noise from the jazz trio and she leaned close to me over the table, her blond hair hanging across her face. "He's from the British Embassy?"

"Who?"

"Your friend."

"Yes."

"I haven't got any friends." Small, rather pointed teeth, a shred of tobacco on her lip, smoke curling as she spoke. "I talk all the time about getting across, and it bores them."

"About what?"

"Getting across." She leaned closer, spoke louder. "I'm completely fed up, you know? They call this a workers' and peasants' state but it's a two-class system—you've got West German currency or you haven't. The roof of the Metropole's full of Lancias and BMWs and all most people can afford is a Volkswagen. You're not here looking for somebody?"

"No." I wasn't certain she meant a girl.

"I thought you might be."

"What would you like to drink?"

"I've had too much. You can't tell?"

"It doesn't show." If not a girl, then who?

"You know what I think? I think Moscow ordered a boycott of the Olympic Games in Los Angeles because they knew the GDR would beat them hands down."

"It wouldn't surprise me."

"Are you frightened of AIDS?"

"No."

"That means you're either married or careful."

"Careful."

"Isn't it terrible, though? Everyone's too scared even to fuck."

"Why did you think I was here looking for someone?"

"I thought—I was mistaken, that's all."

Her eyes didn't make any connection with mine; she looked as if she were speaking on the telephone. She could be stoned. I tried a long shot.

"When did you start working for the KGB?"

"For what?" Smoke curling out of her mouth, her eyes meeting mine but without any expression.

"The KGB."

"Are you out of your mind?" But they still didn't change; she was like a talking doll. "I saw a Soviet military truck make an illegal U-turn today across Unter den Linden, and one of our Vopos stopped him—but he didn't get a ticket. I *hate* those people; it's like they *rape* us every day. You're not looking for Volper?''

''Who?''

''Horst Volper.'' Her eyes blank, indifferent.

I said: ''No.''

Pulling another cigarette out, ''You want one?''

''I quit.''

''I don't know how I'd live without them.''

I was losing a word now and then because of the noise. ''Have you got relatives over there?'' Across the Wall.

''Yes.'' A flicker of emotion came into the ice-blue eyes. ''My father. I've only seen him three times since I was five. Don't you think that's terrible?''

''He came through to see you?''

''Yes. God, it's like I'm in gaol, isn't it? But then I suppose I am. You know the worst thing? To me, the GDR is Deutschland. West Germany isn't a foreign country—it's German, and so am I. It only feels foreign because I can't go there. Don't you feel that?''

''I've got used to it. And we shan't have the Wall forever. Who knows, Gorbachev might pull it down one day.''

''I can't see that happening,'' she said, ''in my life-time.''

It was another hour before she said goodnight and left the club and I waited three minutes and went up the steps to ground level and saw her getting into a dark-coloured VW with a front wing smashed in and covered with adhesive plastic with the headlamp poking through. Five minutes later I was fifty yards behind her along Französischestrasse with a taxi between us and nothing in my mirror, the streets quiet and access to the target for *Quickstep* depending on the thin thread leading me through the night as the twin rear lamps moved ahead of me and I sped up or held back, keeping them in sight.

North-east along Werder-strasse with the same taxi and a small pickup truck between us, a black Audi in the mirror: it had come up behind me from a sidestreet and I discounted it because we'd gone two miles from the club and it was the first I'd seen of it.

Turning right onto Spandauer-strasse with the clock on the dashboard moving through 12:35 into the early hours and the Audi closing up a little: it had turned right as we had but I still couldn't take it seriously because it was too close. It couldn't be one of Yasolev's people because they'd have tagged me to Charlie's Club and I'd checked when I got there, taking a lot of care. Cone wouldn't have put anyone on to me unless I'd asked for support or unless he'd thought I was going to need it.

Left onto Gruner-strasse with the taxi peeling off and moving down a side street, leaving the pickup ahead of me and the rear lights of the Volkswagen showing whenever I veered far enough in the traffic-lane to make a check. There was almost no traffic at this hour and the only police car I'd seen was stationary, three blocks behind.

Eyes watering a little from the thick cigarette smoke at the club, the smell of it on my coat, 12:41 and the thought persisting that I'd handled things correctly, holding off when she'd mentioned Volper, giving her nothing.

I mustn't lose her.

Right onto Karl Marx Allee, 12:45 and the streets almost deserted; another police car cruising north, passing us on the far side. The Audi was still with us but it peeled off a block later, leaving the mirror blank.

12:49.

"98.3."

It can't be ninety-eight point three. That isn't any kind of time at all.

"Pulse normal."

The smell of cigarette smoke on my coat, and of something else.

"Blood-pressure 125 over 83."

Antiseptics. Smell of antiseptics.

Terror.

"All right, you can take him off the drip."

The terror of disorientation, of not knowing.

"Lights," I said. "Can you turn off the lights?"

Blinding me. I was enveloped in some kind of passive restraint. Blankets.

"Did he say something?"

Cone's voice.

"Yes, he's conscious now."

Conscious? Jesus Christ, of course I'm *conscious*.

Said: "Of course I'm *conscious*."

It had gone almost dark now, just one lamp burning, like a moon in haze.

"Feel all right?"

Cone's face with its eyes squinting and its gash of a mouth, hovering over mine.

"God knows what I feel." I tried to sit up but the girl in the white linen coat put her hand on my shoulder and I wasn't strong enough to resist.

"You can't get up yet," a man said in German. Also in a white coat.

"Are you a doctor?"

"Yes."

Someone else standing there looking down.

Yasolev.

Said: "Is this a hospital?"

"Yes," the doctor said.

Some kind of amnesia, then.

"Am I functional?"

"Please?"

"*Functional*, for God's sake. What *injuries*?"

"Take it slow," Cone said. "You're all right. There's nothing broken."

Furious now. Panicking. "Tell me what *condition* I'm in."

The sharpest fear of the executive: to become unfit and lose the mission.

"You've come out of hypothermia," Cone said, "and there was some concussion and various bruises and some skin ripped off. There's nothing serious."

"Hypothermia. Cone, fill me in, will you?" Excessively polite, monumentally patient, because my head was full of bells ringing and lights flashing and fireworks going off—the nerves, in other words, had been rubbed raw and the brain was screaming out for information so that I could find my place again in reality. So I had to keep the lid on things, strictly essential.

"You were nearly drowned," Cone said. "The police pulled you out of the Spree. The other man was found floating."

Sensation of black water rising against my face, filling my mouth, blocking my throat—*Oh Christ*—

"Nurse—"

"Yes, Doctor—"

"Take it slow," Cone said and the nurse held me by the shoulders, some sort of paroxysm, choking fit, hadn't expected it. "You swallowed the wrong way, that's all."

It was a minute before I could speak. "Out of the *Spree*? What was I doing there?"

"We're hoping you can tell us."

There was a sense of oblivion coming over me, of a

void. It was enough to chill the blood and I stayed with it alone for as long as I could before I asked for help.

"Doc," in German, "I had concussion, is that right?"

"Yes. Mild concussion."

"Any shock?"

"Shock too, yes. Because of the hypothermia and because of the other trauma."

"I see. Well I—listen, what about retrogressive amnesia?"

"You're having difficulty in remembering?"

I didn't answer right away. When it's necessary to fight panic off you can't think of anything else. It came at me in waves, freezing the blood, stilling the mind, blocking the breath. After a long time—

"Cone."

He leaned closer.

"The last thing I can remember was looking at the clock on the dashboard, at 12:49."

He watched me for a moment. "That was twelve hours ago."

Mother of God.

"What is being said?" In Russian.

Cone turned to Yasolev. "He's got a memory lapse."

The doctor glanced at them, not understanding, and I remembered I hadn't answered his question. "Yes," I told him, "I'm having difficulty recalling what happened between 12:49 this morning and when I came to a few minutes ago."

He opened his hands, fingers spread. "It sometimes happens after an accident. The mind protects itself from unpleasant memories. I wouldn't worry. Perhaps nothing very important happened."

But Jesus Christ I'd been tagging someone who'd connected me with Horst Volper and she could have led me straight into access to the target and it would have swung the mission from phase one into a totally new situation with a chance of going in and reaching Volper and completing *Quickstep* in a matter of days, hours, *nothing very important*?

"Cone. You said 'the other man.' *What* other man?"

"We don't know who he is."

It was for me. For me to know.

"Where is he?"

"In the mortuary."

"Aren't you trying to find out who he is?"

"Yes."

"What time did they find us in the river?"

"It's down on the incident report as 01:15."

Twenty-six minutes. That was the gap.

"Where was the car?"

"Your car?"

"Yes."

"Two blocks away, in a side street off Karl Marx Allee."

"But that's—what d'you mean, *my* car? Was there another one?"

"You must allow him to rest now, please. He—"

"You mean I *walked* as far as the river? But that's over—"

"There was a car in the river, where you were found."

"In the—I got into someone *else's* car?"

"We think so. A Mercedes."

"So why did it go into the river?"

"We don't know."

"But for Christ's sake, were the tyres shot off, was it hit by another—"

"That is enough." The doctor stepped between Cone and the bed and signalled the nurse. "Gentlemen, you have to leave now. My patient needs to rest."

Yasolev said something about getting a tape-recorder but Cone interrupted him.

"Doc, this is very important. We need—"

"*Nothing* is as important to me as the welfare of my patient. Please understand that."

"Give me thirty seconds more," I told him, and he looked down at me.

"Very well. But don't get excited, please."

"Cone," I said, "call the doctor at the embassy and ask him if he's ever used hypnosis. If he can do it for me, I'm ready. I'd ask this man, but it's got to be in my own language. It's the *only* chance."

"Pretty long shot."

"Look, it's all *in* here, inside my head, and all we've got to do is get it out. Nothing's *lost*."

Cone looked at Yasolev and said in Russian, "Hypnosis. What do you think?"

"Yes," nodding emphatically, "yes, yes."

Cone picked up the telephone and asked the operator for an outside call.

"Can you take yourself down to the alpha level?"

"Yes."

"Good. You've been hypnotised before?"

"Couple of times."

His name was Cosgreave, been at the embassy six months or so, "won't have me in the West, I'm too Commy for their liking," not a smile in him anywhere, very intent, dark, still smouldering from some kind of conflagration in his past. What were they thinking of, for God's sake, keeping a leftist at the embassy *this* side of the Curtain? I suppose he'd been to Cambridge, one of us, you know.

"Have you any ideas on induction?" he asked me.

"I use the image of a brass pendulum."

"Never fails. Big, slow?"

"Yes."

"All right, are you comfortable?"

"Let's hit those lights."

He signalled the nurse. "You want her to stay?"

"I don't mind."

The main light-tubes went off and I felt the eye muscles relaxing. Still smothered in blankets but not too hot any more; a sense of overlying comfort with a tendency to break through it and worry, worry like hell because this might not work and if it didn't God knew what we were going to miss but it'd be something vital: *who was the man in the Mercedes and what had he said to me?*

Cosgreave pulled up a chair. "When you reach alpha, just lift a finger."

I closed my eyes and relaxed, went limp, listening to the settling of the pillow as the neck muscles lost tension and the head grew heavy and the brainwaves slowed and the ticking of a watch came in and I eased it away to silence, silence and the deepening dark as the mind drifted, floated, drifting, floating as I lifted a finger and let it fall again, floating, drifting . . . as his voice came in quietly . . .

So you're watching the big brass pendulum . . . swinging . . . swinging to and fro . . . to . . . and fro. . . . with the light catching it as it swings . . . the light flashing softly . . . flashing softly as it swings . . . to and fro . . . to . . . and fro . . .

My head settling lower on the pillow, lower, as I drifted in the darkness, drifting, floating, his voice still soft but clearer now, my mind opening gently, intent, attentive.

What is the last thing you remember, then? It really doesn't matter if you can't think of it; we can always try again later.

A street. Karl Marx Allee.

You're walking along the street? You're—

Driving. Driving along Karl Marx Allee. I'm following another car, with a woman driving it.

What do things look like? Feel like? It really doesn't matter if you can't remember.

There are just the street lights, and sometimes the reflection of my own lights in a shop window at the intersections, the sound of the engine and the smell of cigarette smoke, that's about all. We'd turned onto the Allee a few blocks ago, and the time on the dashboard clock was 12:45. Not much in the streets, not much traffic. Police car cruising the other way. There was another car behind me, a black Audi, but it peeled off after a while and left a Fiat in the mirror. When I looked at the clock again it was 12:49.

Silence.

12:49.

Aren't you going to ask me anything more?

I don't think so. It's really not important. Just go on talking, if you want to. Just go on talking.

12:49.

If you like, but I'm not sure—

Just go on talking.

We were driving along the street, that was all. I'd fallen behind quite a bit now because the taxi had peeled off earlier and I didn't want her to see me close enough to identify the front-end profile. Then I looked at the clock again because I wanted to keep a check.

What time was it?

12:49. No, 12:50.

Good. Go on.

I was just keeping station. It was a routine tag. Then she began slowing, soon after Strausberger-platz, and turned right onto a side street, Andreas-strasse. I sped up and swung onto the same street and saw her tail-lights ahead of me as she turned left into a car park.

This was tricky because I wasn't certain she was going to park there but I took a chance and put the nearside wheels of the Lancia onto the sidewalk and switched off and got out and began walking, listening as I went, and heard the engine of the VW throttle up and then cut off.

Slam of a door and then she was within sight and I held back and used a rubbish-bin as cover. She was walking away from the car, not hurrying, not looking around her, and I closed the distance to something like a hundred feet before she picked her way across a vacant lot and turned into an alleyway with one street light at this end. I was fifty feet behind her and using cover as I went—doorways, rubbish-bins, a section of fallen fence—because if she turned she'd see me. There were brick walls on each side now, high ones, with almost no cover, and I held back, taking the risk of losing her if she went into one of the doorways farther down. It couldn't be helped and in any case it made no difference because the sound of an engine exploded in the silence and I spun around as a flood of blinding light leapt in a wave against me.

8

SKIDDER

There wasn't a chance because the width of the car was filling the alleyway and there was no door I could reach and the walls were too high and there was nothing to climb so I waited until the headlights were close enough and then jumped and hit the bonnet with the flat of my hands and pulled my legs up and got thrown against the top of the windscreen and over the roof, hitting the CB antenna in the centre of the boot and feeling it flex and break but the base held and I got one foot against it and used it for leverage and smashed the rear window with a heel-palm and got a grip on the frame and held on while the car accelerated through the alley like a bullet down a gun-barrel and burst into the street and began weaving from side to side with the tyres shrilling and the suspension taking the shock and the bodywork heaving and recoiling

and heaving and throwing me from side to side as my foot
lost its hold against the base of the antenna and I clung on
with one hand, side to side, weaving and bucking as he
sped up and zig-zagged from kerb to kerb.

He'd been sure he could shake me loose but I found
purchase again on the antenna base and he went down on
the brakes and my shoulder hit the window frame and I got
both hands on it now but he was going to pull up and get
out and come for me and he'd have a gun and if I dropped
off and tried running clear he'd shoot me down at close
range and my skin began crawling because this was going
to be it, *finis*.

Lights.

They swept across the street's facade and flooded the
rear of the Mercedes and he came off the brakes and hit
the throttle and the tyres spun and then gripped and the
rear went down and all I could do was hang on because if I
dropped now I couldn't deal with the speed and there'd be
no chance of shielding my head. A siren had started up
and the flashing lights came on from behind us and the
Mercedes began slewing again from one side to the other
because this man's orders had been to wipe me out and
this was the priority he wanted to take care of before the
police could close in.

It carried the same signature: they'd gone for Scarsdale
in the same way but this time they'd assumed I'd be more
difficult so they'd chosen the alley and set up the kill with
the girl for the lure and the timing precise and it must have
looked certain and would have been certain if I hadn't got
things right.

I couldn't see where we were going, couldn't see street
names because I was prone with my face down, one cheek
sliding across the paintwork and my foot slipping, catching
again and slipping with both hands burning on the chips of

glass in the frame. I didn't know what the speed was in actual figures but he was moving flat out for the terrain and hitting the kerb and bouncing with the springs heeling, straightening and heeling as he shook the car like a ship beam-on to a running sea, the siren howling close behind us now and the reflection of the headlights dazzling on the bodywork against my eyes.

We turned and the car slewed through an intersection with the tyres sending out a long-drawn whimper that echoed from the buildings and my weight shifted under the pull of the centrifugal force and my foot lost its purchase on the antenna-base and my legs swung clear and one hand was tugged from the windowframe and I half-rolled with my hip smashing against the bodywork as the brakes came on again and the lights of the police car grew suddenly intense and then swung away as it lost traction in a slide that took it across the kerb and into a glass window and the thought came into my mind that this would be a good place to chance it and let go and try to roll and minimise the damage because he wouldn't stop and come back for me with the police here and they'd pick me up and get me somewhere if I were still alive.

But I had my priorities too and the chief of them was to move in on this man if I could and force something out of him, even if only a name, one name, or a clue, one clue that would take *Quickstep* a stage farther towards the access I *had* to have, the access to Horst Volper.

A siren sounded again, a different one from somewhere ahead of us: the Vopos had been using their radio and calling in some support and at this hour with the streets almost empty there'd be patrols cruising the city with nothing to do. Lights swept the intersection ahead of us and the driver braked and swerved to the right and hit the kerb and bounced into a wrenching U-turn and my legs were swung back and my foot caught the antenna-base and I got my other hand back to hook onto the edge of the window but I began worrying about muscle fatigue setting in before we hit something and I could move into close quarters with the man at the wheel. I was also worrying about the Vopos because if he smashed up the car and they came for him he'd probably pull his gun on them and then he wouldn't stand a chance because he'd be outnumbered and they'd blow him away and I'd never be able to ask him what I wanted to know. I was within minutes, inches of forcing answers out of him that would give me access to the objective but he was pushing himself closer and closer to death and taking me with him.

Headlights in front of us and a siren howling and he swerved and grazed a lamp-post and the Mercedes shuddered, rocking on its springs and heeling to one side before it hit the police car at an angle and the deceleration forces pushed me forward and I kept my foot hooked against the antenna to anchor me but it slipped free and I hit the body-work with one shoulder and lost all conscious thought for a while because the metal shrieked as the two cars glanced together and glass smashed and threw a shower of fragments across the Mercedes in a sudden hailstorm and the siren's volume rose until the ear-drums went dead and all I could do was hang on and wait till it was over. A man shouted something and then we were clear and slewing across the road surface and swinging at right angles into the intersection, bouncing against the kerb and straightening with only the street lights ahead of us because one of the headlamps had been ripped away and blown a fuse and shut the other one off. Stink of burnt rubber on the air from the torn treads of the tyres.

He could see me in the rearview mirror and one of the things I expected him to do was get at his gun and snatch a half-second to swing round in his seat and fire into me and there was nothing I could do to stop him except let go and drop off and leave it to happen that way instead of with a bullet. He was having to concentrate on driving clear of the tightening police net and he was hoping he could shake me off at some point along the way and leave me lying at the front end of a long red smear on the road surface but even so I was beginning to wonder why he didn't go for his gun and one answer could be that he didn't have one: he could be a specialist with the hit-and-run routine and have a certain degree of contempt for side-arms just as I do.

We were going very fast now and the street was wide and I thought it could be Karl Marx Allee again. They'd flushed him out of the side streets into the open and that was another worry because he was a clear target and they could bring in a dozen more patrols if they wanted to, fifty if they wanted to, and fill the whole of the avenue and shoot his tyres off and wait till he spun and crashed. The speed felt like something close to a hundred kph and the backwash of the slipstream was tugging at my clothes and I thought that if he smashed the Mercedes now there wouldn't be any question of forcing anything out of him and I had a sudden feeling of rage because we were only two days into the mission and Shepley was manning the signals board for *Quickstep* and all he'd get from Cone was the routine phrase for a terminal situation, *Shadow down*, and upstairs they'd punch the uncoded equivalent, *Executive deceased*.

Sirens were sounding everywhere now and sending echoes from the buildings and there was a wash of headlights flooding the street. He gave it one more block and hit the brakes and brought the speed down and then used the throttle to swing into a side street but we were still going

much too fast to do it cleanly and he lost the rear end and
it hit the kerb and bounced back and hit it again as he tried
to correct and then we were skinning the shop windows
with a scream of metal against stone and glass that hollowed out the night and left conscious thought blanked off
because of the overload. Then we were clear again and I
caught a glimpse of a street sign and saw that we hadn't
been in Karl Marx Allee before we'd changed direction
because this was a side street off Stralauer and we were
turning back in our tracks. We'd lost the Vopo patrols but
I could still hear some of their sirens in the distance and
it'd only be a matter of time before they picked us up
again.

I was having to get my mind off the fatigue in the wrist
muscles because they were burning now and unless I could
shift forward and get one elbow inside the window I
wouldn't have more than a minute, a minute and a half
before I had to let go and drop. I waited for him to use the
brakes and let the momentum take me forward but he was
accelerating the whole time now and the strain on the
wrists was intensified and there was another factor coming
into play—I was beginning to lose the ability to process
the data coming in because I'd been bombarded with a
massive input of light and sound and movement for a long
time now and the stress was nearing the point where I'd
start hallucinating and that would be fatal, *finito*.

Thing was to hang on. Thing was to focus the sense of
reality on this one objective, to forget why it had to be
done, to ignore all other considerations and reduce everything to the simple facts: these are my hands and they must
keep their hold on the edge of metal here and anchor
themselves to it and become one with it, *my fingers are
made of iron and nothing can bend them*, the car swinging
wide suddenly and lifting on one side as he tried again to

shake me off, *my wrists also are made of iron and they cannot tire so I have no fear,* the momentum of the swing taking us against a parked car and slamming us sideways into it and bouncing off again with one fender torn half away and caught against a tyre, *there is nothing the organism has to do but remain where it is, with its iron fingers hooked over the metal and its iron wrists taking the strain without effort,* a sudden burst of acceleration with the rear wheels spinning and then some kind of shout from him, from the man at the wheel, before the front end tilted and a strange quietness came in with only the singing of the torn fender against the still-spinning tyre and the dying note of the engine and the sensation of flight, of weightlessness and then a waste of still water as the car tilted and went on tilting, a waste of still water with distant lights reflected in it as we dropped and hit the surface and I was flung away from the white explosion of the impact and instinctively began treading water.

"I don't know."

"Volper? Is his name Volper?"

"I don't know."

I pushed his head down again and he began struggling. It was like drowning a dog.

Cold. Freezing cold.

Sirens in the night, sounding a dirge, their cadences orchestrated, rising and falling and rising, their echoes wailing across the flat still water. I thought I could see the humped roof of the Mercedes in the shallows near the bank of the river, and they'd see it too before long, the Vopos, so I'd have to hurry because once they found us he'd be taken out of my reach.

"What's your name? *Your name?*" In English. I'd started in German with him but he hadn't understood.

"Skidder."

Nickname. "Listen, I want to know who's running you."

He didn't answer. I pushed his head down again and felt him struggling under my hands. It's not an exact science, half-drowning a man to make him talk, and even a doctor wouldn't have known exactly when to stop, when to let him snatch another breath. He'd been much stronger, before, when I'd found him swimming towards the bank, and he'd thrown an arm round my neck and forced me below the surface—a big man, he was a big man, and frightened because of the sirens—and I'd had to work on his nerves with knuckle strikes to get him docile.

Struggling like a madman, not frightened by the sirens any more, frightened of drowning, dying. I let his head break surface and waited until the worst of the choking was finished with.

"Skidder, I want information and you want to live. *Is it Horst Volper you work for?*"

I think he was trying to nod and it sounded like *yes* but it could have been his breath hissing as he tried to snatch at it. I would ask him again later. "Skidder. Who is the target?"

Oh Jesus *Christ* it was *cold* in the water here, *it was cold enough to kill*. He didn't answer so I pushed him down again. *God damn his eyes* he was wasting my time and freezing me to death. *Struggle*, then, go on, you'll get the message quicker this way. Five seconds, ten . . . *Up*.

Blowing out water, half-choking.

"Who is the target? Come on, who is the target?"

He made a sound.

"What?"

"Gor—chev—"

"Gorbachev? *Did you say Gorbachev?*"

" 'Ess," nodding, " 'Ess," choking up water.

He was getting heavier and I was warned. Our feet were grounded in the shallows so I didn't have his full weight on my hands but he was weakening and I'd have to watch it because this half-drowned hulk could give me the access for *Quickstep* and perhaps save time, later, lives, later.

"What's the operation, Skidder? *Listen,* you give me some answers and I'll pull you out and get you to a hospital but if you waste any more of my time by *God* I'm going to push you under and keep you there, *now do you understand that?*" Heavy on my hands, now, he was heavy. *"What is the operation?"*

The sirens were louder now and I could see headlights slanting across the water as one of the police cars swung in this direction.

"What?"

He'd said something.

I waited but he didn't repeat it so I pushed him down and dragged him up again.

"Come on, Skidder, I want information."

But I wouldn't have to push him down again if it came to that, and I didn't think it'd do much good if he told me what I wanted to know and I got him to a hospital; he was a dead weight on my hands now, with his legs jack-knifing under the water. I was losing alertness myself by this time: the water was freezing the blood, numbing the limbs, and all I could think about was getting out while there was time.

I waited but he didn't say anything more.

"Come on, Skidder!"

Didn't say anything more.

Sirens close now, and headlights along the river, a mobile spotlight throwing a beam across the water, passing over the hump of the Mercedes and coming back, fixing on it and then moving again, sweeping, suddenly dazzling, blinding.

"*Skidder!*"

Anything more.

There was just the white flare of the light playing on us and his face, Skidder's face close to mine with its eyes open and its mouth hanging slack, his dead weight on my hands, and voices now, voices calling from the top of the bank, a door slamming and a man running, more lights as another car swung from the higher road and pulled up with its siren dying.

Conscious thought slipped into illusion: I was aware of the police cars and the men coming down the bank and the man in my arms and the dark flat surface of the river reaching forever beyond the brilliance of the lights, but they were all unreal, a chimera, and the only reality was this gripping cold, sapping the strength and numbing the mind, turning me into something immovable, an entity that was losing its significance—*watch it*—and now the beginning of euphoria as the will to move gave way to the comfort of deciding to make no effort—*move, for God's sake, move*—no more effort, just the feeling of letting go, with the water lapping against my throat now, against my mouth—*move move move you're drowning*—and a man with a peaked cap and other men, uniforms, *it's all right, we've got you, hang onto me now*—and the bright lights spinning and the man's face watching, watching me from slightly above, nodding, making a note.

"You were pretty far gone, yes, when they found you."

"*Oh Jesus,* it was so *cold,* I tell you."

Nodding again. "And you remember being brought in here?"

"Yes. Most of it. I mean there was nothing very specific about it; I knew they'd dragged me out of the river but I was shaking badly and I didn't want to take much notice of anything. Hot drinks, beef broth, I think.''

''They did a good job.'' He switched off the recorder. ''How d'you feel now?''

''All right.''

Not true, of course, not absolutely true. The psyche was under the assault of varied reactions and I felt rage that I'd misjudged things, forced that man too hard and got nothing from him, or next to nothing, *rage, too, about what Cone had done,* rage and depression because of a death on my hands, and above all the knowledge that because of all these things I'd left *Quickstep* to founder out there in the night-dark waters of the river.

9

TEA

"Umdrehen auf dein Magen, bitte."

I turned over onto my stomach and she began again, a huge woman, huge hands, but experienced, feeling the exact degree of pain she was giving, keeping it under control.

"No. Not for a few days."

Cone was sitting on the edge of the chrome-framed vinyl chair near the bed, the phone in his hand.

"Entspannen, bitte, loslassen."

I went as limp as I could. It was mainly the right shoulder, where I'd been thrown against the bodywork of the Mercedes. The rest consisted of abrasions and wasn't serious, wasn't hampering.

The curtains were open and the glow from the floodlit Wall was on the ceiling, like the reflection of snow.

"I'll ask him, sir." Louder—"Morale?"

"Not very high," I told him. "We'll have to talk about that."

I couldn't see his face from where I was lying on the massage table but he was quiet for a moment before he spoke again, repeating what I'd said to Shepley. A bruised shoulder and a few abrasions and the lingering effects of hypothermia didn't amount to anything major, considering how close I'd come, but the morale of the executive in the field is vital to his operation and if I couldn't deal with the angst it was quite likely that Shepley would pull me out and replace me before I endangered *Quickstep* and the critically sensitive Bureau-KGB relationship.

"*Bleiben enrspannen fur zehn minuten, bitte.*"

"*Ya. Danke, Fräulein.*"

"*Bitte.*"

I rolled off and went over to the bed and lay there while she folded the legs of the portable table and went lumbering out with it.

That *bloody* Audi: he'd have to explain *that.*

"Sir? No, the opponent was lost. Yes, I'll be getting a report for you. No, the only product amounted to a few words. There was—" he broke off and listened and then said, "Ash, can you take the phone?"

I sat up on the bed and he gave it to me.

"Executive."

"What did you get out of him?"

This was going over scrambled: that man Binns had hooked up a T3 to the phone. "He said the target is Gorbachev."

"And that is all?"

"Yes."

"Do you consider it was worth the consequences?"

He meant Skidder's death. "It confirms who the target is

and it's knocked out one of their hit-men.'' I thought I was going to stop at that but the anger needed relief. I didn't raise my voice. "If you think I should have got more out of him I'll remind you that we weren't sitting in a cosy interrogation room; we were up to our necks in freezing water and he didn't break easily."

"I implied nothing. Have Cone come to the telephone again, will you?"

I passed it to him and tuned out what he was saying. It wasn't totally unlikely that Bureau One would order him to pull me out of the mission for mishandling the Skidder thing and letting it affect my morale.

"Something for us to work on," Cone said when he'd put the phone down. "One of our sleepers out here got his wavelengths crossed with someone's transmitter and picked up Werneuchen Luftwaffe Base as the site of a clandestine operation. Mr Shepley suggests you do some work on it."

I opened my eyes. "Volper's operation?"

"They don't know."

"Werneuchen," I said, "is a bomber base."

"See what you can find out. But I need your report before we do anything else. Feel up to it?"

I said yes and he got the recorder and put it on the edge of the bed and pulled his chair closer and switched the thing on and said, "Report on terminal incident, DIF Cone, executive Quiller." He gave the time and the date and sat back.

"The loss was unintended," I said into the recorder. "I had to judge how far to go with the subject, and how fast. This was difficult because there was very limited time and we were both feeling the onset of hypothermia."

His blunt, heavy face bobbing at the surface of the water, his eyes not looking at me, though we were face to face.

"There was no personal element involved. It's my feeling that if I hadn't pressed him he would have lost consciousness before I got anything out of him at all. Or he would have gone on blocking."

The weight of his body under my hands as we swayed together in that freezing river, both of us near death, thrown together like flotsam on the tide of circumstance and performing our little *danse macabre* to the tune of sirens in the night.

"I have no compunction. I feel no remorse."

But I'm depressed, I tell you, I'm bloody depressed.

The compunction-and-remorse bit's always asked for in these reports because some of us can take a man's life like swatting a fly but others find it affecting their work, the mission, and they're often pulled out.

"The subject had been trying hard to kill me and that had been his intention; the trap had been set specifically to accomplish that. Hence no remorse. I regard it as having been in the day's work, but I admit to a feeling of depression and this is normal for me after a terminal incident."

Words, words, oh my God *words,* it *does* matter when you cut down a human life and the fact that he was trying to wipe me out has got *nothing* to do with it. There was that awful sound, the gurgling, and *that* has got everything to do with it, the sound of someone drowning like a dog while I went on pushing him under and blocking the force of my natural instinct to save him.

"I contend that I got as much information as was possible in the circumstances, and that I didn't hasten the loss by poor judgement."

Bullshit, but they wouldn't know that. All those snivelling bloody clerks want is what they call a clear picture, just give us a clear picture, old boy, can you, so they can peck it all down on their neat little keyboards and go home to their steak and kidney pudding and watch the telly, *damn* their eyes, do they *really* think you can give them a clear picture when you were up to your neck in a river and freezing to death and trying to decide just how much to put the fear of Christ in a man to make him squeal? They don't—

"Anything else?"

"What?"

"Is that all?"

"Yes." A killing, nicely wrapped up. Oh my God how I hate bureaucrats.

"Did you look for any identification on him?"

"No. There wasn't time—the Vopos were coming."

In a moment: "How do you feel now?" But I noticed he'd switched the thing off before he said that.

"Bloody awful."

Rather vague, yes. This man was my director in the field and it was his job to support, nurse and succour his executive, test him out at every major phase of the mission and decide whether he was still operational, still competent to go ahead, unaffected by fear, guilt, remorse or emotion of any kind. And if he thought fit, to warn London to pull him out.

"What sort of bloody awful?" Squinting at his nails.

It'd need time. I got off the bed and moved around, checking things out—pain in the shoulder but only when I moved it; other areas, left thigh, left shin, rib cage, where I'd been flung around on the back of the Mercedes; but nothing wrong with the feet or ankles: I could still run flat out if I had to and that's the first thing you worry about when you've come through the wrong end of the mangle— whether you can still run fast enough if you've got to.

"For one thing," I said, "I'm pissed off. Was that *your* Audi?"

"Which one?"

"Look, when I went to meet Pollock at Charlie's Club I checked the area *very* carefully and it was clean. So how did you know I'd gone into the river?"

"We don't use an Audi, as far as I know."

"It was a blind?"

"It could have been."

"So you *did* put a tag on me?"

"Yes."

Gott straffe the bastard.

When the traffic conditions are too light for comfort in a vehicle-tag operation you can slip a third car in the middle with instructions to stay there until some innocent vehicle gets in between, and then peel off and come back when it's needed again. The object is to make sure there's always something between the tag and the target and that could've been why the Audi had gone down a side street when the Fiat had come up, but it was academic now: Cone had said yes, he'd ordered someone in.

"When did the tag get onto me?"

"When you left here."

"Shit."

I'd checked for tags when I'd got to the Club but not when I'd left, because I'd been too busy watching the girl and keeping her in sight.

"Why did you have me tagged?"

"You told me you were expecting Volper to have a go."

"Then why didn't you tell me?"

"You wouldn't have liked it—" looking up from his nails—"would you?"

"Oh for Christ's sake, let's get some tea sent in." Whatever they'd given me to pull me out of the hypothermia thing had left me as dry as a husk. "If I'd wanted someone in support I'd have asked for it."

"It's not like that," he said, "this time," and picked up the phone.

"It's so bloody dangerous."

When your own cell puts some kind of support in the field without telling you it can lead to a whole lot of trouble: three years ago in Mexico City I'd spent half the night coming round full-circle on a tag and when I'd got him on the floor of a hotel boiler-room with a near-lethal lock on his throat and started asking questions he'd turned out to be an extra-curricular peep tacked onto me by an over-anxious local director and it'd set the mission back by two weeks because I'd lost track of the objective.

"It's a calculated risk," Cone said, and switched to German and asked for some Earl Grey, putting the phone down and getting out of his chair and standing with his shoulders forward, leaning into that bitter wind of his. "My instructions are to protect you whenever I think it's necessary."

"I can look after myself. You know my record."

"You've survived very well, so far. But you've been lucky."

His eyes came to rest on mine, which was unusual. He'd won a major point and I think he was watching me for my reaction.

"We all need luck when a wheel comes off but that doesn't change anything."

"It does, this time. This time, it's Mr Shepley."

"He's a soldier, and they can only think of making a move with a mass of troops in the field."

It looked something like a smile; the skin tightened on his face and his eyes lost their look of unbreakable concentration just for a second. "I wouldn't call that man a soldier, not the way he works. What you've got to realise is that this time we're expecting you to cooperate with us.

I know that doesn't come easy, but *this* time we're trying to protect one of the two most powerful men on the planet. It'd be nice if you could get perspective on that.''

I gave it some thought: I had to. It was no good asking what the KGB was doing if their top kick needed protection because I knew what they were doing: they'd sent Yasolev in to ask us for liaison. Volper was a British national and the Bureau was digging up enough ground in London to bring the place down before they could find his tracks. What Cone meant was that I still hadn't got a grip on the size of this thing and he could be right, but there was only one way I could work and they'd known that when they'd called me in.

"All right, try this. Whenever you put someone in the field with me I want to know about it. I want to know who they are and where they're deployed and what their instructions are.''

"That's a tall order.'' There was a knock on the door and he loped across and opened it and we didn't say anything before the boy had left the tray on the round plastic-topped table and gone out again.

"No, I mean in the field with me *actively*. I know the place must be full of lamplighters.''

"You wouldn't believe how many. You want it straight up?''

"Yes. *Actively*—all right?''

He brought my tea over and I went halfway to meet him and wondered if he caught the symbolism.

"All right, you'll be told. There's got to be trust, hasn't there, like with Yasolev. Got to meet each other halfway.'' The skin tightened again and a spark came into his eyes and I had the impression that this man Cone was deeper than I'd thought, quicker, harder, more implacable, and with the power, perhaps, given only to people in the very top echelon: the power to break me in an instant and throw me to the dogs if he thought I looked like endangering the mission. It occurred to me that the KGB connection wasn't the only thing that could cost me sleep: I was expected to "cooperate" right across the board, and I could believe they'd given me a director in the field who'd wipe me out if I didn't. This time, yes, things were different.

He held his cup in both hands, stooping over it, though it wasn't cold in here. "And that works both ways, doesn't it? If you make any kind of move where you think you're going to need some luck, I want you to tell me."

"I don't have to. They'll come for me again, whether I make a move or not."

"That's how you see yourself? A sitting duck?"

"Don't you?"

"Yes." Squinting down at his tea. "That's unavoidable. And you're prepared to draw their fire?"

"It's the only way in. I've done it before." Moscow, West Berlin, Prague. "It's a classic, you know that. It's the *fastest* way in."

"They'll want," he said, "to make sure, next time."

"The greatest risk is that one of your people gets in my way. The whole thing's very hair-trigger and I could lose him by a knee-jerk reaction before he'd got time to identify himself. I wish you'd see that."

He put down his tea by the phone and got his briefcase and found an envelope and ripped it open.

"I've got five men on standby. Here are their faces." He gave me some photographs. "I don't use them all at once. There was only one of them behind you when you left that club. Keep these somewhere safe."

"What are their code-names?"

"You don't need to worry about that. They won't ever

come out of the background unless something happens, and then you won't be interested in their names.''

I put the prints away. "All right, that's a help. D'you think Yasolev's got people out there too?"

"He gave you his word. I don't know how much it's worth."

I let it go. "What about the police?"

"We haven't asked them to look after you. He might have."

I got myself some more tea. "What are they doing about the Spree thing?"

"Yasolev asked them to put out smoke. They did. You won't be questioned."

"But it's woken them up, hasn't it? He wiped out at least two of their cars and finished up on a slab."

"We can't help that." The phone was ringing. "We've got to leave the HUA to Yasolev." He picked up the receiver.

I was getting gooseflesh, the more I thought about it. Cone had got five men in support and the Spree thing had shaken Yasolev badly and he could easily decide to bring in some KGB support of his own and on top of that the East German police could just as easily decide to take an interest in me after what had happened, despite Yasolev's request to leave me alone—this was their pitch we were playing on. But the only way we'd got of reaching Horst Volper was by letting him come for me again and he wouldn't do that if it meant taking on an army: he'd realise I was bogged down and no longer a danger.

I'd known I'd have to find a safe-house and go to ground and work *Quickstep* solo, but I didn't know I'd have to do it so soon.

"He wants to see us." Cone was putting the phone down.

"Yasolev?"

"Yes. Sounds worried." He loped across and took the lid off the big brass teapot to see how much there was left.

"What did he say?"

"Just wants to talk." He went to the door and opened it and left it like that, a small gesture of courtesy. "He's on his way."

The chrome *art déco* clock on the wall was at 11:05. An hour earlier Yasolev had phoned us and said he was turning in.

"He must have had some kind of signal."

"That's conceivable." He lowered his voice. "Before he comes, there's been another instruction from London. We're to check on Cat Baxter. She's coming out here."

"The rock star?"

"Yes."

"Why do we have to check on her?"

"Now that's a very good question." He took his cup into the bathroom and rinsed it out and dried it on a towel and came back, and then Yasolev was suddenly in the open doorway in a worn red dressing-gown, his thin hair untidy as he looked first at Cone, then at me.

"I have just received information that General-Secretary Gorbachev—"

"Door," Cone said and jerked a hand.

I went past Yasolev and shut it and came back.

"Thank you—that General-Secretary Gorbachev will make an informal visit to East Berlin."

"When?" Cone asked him.

"He arrives on the 17th of this month."

In a week from now.

"There's some tea," Cone said, "if you'd like some."

10

LIBIDO

"They shot him."

Closer, now, the Wall.

"They shot him in the back."

Looming against the south sky, the Wall.

"What made him do it?"

It was all you could see through the window here: the Wall, floodlit, towering, though it's not all that high, fourteen feet, but towering because of what it is, what it means. And because of the barbed wire, the watchtowers, the machine-gun posts.

"I suppose he wanted freedom," I said.

He took another gulp of *schnaps*, puckering his mouth over it, squeezing his eyes shut, a drop of clear mucus gleaming at the end of his nose under the bleak white light. You could even see the reflection, in the glass of the china cabinet opposite the window, the reflection of the Wall. It shut us in, squeezing us into the small overheated room between its floodlit expanse against the window and its reflection on the cabinet. It was all they talked about in these rooms, these buildings, along these streets: the Wall. Twenty-seven years ago it had leapt like a tidal wave and frozen solid, cutting a city in half.

"It's not so bad here," he said.

Gunter Blüm, sixty, cab-driver.

"No."

"We're better off here than what they are in Poland or Czechoslovakia. There's industry here, goods, stuff in the shops. You can earn a decent living." He wiped his nose on the back of his hand. *"So why did he do it?"*

"Those things aren't freedom," I said. "Perhaps that was what he wanted. How old was he?"

"Thirty-two. *Still a young man.*"

This place was near Spittelmarkt, and we were on the second floor. The other apartment was next to this one, next to his. He just had the two.

"When did it happen?"

"Three years ago. Three years and seventeen days." He rubbed at a blister on his hand. "She tried to kill herself."

"Your wife?"

"His mother. More his mother than my wife, you know? He was everything to her." Small jerk of his head. "It's the way it is, sometimes, mothers and sons."

This was the fourth place I'd seen. I hadn't looked at the small ads in the local papers because I wanted somewhere close to the hotel, close to the embassies. I'd spent two hours getting rid of a tag, not one of Cone's people because his face didn't match any of the photographs, possibly one of Yasolev's if he'd decided to break faith, possibly one of Horst Volper's. Then I'd gone on foot, looking for the *Zimmer zu Vermieten* cards in the windows.

"Where is she now?"

There was no sign of a woman here.

"She's living with her sister in Strausberg. She—we couldn't get on, after that." Jerk of his head. "She shouldn't have tried to do such a terrible thing. I didn't, and he was my son too, wasn't he? She still had me, didn't she?"

The cheap schoolroom chair creaked as he tossed back the last of his drink; he was a big man, his arms tattooed, his fists resting on the table, bunched, angry, his eyes glancing up at the window every so often as if he were keeping watch on an enemy.

"I read about it," I told him.

"A lot of people did. It caught attention." He reached for the bottle of *schnaps* and then changed his mind, looking at the tin-framed clock on the shelf over the sink.

The story had caught attention because of its irony. Paul Blüm had almost made it to the West: he'd been poised on the top of the Wall when they'd shot him, and it was only his body that had dropped to freedom on the other side.

"Why did he do it?" Couldn't get it off his mind.

"He was making a statement," I said.

"They don't shoot to kill, these days. If only he'd waited."

"His statement still stands. There are plenty of others crying out for freedom. He spoke for them too."

"Hero, then. He's a hero? They didn't think so when I went to the checkpoint. I didn't know he'd been going to try it. I saw the papers, next day, and I went to the checkpoint, out of my mind, hit some of the guards, went crazy." Eyes on the window again. "They beat me up and shoved me inside for twenty-four hours. Common criminal they said he was, a criminal, betraying the cause, all that

Party bullshit.'' His glance was on me, now, wary. "I
don't know you, don't know who you are.''

"They're no friends of mine. I'm in the market.''

He looked away. "Do a bit myself.''

They all do. "So you never see your wife?'' I needed to
know.

"Once in a while.'' Jerking his head—"I still love her,
but I'm not sorry she keeps away. Breaking her heart, you
see, and I can't stand for women to cry. Wants to visit his
grave. I think if she could ever do that, she'd start
mending.''

"They buried him over there?''

"I've got a cousin. I sent him the money. He sent us
some pictures—Paul's in a cemetery in Grunewald. Pictures aren't the same as seeing, though, being there. I'd do
anything, but they won't even look at our applications. He
was a criminal, is how they think of him. God in heaven—''
he hit the top of the table with the flat of his hands and got
to his feet and kicked the chair aside—"he was *born* there,
you know that? They killed him trying to get into his own
country!''

He moved in the room like a creature tethered, going in
lumbering circles, trapped, his big hands hanging with
their fists still bunched, his breath heavy, his mouth
puckered.

"Do you think she'd come back to you,'' I asked him,
"once she'd seen the grave?''

"Or stay over there. Either way, she'd feel better, start
mending.''

"Why haven't you moved away?''

He stopped dead. "Where to?''

"Just away from the Wall.''

He faced the window again, his square head going
forward. "No. I'm not turning my back.''

I got out of the worn Leatherette armchair. "He wouldn't want that for you."

"I want it for myself. I want to go on *hating* them."

I let him talk some more, enough to do him a bit of good; then I got out my wallet. "I'll take the flat," I told him, "for a month."

"The flat?" He'd forgotten why I'd come here.

It'd be as good as I'd find and I'd run out of time; it was three days since Yasolev had told us Gorbachev was coming to East Berlin and we'd only got four left. From this floor there was an easy drop into the small littered yard behind the building, and the window at the front wasn't overlooked—there was just the Wall. There was a staircase instead of a lift and good enough cover in the street outside: vans standing opposite the paper mill, loading and unloading; five doorways within plain sight and a long shop window diagonally opposite with a wide angle of reflection; a high fence alongside a demolition site where they were knocking a three-storey building down.

I got out some money. "I'll want privacy," I said, "just as you want yours. I'm not into anything risky, I just want to keep myself to myself. Is that understood?"

"I'm not interested in other people's business." He picked up the money.

"I'm going to rely on that. Give me your wife's name and her sister's address, and by the end of the month I'll see she gets a permit to visit the cemetery on the other side."

He swung his head up. "You can do that?"

"I guarantee it. If you'll look after me well."

"Got my word."

Safe-house.

"Didn't you see me?"

She was in Luftwaffe uniform, the greatcoat buttoned to

the chin against the freezing wind, her hands gloved. 1st Lieutenant's insignia.

"It was the brakes," I said. "They've been giving me trouble."

"What did you say?" She stood closer, pitching her voice above the din of a truck going past, its wheels churning through the slush. There'd been snow last night.

"Brakes," I said. "They don't work."

"You admit responsibility?"

"Yes. You'd better shut your door." She'd left it open when she got out of the car to look at the damage. It wasn't much more than I'd done to the other two cars the night before: creased rear fender, smashed tail-light.

She went back to the pagoda-top Mercedes and got a black briefcase and slammed the door. "Show me your driver's licence and your insurance, please." A bus came past, throwing out a wave of slush, but she didn't move when it hit her jackboots, knew how to concentrate.

"Let's go in there," I said, "or we'll freeze."

She glanced at the steamed-up window of the restaurant, then at her watch, then back to me.

"Let me see your identity-card."

I showed it to her, the official one with the HUA insignia, and she gave me a closer look, dark eyes, pale skin, a hard straight mouth. "Very well, Captain."

The place was almost dark inside, either trying to look like a night-club or keep down the electricity bill. She put her briefcase onto a bench inside the door and zipped it open, her hands ungloved now, her movements deft. The other two women had been slower, less controlled. "Here is my licence. May I please see yours?"

We exchanged notes; one of her gloves dropped and I picked it up; she didn't thank me. The window shook as something big went past, and a man in a moth-eaten fur hat came in and slammed the door and banged his feet up and down to get the slush off; but I was more interested in the woman—First Lieutenant Lena Pabst, Werneuchen Airforce Base, thirty-two, status unmarried—and the way she wrote, quickly, vertically, the way she stood, straight, balanced, totally confident.

"Thank you, Comrade Captain."

"I haven't eaten since this morning," I told her. "Will you join me for a meal?"

I think I got the tone right: it wasn't an invitation, only a suggestion. We weren't so much a man and a woman as a secret-police captain and an air force lieutenant in a communist state; she'd pay her own bill when we left, if she decided to stay.

"Very well. I have time."

The other two had been more feminine, more relaxed, and neither of them had known anything about Moscow, hadn't particularly cared, and that was why I hadn't gone any further with them. This one was into a fairly sophisticated summary, halfway through the meal, of her thoughts on the future of Europe.

"It's impossible for Greater Germany to remain bifurcated for much longer, given the climate of world political thinking inside the Kremlin—given the undoubted genius of Gorbachev. And it's impossible to conceive of the new Germany following the corrupt and bourgeois system of the decadent West. The direction we shall be taking is obvious."

We hadn't ordered wine. *I'm driving. But when I get to my apartment I shall drink Underberg.* She hadn't said *when I get home.*

"Have you been in the West?"

"Only for a few days," she said, "to the other side."

"You were allowed to cross?"

She moved her head quickly to look at me. "A group of

us made a request to go there, for educational purposes. It was granted. There was no question of 'being allowed' to go.''

I'd made a slip and she'd picked it up at once; I was thinking like a Westerner and I'd have to watch it.

"And how did it strike you?"

"Have you been there, Comrade Captain?"

"My name's Kurt, as you know. May I call you Lena?"

It stopped everything dead and she glanced down, and when she looked up again her eyes had changed. I'd thrown a personal note into the relationship, and her reaction was the same as when I'd suggested we have a meal together, but stronger, and she held my eyes for a moment, watchful, engaged.

"Very well, you may call me Lena."

"Thank you. Yes, I've been into West Berlin."

In a moment, looking down again, her strong fingers toying with a crust, "I found it pathetic. I don't think it's important that people can drive up to a bank and do business without having to get out of their car. I don't need the choice of a dozen different brands of breakfast cereal, all of which contain fifty per cent of refined sugar. I need bread. Bread, food, work to do for the world. But the difference between the East and the West isn't really significant. The people wear much the same clothes, have children, go to the movies, drive cars. War springs from fear, not from the slight difference in ways of life, and while there are these two all-powerful nations pitched together on the same planet there's bound to be fear. We need one world, not of nations but of people, earthlings, living in harmony, working for the future, poised on the threshold of space, the ultimate adventure. To achieve that, a last war is necessary. My air base, Werneuchen—" she twisted in her chair to face me—"is in the front line of that war, and the thought excites me beyond all wôrds. *I am in the front line of the last war on earth, and when it's over I shall still be here to see the dawn of the new world. When I think of it in the night it's like an orgasm.''*

The dark eyes liquid suddenly, shimmering, the mouth parted and the tips of the sharp teeth touching together, the small face drawn into a rictus, fierce, vulpine, carnal.

"I can imagine," I said.

Third time lucky: I'd creased the rear ends of a Fiat and a VW last night and toyed with *schweinefleisch und sauerkraut* in two shifts and hadn't got anywhere, but this was the one I wanted, manic, obsessed and pro-Gorbachev.

"That surprised me." She was still twisted in her chair, watching me.

"What did?"

"My reference to orgasm."

"When feelings get intense enough, there's nowhere else they can finish up."

"You don't seem," she said, "the kind of man who lets his brakes fail."

Still watching me, her eyes dipping to my mouth, lifting to my eyes again.

"It didn't have to look like a pickup."

"But that isn't all it is."

"No."

The man in the moth-eaten fur hat had been sitting opposite, under the portraits of Lenin and Honecker; now he was leaving, shrugging into his coat. I'd been checking him, because he'd come in here soon after I had; but I was satisfied; he'd sat too close, and was known here, a regular. And Werneuchen Airforce Base was eighteen kilometres from Berlin and I'd driven here with enough feints and detours to arrive totally clean. That was essential. Back in Berlin I would have to leave myself open

again, but I was here to get information and I didn't want
to be disturbed.

"I'm not the type," she said, "that men want to pick
up."

"Most men are conservative."

In a moment, her eyes still on me, "I think we have a
lot in common. You're very disciplined. So am I."

"I don't take punishment. But I could give it."

"I'm more complicated," she said, "than that."

I looked for the boy in the apron. "Would you like
some more coffee?"

"No. I'm going now. Will you come with me?"

"Of course."

Underberg, black, bitter, gold-rimmed on the surface, the
German version of Fernet Branca, lighter but not much, in
a shot glass, scented, viscid.

Light came from slits in a shutter, blue light falling
across black leather, black silk, turning the smoke milky,
the tendril of smoke curling from the incense in the black
lacquer bowl. A single gold eye, fixed in the brow of a
mask on the wall, watched.

"There are these," she said, the blue light dwelling on
pale skin and the darkness of coarse hair, the shadows
sculpting the long lines of muscle.

Metal glinted, chased, knurled, cloisonné; the smell of
leather came into the air, underlying the sandalwood and
the emanations from her body.

"Where did you get them?"

"I collect them."

It wasn't an answer. Heat came in waves from a floor
unit, the thermostat cutting on and off.

"How did you get them through customs?"

"Are you serious? They were smuggled in from Poland."

Faintly, from inside the building, the voice of the guardian. Someone coming in late.

"Feel this," she said. "Feel it now."

The thermostat cut on, cut off. *Try this one, look how they made it. Have you ever seen such imagination?* There was no fierceness in her now, in this different aspect of her obsessiveness; she became loosened, languid, pliant. I wasn't uninterested; the libido is linked with the urgent needs of the psyche, not the body, and there were the same dark reaches in her that were in me, the same urge to go beyond the knowable. Here was the domain not of Eros but Thanatos, and this had nothing to do with the creation of life, but with the expression of the fear of death.

She masked herself and unmasked, during the night hours, revealing herself, her psyche, in a way that left her with a nakedness that seared the nerves.

I'm taking so much risk, she said again and again, and this was the nucleus of her innermost identity, the dark heart of the vortex: she talked of risk as she talked of love, and I had the thought, at some time before dawn, that in this brief exposition of her psyche she was expressing the same pathological drives that had goaded me into mission after mission, each time seeking the ultimate experience—a kiss from death.

She made coffee and we drank it in the first pooling of daylight that came through the shutters. She looked sated, drained, liberated.

"This brave new world of yours," I said, "isn't some kind of facade?"

"I know it seems contradictory, but no, it's all I live for. It's an intellectual concept, nothing to do with—what goes on underneath."

So I told her there was a major threat to General-

Secretary Gorbachev and that she could help to defuse it
by tunnelling immediately into the substructure of Werneuchen
Airforce Base and looking for any changes of plan in its
routine training operations during the next four days. I
gave her the number of my room at the hotel and told her
to use the code-name Renata.

11

MIRROR

12 noon: meeting with Yasolev.

I'm not absolutely sure, but at that time I think he was ready to cancel *Quickstep* and tell us to get out of Berlin.

"We wanted information." Standing with his feet placed solidly apart to balance him. "We now have information. We should act upon it." Thick square hands chopping at the air.

"It's not exactly information," Cone said quietly.

"It has been confirmed that the target is Gorbachev. Your department has alerted you to Werneuchen Luftwaffe Base and its bombers as a possible threat."

"It's just possibilities, Viktor, not information."

"In any case," I said, "I've got someone working for us at Werneuchen."

"Who?" His eyes sunk deep under their brows, defen-

sive, impatient. I believe he might have thought we were
trying to play down the few shreds we had to work with,
for our own reasons. Yasolev hadn't been trained to trust
people.

"One of the officers," I said, "in their administration."

"An agent-in-place?"

Cone looked down. I didn't answer. Yasolev tilted his
head, didn't persist. London and the KGB were working in
liaison for a single mission, and that didn't mean exposing
our networks. Nor was I going to blow "Renata."

"I can send *ten* agents into Werneuchen."

"We know." Cone, hunched forward, hands lost in his
pockets, watching Yasolev intently. "You can send fifty
in, and the whole of the personnel is going to close up like
crabs, and you—"

"Going to shut their mouths," I said, because Cone's
Russian was patchy and he'd meant clams—*molluski*—and
I didn't want any misunderstandings. Yasolev was tricky
enough to handle as it was.

"That's right," Cone said, "and you wouldn't get anything out of them."

Yasolev was quiet for a bit, looking anywhere but at us,
at the Wall through the window, at the tea-tray with its
cups still upside down, at the carpet with its cigarette-
burns and its worn threads. We hadn't poured any tea; we
didn't even sit down; the tension was keeping us on our
feet like puppets with their wires jammed.

"You know my responsibilities." Not chopping now;
motionless, sunk into obduracy. "The welfare of the
General-Secretary is in my hands. *My* hands."

"We think we all need him," I said, "or we wouldn't
be here. There's more at stake than your neck." I didn't
use those exact words, but that was the tone. But the stand
he was making wasn't entirely because he'd be shot at

dawn if anything happened to his General-Secretary; he was a KGB man and when the KGB wanted information they normally sent in a regiment and turned the building upside down and beat on the sides.

"You seriously believe that one agent can do as well as ten?"

"One whiff," Cone said, "of any KGB action inside Werneuchen and they'll shut their mouths and Horst Volper will immediately make an alternative plan. We've got to go very careful."

"Then I will send *one* of my agents in. *One.*"

"All right," Cone said quietly, "then we'll wrap up the mission and go home."

That surprised me. But we'd got less than four days left and Yasolev had called us in to do the job our way and that was how it would have to be done.

"That is putting the matter too *strongly*." Chopping at the air again, and I was glad my hand wasn't in the way. "We agreed to liaise with each other, on the understanding that—"

"Viktor." Cone's voice was as quiet as Shepley's. "If you won't stick to the rules, we're going home."

Yasolev swung his body to one side and then to the other like a trapped bear, and I had a flash of what he'd be like when he lost patience and gave the order for someone's destruction.

"You will not see my point of view."

"I see it very clearly," Cone said. "And I want you to see ours. You guaranteed that while the mission was running the KGB wouldn't interfere."

We waited.

"But you fail to understand the *weight* of my responsibilities. If—"

"You knew how heavy they were," Cone told him, "when you first approached London. Nothing's changed."

"But of *course* it has changed. The General-Secretary is now to make a *visit* here."

That was true and there was only one way out. "Do you think," I asked him, "there's any threat to the General-Secretary from Werneuchen Airforce Base?"

"But of course. Your department in London spoke of it. Isn't that so?"

"Yes. So the day before Gorbachev lands in Berlin you can send as many people as you like into Werneuchen and close the place down and ground all the bombers and lock up all the pilots. Your General-Secretary isn't at risk until his plane touches down here, so until then we want you to leave us alone."

1:15, lunch with Pollock at the Steingarten.

"It's just that I can't work up any interest in soccer. Can you?"

"Not really," I said.

"I don't imagine. Nothing like cricket, is there?" Spoken with passion. "I spend most of the winter replaying the Test on the VCR. Anytime you'd like to watch, give me a buzz."

"I'll do that."

At 2:15 I would walk into the street.

"But even with the videotapes it seems an awfully long time till May."

"May?"

"When the cricket season starts again."

"Ah, yes."

Walk into the street, if I could face it.

He'd told me he'd only got an hour for lunch, awfully sorry. "Miki's" visit had relegated all other business to the back burner. That was why I would walk into the street

at 2:15. And there wasn't any question, really, of not
facing it. They expected it of me: Shepley, Cone, Yasolev.
I expected it of myself.

"Losing your appetite?"

"I had rather a late breakfast."

"Ah."

I had asked Pollock to lunch because Horst Volper
would have stationed a permanent watch on him. So far I
hadn't found a tag on me when I'd left the hotel. So far the
safe-house near Spittelmarkt was unblown. Unless Cone or
Yasolev had been picked up, Pollock would unwittingly
provide Volper's cell with a potential contact with me, and
they'd go wherever he went. They would have come to the
Steingarten. They would be waiting outside.

It was beginning to feel hot in here, and this was
normal; in fact the place was underheated.

"Well, well." Looking at his watch. *"Tempus fugit."*

I got my wallet out but he put down a 1,000-mark note on
top of the bill. "Honoured guest of the Embassy." Clean
white smile, lowering his voice. "Not often we get anyone
out here with your kind of credentials."

I thanked him.

"Are they looking after you at the hotel?"

"No complaints, except for the view."

"Oh yes, you're at the front, aren't you? It's a bit
sinister, I know what you mean. I'm not really used to it
myself, yet, and I've been here three years. Kind of
presence, isn't it?"

"I'm rather relieved. I thought I was being oversensitive."

He got up and fetched his coat from the rack. "Oh no, it
gives most visitors the willies. I send quite a few of them
to that hotel, visiting artists, culture vultures. I've booked
Cat Baxter in there." Chasing the sleeve of his coat. I
helped him. "Thanks."

Rock star.

"When is she coming?"

"Tomorrow."

"She's bringing her group?"

"Yes. Got a concert scheduled, big one. God, I hope she's going to behave herself—she's worse than Vanessa Redgrave, except that Cat's thing is human rights. Share my cab?"

"I'm not going far."

Hoped it wasn't true. Hoped very *much* it wasn't true.

"Take care, then, and you know where your friends are if ever you need anything."

"Yes."

And where my enemies are.

Outside.

I found a telephone near the rest rooms. Cone answered at the second ring.

"For what it's worth," I told him, "Cat Baxter is bringing her rock group here tomorrow. The Embassy's putting them up at our hotel."

"Well, now."

"I suggest you tell London. How is Yasolev?"

"I don't know. He's across at the Soviet Embassy."

"Do you think he's breaking up under us?"

"I don't know. He's a very tough bloke, but he's got a very tough assignment. Thatcher and Reagan are one thing, but Gorbachev's turning half the world inside out and we don't want anyone to stop him. But that's my worry. You're still with Pollock?"

"He's just left here."

"The Steingarten?"

"Yes."

"And when are you leaving there?"

"Now."

"Immediate plans?"

One, two, three—"I'm going to see if I can get them interested."

He didn't answer right away. "You'll have support."

Not really.

I said: "Understood."

"I want you to keep in contact."

Said I would. What else could I say? If I made contact with him before this day's end it would simply mean I was still alive and had access to Horst Volper. If I didn't make contact he'd have to signal London: *Shadow down*.

I dropped the receiver back and walked through the lobby, big poster over the door—*Berlin, capital of the German Democratic Republic!*—they put it everywhere, on posters, book matches, hotel stationery, as if they might be having a little trouble getting people to believe it.

Swing doors, a woman behind me—*Danke schön, Bitte*—and out into the street.

Felt suddenly naked, vulnerable.

The afternoon's operation was simple enough. I was going to make myself conspicuous so that they could catch me in the open and try killing me off as they tried before and I was going to give them a chance because Volper was the target for *Quickstep* and we didn't know where to find him and the only way to do it was to meet with his people at close quarters and ask them questions. It hadn't worked very well with Skidder but this afternoon it might work better. But as I went down the steps onto the pavement and turned west along Dieckmann-strasse I felt so very vulnerable because they'd known I was in the Steingarten with Pollock and they could have got a hunting-rifle set up on a rooftop across the street and they could be lining up the reticule and putting pressure on the trigger spring *now*, and

the air felt supernaturally cold and my body felt strangely
light because whether you are very close to death or only
think you are very close to death the nervous system reacts
in precisely the same way: you go through a subtle shift in
reality and feel poised, floating.

Then it was over and the nerves steadied and the street
came back into focus and I went on walking, keeping up a
good pace, business to do, so forth, because one of the
things I had to do this afternoon was to make them believe
that I didn't know they were there.

Tewson.

He was one of Cone's people, a man I knew, and he
was fifty yards behind me on the other side of the street.

You'll have support.

Cone didn't use amateurs. He would have hand-picked
them as soon as he'd reached Berlin and he might even
have brought some of them with him or sent them ahead.
Yesterday it had taken me almost two hours to throw one
of them off before I could start out to Werneuchen. Today
it would be quicker. I'd made arrangements, because these
streets were strictly a red sector and I didn't want anyone
coming in to help me when I could be into a close hold
with one of Volper's men and getting the answers I wanted.

Tewson wasn't keeping to my pace; he wouldn't have to
shorten the distance before I reached a corner: there'd be
relay men, two, even three, somewhere ahead to take over
and pass me on.

This was all Cone could do. We'd chewed the whole
thing on the mat and he knew I was liable to go solo at any
minute and he could only try to follow Shepley's instructions. Viktor Yasolev had his heavy responsibilities but so
did Cone. He wouldn't be shot at dawn if he failed to
bring me home from *Quickstep* but he'd find sleep hard to
come by for a long time afterwards. He was one of the few

field directors—Ferris was another, and Bainbridge—who took a personal pride in protecting their executives, and he'd brought them home again and again, sometimes from last-ditch situations where other directors would have left them for dead and pulled out. This afternoon he'd try to make sure I was never alone, never without support, but I couldn't let that happen because when it came to the crunch I wanted a clear field to work in.

Charlotten-strasse and I turned the corner and walked north, a damp chill in the air, the river smell drifting through the streets from the Spree. I felt better now; the nerves had reacted to the fear of imminent death when I'd stepped into the street but the gooseflesh had gone by this time and I was walking steadily and the organism was gradually eliminating the excess adrenaline. *Not all of it.* I could need more, at any time.

The relay man was a hundred yards ahead of me on the other side. I couldn't see his face but I knew he'd be there somewhere and I picked him up fairly soon; if I hadn't been looking for him I could have missed him easily: he was using good mobile cover—other people—and had his back to me most of the time.

"How are things, Gunter?"

I got in and slammed the door and sat back straight away. There was a Mercedes SEL behind us and I didn't want to overlook *anything*.

The relay man was at the intersection of Charlotten-strasse and Franz-strasse by now and he'd seen me get into the cab and he was turned away from us and using his walkie-talkie, but there wasn't anything he could do unless Cone had put a vehicle into the field and that wasn't likely with a relay tag in operation.

"I was on time?"

"Yes." He wanted praise, and I should've thought of

that; in this trade we don't give it. "Exactly on time. Take a right and a left as fast as you legally can."

"Whatever you say."

Give me your wife's name and her sister's address, and by the end of the month I'll see she gets a permit to visit the cemetery on the other side.

He didn't think I'd give him a bill. I hadn't put it specifically but I'd given him to think I was what they called a live-body entrepreneur. Ever since the Wall had gone up there'd been a steady trade in people who needed to reach the other side; prices varied, and the cost of getting young people across was higher, their working-life and value to the German Democratic Republic making them expensive: in the region of twenty-five thousand US dollars. For this man's wife the price would normally be a quarter of that: she was middle-aged and a woman. But he didn't think I'd give him a bill because I'd told him there were things he could do for me.

"Get into Unter den Linden."

Nodded his head.

I wanted Unter den Linden because we'd have more room to manoeuvre. The Mercedes had been behind us when we'd pulled out from the kerb in Charlotten-strasse but that didn't mean anything. I didn't think it was Cone's because it was a four-door model and too big, too notice-able for a tracking vehicle and too expensive for the Bureau's economies. It could be Volper's, making a series of sweeping passes ever since I'd walked out of the Steingarten. It couldn't have shadowed Gunter from his apartment because I'd taken extreme care before I'd decided on it as a safe-house. The SEL could have more than one, more than two men in it. The object of their operation was to get onto my track and stay with me until they'd set up the kill and could trigger it but it didn't have to take all afternoon—they could pull into the next traffic lane at any time and come alongside and put out a burst of rapid fire. But I didn't expect that. The streets of East Berlin are well policed and the bleak, quiet atmosphere would deter anyone from calling attention.

And I was beginning to know Horst Volper's style. The first attempt at a kill had been carefully organised, and designed to look like a hit-and-run. He wouldn't start lashing out in a panic.

"Gunter. What kind of car have we got behind us?"

"A VW."

"And behind that? Don't move your head."

He let the cab drift a couple of feet to the left side and checked the mirror again.

"A Mercedes SEL."

"Find me a phone-box."

It took us another three blocks and he pulled into the kerb and waited for me while I got out and crossed the pavement to the telephone and called the Soviet Ambassador.

12
SHARK

"Liaison."

"How can I help you?"

"Is Major Yasolev still in the Embassy?"

"I will see."

It was only three o'clock but the rooftops were already losing definition. Dark would soon be coming down.

"Yasolev."

"Liaison."

"Yes?"

"Have you put a tag on me?"

"No."

The Mercedes had pulled into a space well ahead of us; I could only just see its rear number plate. Within that distance Gunter wouldn't be able to make a U-turn legally and there was no side street. All they had to do was wait, and if I didn't go back to the cab they'd simply deploy people on foot.

"Are you sure?" I asked Yasolev.

"Of course I am sure. We agreed."

"It's not that I don't trust you. I'm just checking."

"Where are you?"

"I'll be in touch," I said and rang off and went across the pavement and got in and saw the small black Audi reflected in a window on the other side. It had swung into Unter den Linden three blocks ago and I'd seen its image in windows at the first and third intersections. I thought it was best to leave it alone and blow the Mercedes.

"Gunter, that SEL is parked about seventy metres ahead of us on this side. When you go past it, put your foot down hard and take a right into Spandauer-strasse and then a left as fast as you can." He started the engine. "If the lights are against us at Spandauer, go when they change and then do whatever you think best to lose the Merc."

"Without doing anything the police—"

"Your own discretion."

"I could lose my licence, and it's my living."

"Absolutely at your own discretion. Just lose the Merc."

He got into gear.

It wouldn't be difficult.

They would let him do it.

Horst Volper knew more about me than I knew about him. He knew I was experienced: witness the Skidder incident. He knew London wouldn't send anyone out here who didn't know what a tag was, who didn't know how to get rid of it: they'd seen me lose Cone's man a few minutes ago. So I had to blow either the SEL or the Audi because that would be my level of street-craft and they'd expect me to conform. The Merc had been with us longer and it was more noticeable and it was slower on the gun than the Audi so this was the better one to go for.

And they'd let it happen because then I'd be lulled, satisfied that we were alone again. I wasn't expected to know about the Audi.

"Yes," Gunter said, "it's just—"

"All right. Turn your head and look at it when you go past and then give it the gun."

But the lights were red at Spandauer and we had to wait till they changed, but he'd gone through the motions and worked up a bit of tyre-squeal and when the green came on he jumped it by a fraction and took a right and two lefts and I told him to slow and take it easy: we'd lost the Merc.

The Audi was still with us.

"Put me down outside the U-bahn station at Alexander-platz. Have you had lunch yet?"

"I eat on the job."

"You did well."

I got out and went into the subway entrance, checking the environment as a precaution, simply as a precaution, looking as if I didn't expect tags now that the Mercedes was blown.

Two men got out of the Audi but I made sure to catch them only at the edge of the vision-sweep; then I went down the steps.

Chicken, I suppose.

I mean going down into the subway. Nerves.

All right, I'm not your bloody hero.

The subways in Europe are normally safe from killing attempts because they're confining and limiting in terms of freedom to get away. You can make the kill quite easily—I've done it twice, but only because I had to do it there or nowhere—but if there's going to be any noise or fuss you risk getting cut off from escape. I'd used my hands on both occasions, in total silence.

The U-bahns in East Berlin are safer places than most others in Europe; as safe as in Moscow. I didn't expect an attack at Alexanderplatz; all I wanted to do was make sure they were still on my track and begin the major work of the afternoon. This was to make it seem that I had a rendezvous to keep, that I realised they were still in the environment and that I couldn't make the rendezvous until I'd thrown them off.

This meant using a phone at intervals, to give the impression that I was having to shift the rendezvous in timing and location because I wasn't alone and mustn't expose the contact. The entire operation for an agent's enticing the opposition to make an attack in the hope of securing one of them for interrogation is in the books at Norfolk but I don't know anyone who's carried it through; the risk factor is exorbitantly high and a director in the field would never ask his executive to do it, because it'd be like giving him a loaded revolver with five rounds in the cylinder and asking him to play Russian roulette.

Sitting with my tea in this sleazy cafe scared to death.

I'd got on a train and got off again at Schilling-strasse and here I was and here they were, one of them at a table across by the door and I couldn't help that because I hadn't wanted to sit there myself: it was too exposed. The other man was in a corner as far from the door as possible, so that I couldn't keep both of them in sight at the same time, which is good close-surveillance practice and very effective.

Scared to death because I hadn't *wanted* to mount this operation and I'd done it reluctantly and you don't do anything reluctantly in hot blood and it's infinitely worse for the nerves. I knew that Shepley was pushing the Bureau to the limits trying to locate Horst Volper and I knew that Yasolev and his cell were doing the same, and at any time they could come up with some kind of access for me that would take me off the street and put me into a new direction. But they hadn't found anything and all I could do was sit here in this bloody place and hope these two would try an attack so that I could nail one or both of them and wring some information out of them, sit here and hope at the same time that they'd decide *not* to attack because it could easily go their way instead of mine and they could walk out of here a minute from now or an hour from now and leave me curled up in the cleaner's closet or one of the cubicles in the lav with my head on my chest and my eyes looking at nothing, nothing at all, while the blood—oh Jesus *Christ* this is the trade you're in and this is the way you want to play it so don't bloody well whine.

Got a bun.

Went and got a bun from the filthy cracked marble counter and paid for it, a huge woman, shut-faced, her eyes already mourning a lost future. I sat down again and started on the thing though I wasn't hungry—I needed fifteen more minutes in here and it was something to do, but at least I'd got a glimpse of him, the one by the door, in the mirror behind the counter, and that was a plus because it could be very important indeed if later the same man—*if I got out of here*—the same man came close to me in a crowd; I'd be able to recognize him and get a chance of jumping the gun.

But let's not talk about guns. Right—I never draw one when I'm going through Clearance because they can be dangerous: it's not just professional caprice. Carrying one of those things can make people nervous and they'll pay you a lot more attention and try for an overkill before you can do any useful work; but let them know you're unarmed and in their opinion harmless and they'll come up quite close and then you can go in with the hands and do a very great deal more damage than a bit of hot copper because you can be selective, picking on the right nerve for the job, producing paralysis or producing pain, the intense pain that's guaranteed to cool them off and get some answers out of them.

But it's like seat belts: they're effective eighty per cent of the time and for the other twenty per cent you're on your own. One of these people could pull something out and use it from where he was sitting, dropping me like a bird off a bough. The risks are calculated, and they're the only kind I ever take.

The one in the corner had gone to the phone when he'd come in here and that was why they weren't making a move. One of two things was on the programme: he'd got instructions to wait here until I left and keep up the tag, or he'd asked for someone else to get here very fast indeed because they had me set up and were ready for the kill.

It really was a bloody awful bun. This was East Berlin, not West, none of your delicate millefeuilles or rhum babas, just this rotten lump of crud straight out of the granary, rat-shit and all.

At 3:16 I began looking at my watch. The time wasn't critical, not important; it was just that the chances of doing anything in here weren't very good. The situation was far too static: when the time came for me to move in on them it'd be when things were suddenly starting to go very fast, so that I could work with reactions and reflexes, find a totally unrehearsed opening and take it on the wing, because the only way you can work this particular operation is in hot blood and with the system full of adrenaline.

At 3:27 I got up and went over to the phone on the wall and dialled at random. The two tags hadn't been joined by anyone: the only people who'd come in here in the last eleven minutes were two women and a man with one arm.

Ringing-tone. Five, six, seven. Not at home.

"I can't be there at the time we agreed on."

Waited.

"I know, Heinrich. I'm sorry. I'll call you again as soon as I can."

I put the phone back and said *auf Wiedersehen* to the big fat woman and walked out of the cafe and turned left without hesitation and had to go half a mile before a bus slowed at a stop and some people got off and it pulled out again and I kept on walking until the rear doorway was abreast of me and I ran flat out and just made it.

"You shouldn't do that!"

Verboten, so forth.

Pitching a bit as the thing changed gear.

"I could have you arrested!"

Abuse of petty authority; it was all the rage because these poor bastards *had* no authority, by grace of their Soviet overlords.

"Have a heart, comrade, my wife's ill and I've got to get home."

But I could have got myself killed, peaked cap and a righteous glare, and then I wouldn't have got home at all, would I, so forth.

Paid the fare and took a seat and used the windows and saw the four-door 230 keeping station at a circumspect fifty metres behind. It had been standing near the cafe in support of the two tags and they'd either climbed in before it moved off or they hadn't; it made no difference: Volper would have a dozen men in the field.

"Is it the flu?"

"What?"

"Your wife."

"Yes."

"It's going around. Plenty of rest."

"That's right."

There was a chance that they'd try driving me into a corner somewhere and make a snatch instead of a killing. Not a big chance but I couldn't ignore it. I'd come out from London and I'd been holed up with Cone and Yasolev and we'd been in signals and Volper might decide I'd be worth snatching first and grilling before he had me put out of the way. It didn't worry me too much at this stage; they wouldn't find it easy and if I got it wrong then I had the capsule and I wouldn't think twice because there was enough information on the Bureau inside my head to blow it clean out of the European intelligence community.

I got out at Strausberger-platz and walked as far as Blumen-strasse and *they came very close* and I felt the air-rush and bounced off the side panel of the front fender and went spinning across the sidewalk while the tyres squealed and someone caught me before I could go pitching down, the rooftops reeling across the vision-field and the stink of exhaust gas and the terrible fear that they'd stop and get out and finish me off, catch me while I was off balance and unprepared.

"Are you all right?"

Said I was, trying to get focus back, trying to get ready in case they stopped and came for me.

"He must have been drunk!"

Eyes watching me, full of concern, hands on my arms in case I fell.

"Yes. Must've been."

"Are you hurt anywhere?"

"No. I'm—"

"You were lucky."

"Yes. I'm all right now. Thank you. Good of you."

"Do you want to sit down somewhere?"

"No. No, thank you."

And at a deeper level of consciousness below the polite exchange the creeping of dread, because it had been extremely close and yes indeed I'd been lucky and if they'd come an inch or two nearer they'd have spun me round with a smashed spine and left me face-down on the pavement with my arms flung out, *finis,* the unfortunate victim of a dastardly hit-and-run accident involving a black Mercedes for which the police are now searching assiduously, so forth, and a signal to London, *Shadow down.*

"Well, I'll be on my way."

"What? Yes. Yes, very kind, thank you."

The creeping of dread because however much you're aware that you're *inviting* attack, however carefully you're playing it by the book, the shock of a close call reminds the psyche that its death is sought, its extermination, eagerly sought; and there's something horribly personal in this, horribly intimate, and it reaches down into the secret confines of the personality and plunders it, and leaves its effect, which can finally be devastating. It's this feeling that brings a man back from a mission with a shut face and slow speech as he sits in one of those small stuffy rooms with his operations director and signs his name on the form, *Request no further action in the field.*

Walking on, bumping into someone—*verzeihen Sie*—then finding equilibrium again, walking past the line at a bus stop at 4:15 in the afternoon with the dark down and the tops of the buildings lost in a creeping fog.

It had been like a shark.

More people in the streets now, the traffic bunching at the lights. Another hour and work would be over.

Like a shark, that thing.

Yes, like a shark, shuddup. The end of the working-day

would be over and they could get into their coats and line up for the buses and the trams and the trains and go home.

With its jaws open when it came past.

Oh for the sake of Jesus Christ shuddup, it's over now and we're still alive, it's not the first time you've come close to blowing it. Stamping their feet at the bus stop, breath like steam, going home, sweet home, with all the evening in front of them, a nice hot dish of sauerkraut and spuds, or would you like to see a movie tonight?

4:20 in the afternoon and this one man moving among all the others, not of them, not of their company but isolated, an outcast, threading his clandestine way through the city on his own surreptitious purposes, while the Mercedes turned again at the Andreas-strasse intersection and started a loop for the second time, and the man in the black wool coat and scarf kept pace on the other side.

I would like to see a movie, yes. I would like to see a movie very much.

Walking a little quicker now; the scenario required it: I still had a rendezvous to keep and I still had to throw off the surveillance before I could keep it.

Waited ten minutes for a bus and got on and saw the Mercedes three vehicles behind and the black Lancia parked near the U-bahnhof with its engine running: I could see the exhaust gas.

This at least I knew now: they wouldn't try for a snatch in the hope of grilling me. They were here for a kill of whatever kind—at close quarters or with a hit-and-run attack or a premeditated set-up involving precision. The shark thing had just been impulsive, but it proved their intention: death in the afternoon.

At 4:38 I got onto a train at Ost-Banhof and took it as far as Ostkreuz, with one of the men who'd been in the cafe getting on soon after me and sitting with his back turned at the end of the compartment, facing a glazed poster with useful reflection. Back in the street at Ostkreuz I walked south along Markgrafendamm with the same man behind me and a BMW cruising in from a side street: the people on foot would have been using their radios but there hadn't been time for the Mercedes or the Lancia to get here—they wouldn't have known where I was until I got off the train and they had the signal. They'd brought in the BMW from somewhere closer; it had pulled into the traffic twice and stopped twice, keeping its distance.

At Stralauer Allee I went into a cafe and used the phone. Steamy windows and the smell of stale cigarette-smoke and a litter of crumbs and slops on the plastic tables, two cab-drivers with a jug of coffee and a sandwich from the machine, a man in the corner, possibly a tag, his attitude too casual, a man coming in, certainly a tag, the one who'd been on the train.

"Hello?"

"I still can't throw them off."

"What? This is Frau Hauffman."

"All I can do is phone you when there's a chance."

"Who are you, please?"

"Don't leave the phone; I'll call you again soon."

I believe you have the wrong number, so forth; neither of them moved when I walked out of the cafe into the Allee and across to Elsen-strasse and the bridge.

The feeling of dread persisting, haunting the nerves, the bruise on the hip a reminder of how close they'd come, how close they would come again.

The traffic across the bridge was light; there was no one walking: it was too cold. Below the balustrade the black waters of the river glittered from bank to bank with the lights of the city, and the air was freezing here, in the open away from the buildings. I walked steadily, meaning to go

as far as Puschkin-allee and then make a loop and turn back
on my tracks and make a run for it, a very fast run that
might bring just one of them, only one of them close to me
where I could work on him; but they were getting impatient now and I could see three of them ahead of me at the
far end of the bridge and when I looked behind me there
were two more and the profile of the BMW gathering
speed and I felt the rush of adrenaline and the sour taste in
the mouth as the onset of fear triggered the organism as I
reached the middle of the bridge and they began shutting the
trap.

13

PICKPOCKET

Smell of burning flesh; it clung to my coat.

"Have you got anyone in the field?"

More police cars were going in to the bridge; I couldn't see them from here but I could hear their sirens.

"I did have."

Cone.

There was still the glow of the fire on the wall of the building opposite.

"Have you got anyone in the field *now*?"

I was furious.

"I can't say."

Bastard was stonewalling.

People standing outside the apartment block, staring in the direction of the bridge, the light of the flames on their faces.

"Look, I want an answer."

"I haven't got one."

The more you push Cone the harder he is to move. But then they're all like that, the directors in the field, because part of their job is to handle their executives when there's a flap on and they're halfway up the wall.

"Why not?"

"You got rid of one," he said quietly, "but there might be a few others in your zone. I can't say for sure unless one of them signals. What happened?"

"One of the tags got snatched."

"One of *their* tags?"

"Yes."

In a moment, "How close were you?"

"I was halfway across Elsenbridge and they got him at one end."

"Car?"

"Yes."

"Police car?"

"It could've been, yes, unmarked."

I hadn't seen anything close. The car had come past the BMW accelerating hard and then it had slowed to a halt by the three men and then there were two. The BMW had done a lot of wheelspin and got there in time but the other car had swung full-circle and hit the tail-end and sent it rolling, and that was when the tank had gone up.

"Was there any other action?"

I told him.

"Do you think they might've been going to rush you?"

"Possibly."

"Then what are you complaining about?"

"Oh for Christ's sake, you know the operation I'm doing and you know how it works. If—"

"I haven't got a vehicle of any kind," he said, "in the field."

"Then it must have been Yasolev."

"Not necessarily."

"Who else?"

The glow had gone from the building, and the people were going back into the apartments. But that awful smell was still on my coat, sickening me. I'd walked past the burning car on the other side of the bridge when the fire crews were working there, and the air had been heavy with smoke and fumes. One of them had been trapped inside, one of Volper's men.

"I don't know who else," I heard Cone saying, "but we've got a lot of interested parties, haven't we? The KGB, the HUA, and whatever other enemies Horst Volper might have in the field. We can trip over anyone at all in the day's work."

It sounded as if he were putting smoke out, covering tracks, steering me away from the subject. I didn't know Cone very well but it sounded like that.

"Look, I want you to see Yasolev. I can't talk to him direct because I haven't got time. There are three tags still with me and I'm going on trying."

One of them across at the intersection using a parked van for cover; two of them in the opposite direction, a little way along Puschkin-allee, one on each side of the street.

"What do you want me to tell him?"

Yasolev. "This is the thing: he could've decided to use me as a decoy to draw those people into the street, with the idea of snatching some of them. That's what might have happened just now on the bridge. The man they took is probably in an interrogation room now, being worked over. If that's what Yasolev is doing I want you to tell him he's cutting right across my operation and breaking our agreement. Tell him that we'll stay out here for just as long as he keeps his word and no longer."

An ambulance turned off the bridge and headed south from the intersection; it wasn't using its lights; there'd be only the burned corpse inside. I didn't know whose it was, who the man had been, but he was possibly one of the tags I'd seen before on foot, or one of the two who'd followed me into the cafe. Life was that short, this afternoon, and the work wasn't finished yet.

"Would it be that bad an idea?" Cone said.

"Using me as a decoy?"

"Yes."

"If all Yasolev wanted was a decoy he could've used any one of his peons, half a dozen at a time if they got wiped out."

"But they wouldn't, would they? They wouldn't have your status. Volper's afraid you might infiltrate his operation and destroy it, so he wants to get you first—it's that simple. So you're the only decoy worth sending his people out for."

"That's all I am, then? A fucking duck?"

"Now there speaks a proud man."

God *damn* his eyes.

"I like to think," I said, "that I've got more effective uses." But it didn't carry conviction because he was right: my professional pride was getting in the way.

"Look at it like this," Cone said quietly. "You didn't get much out of that man Skidder. I think Yasolev feels that one of his people could've got more. You stand a chance of nabbing one of those tags today and grilling him, but so does Yasolev, if his idea is to do it first, using you as the decoy. And I'm not sure you'd agree that the KGB doesn't know how to interrogate people."

Cold. By Christ it was *cold* standing here at this bloody telephone, the air coming in waves from the freezing river. But that wasn't the worst of it; the worst was the chill of horror creeping through the nerves—not horror, quite—revulsion; a feeling not coming from the brain-stem but the neo-cortex, philosophical, sophisticated, an awareness of the difference between driving *myself* to the brink of extinction on my own responsibility and being driven there by someone else, Yasolev, as a matter of cold-blooded expedience.

"You've got a point," I said, "but if that's what Yasolev is doing he should have put it to me first and asked for my approval instead of breaking our contract. Tell him that. Tell him my life's on the line and not his. And tell him that if he wants to use me as a pawn across the board he's got the wrong man and he'll have to get another one for *Quickstep*—if he can."

Silence for a while, except for scratchy background on the line. The tag on the other side of the intersection wasn't alone any more.

"Understood," Cone said at last. "But I've got a question. What are you going to do now?"

"Keep going. I've got them in the zone and there's still a chance of bringing one of them down."

"Keep in touch," he said and rang off.

It was past ten o'clock when they tried again.

Earlier, I was hungry, and had some potato soup in a place in Baum-Schulenweg farther down the river. Earlier, I was cold and afraid, and went into a library for warmth, to experience the feeling of air that didn't paralyse the face, and to experience the atmosphere of the social norm, wherein ordinary people sat reading books or the papers instead of seeing a movie, or instead of walking the streets from shadow to shadow, cold and afraid.

By ten o'clock I'd gone from Treptower Park to Konigsheide and north again to Baum-Schulenweg, waiting for

twenty minutes in a U-bahnhof and checking my watch,
making it seem that I was so desperate for the rendezvous
that I was taking risks, making three phone-calls and
speaking the correct lines from the scenario because an
efficiently-trained tag is taught to lip-read.

I still can't throw them off, so forth, *I'll make contact
when I can.*

And now I was in a crowd outside a bowling-alley,
huddling among the people for warmth and company and
the chance of a close encounter that could give me what I
wanted: information.

"I don't know," I said. "I think there's room for fifty
but they're short of bowls."

"Well I'm not surprised. They're always short of something." A man in a leather jacket ripped at the shoulder,
his hands dug into his pockets to keep them warm.

"They should either let us in or tell us how long we've
got to wait." A thin girl half-buried in her boy-friend's
arms, her nose raw from rubbing with a handkerchief.

Another bus stopped and people got off, some of them
joining us, blowing into their hands, jogging up and down
on the cold pavement.

"Can't get in?"

"They said they're short of equipment."

"Then why don't they—"

I didn't hear any more because someone had moved
against me and I brought an elbow down on that side and
paralysed his wrist but the knife had already gone in and I
could feel the warmth oozing under my clothes. Minimal
pain because the shock had brought the endorphins flooding to the site.

I hadn't expected a knife in a crowd because it'd be
difficult for anyone to get clear but he'd taken the chance
and we were still close together—he was in a half-crouch

because of the pain in the smashed wrist-bone and the knife was on the ground. He came up at me and I'd been waiting for it and I dropped him with a jab to the carotid nerve and he sank down again with his knees folding and I began easing my way out because there was no chance of getting him away for questioning—the others would be too close.

"What are you—"

"Pickpocket—he's a—"

"Is it a heart attack?"

"Tried to pick my pocket!"

"I think he's ill—"

"I'll get an ambulance—"

"Look, there's a knife—"

Everyone fussing and it kept them busy and I got to the edge of the crowd and kept walking, pain creeping into the nerves on my right side—he'd gone for the liver and it could have been penetrated for all I could tell because the effects wouldn't be immediate, just a feeling of violation for the moment, dark physical mischief: I never see action with a blade of any kind without thinking of Macbeth and his mad frenzied thrusts in the lamplit chamber because a knife is so very personal, so very intimate, a feeling of violation, then, as I walked to the corner and turned, keeping to shadow, a hand pressed to my right side, how sordid, if this were going to be the last of this lone ferret, a knife-wound received in a crowd outside a bowling-alley on a dirty winter night, felled by a chance hit and not even ready for it, *shadow down* and how ignobly, but what do you expect in this trade for Christ's sake, a volley of grapeshot as you stand with breast bared beneath the tattered banner at the barricades with time for the utterance of your famous last words?

In this game you get what you pay for and life's cheap.

Not oozing any more, or I wasn't aware of it, was perhaps getting used to it, the slow letting of blood. It was venous, not arterial, otherwise I'd have been soaked by now and weakening. I tried to walk as upright as I could because they might not have been near enough, the others, to know what had happened, but they'd catch on soon enough if I looked winged and then they'd make a rush to finish me off while I couldn't defend myself, though they'd be wrong there, my good friend, you will kindly refrain from composing my bloody epitaph while I'm still on my feet, and if you've ever tried chewing on a turkey's gizzard you'll know what I mean.

Narrower streets, these, running off Treptower Park, with the Wall half a mile away, less than that, a floodlit concrete dam strong in the night, strong enough to hold back the flow of humanity that would otherwise surge to meet its kind. If only someone would blast a hole in that bloody thing and let the world get on with its business, no one behind me when I turned a corner and looked back, *no one*, and that was a worry because there was no reason for them to leave my tracks; even if I'd gone for the throat instead of the carotid and dropped him to a quick death they wouldn't have gone near him: casualties were to be expected on this busy night.

A vacant lot with a big rubbish-bin against a rotting fence, and I moved into its shadow and sat on the frosty dirt and made a wad of my handkerchief and opened my coat and pulled up my sweater and put the wad over the wound in my side and held it there until it stuck to the blood; I wouldn't see much if I tried to look: a wound is a wound and if it looked big enough to need medical attention it'd have to wait in any case until this night's work was done.

I still couldn't see them anywhere near; in the sour light

from the street lamps here I would have picked out movement but there wasn't any. I was alone.

I was alone and one of two things must have happened: either I'd put too much power behind the half-fist when I'd gone for that man's carotid nerve and he'd never got up again and they'd decided that two dead in the field was enough, or Yasolev had ordered another of them snatched and they'd been called off, *which was exactly what I'd warned Cone could happen, Gott straffe them*, this was a *solo* operation and I didn't want any interference.

It was half-past ten and I moved from the shadow of the rubbish-bin and crossed the street and found cover at the corner of Richter-strasse and checked the environment *and it was blank*, still *blank*. But the light was tricky because at some time or other there'd been a spate of escape attempts in this area and I was within a couple of hundred yards of the Wall and the searchlight they'd installed there was sweeping the ground and flickering across the buildings and the gaps between them with the intermittent effect of a strobe.

There was a parking area with twenty or thirty vehicles in it, all of the same type standing in rows, the nearest one with a crest on it, *City of Berlin*, street maintenance department. I moved between them and then stopped and checked the environment for the last time to make certain.

Flying glass and I dropped flat.

14

RUN

Headlamp.

The spotlight swept the ground, the vehicles.

I didn't move, lay flat. I was in shadow.

The shot had gone into a headlamp close to where I'd been moving and there was blood on my face from the flying glass.

A rifle, nothing smaller; a long-distance shot that hadn't made any noise. He was using a silencer.

The tags had been called off and this was why. For the whole of the long afternoon they'd kept me in sight and waited for the right time and the right place, which was here, which was now. The two attempts to kill me had been made on impulse, a chance taken on the wing in the hope of an easy kill and the kudos it would bring. But this had been the predetermined operation and now it had begun.

The smell of oil as I lay with my face close to the ground over a patch of crankcase droppings. Very little sound; no traffic; there was no checkpoint here, nothing between Oberbaumbrucke to the north and Sonnenallee to the south. A wash of reflected light came from the concrete sweep of the Wall itself but the rotating beam was infinitely more intense and the shadows between the vehicles in the parking area were black in contrast.

It wouldn't have been a single attempt. He would run through a whole ammunition-belt if he had to. He wouldn't have to; it would be a question of time, of number, the number of shots required.

He'd be in no hurry; he had from now until dawn. But he wouldn't of course be alone; there'd be others in the environment, stationed strategically so that I couldn't make a headlong run for it and with luck survive. I couldn't see them from where I lay. All I could see were wheels to the right of this position, dark rounded blobs below the vehicle that sheltered me. On my left there were the others in orderly rows, parked for the night. More of them were ahead of me, and beyond them the lights of a street. Behind me there was another street but I was cut off from that; the sniper was in that direction, posted on a height of some sort, in the window of a building or on a fire-escape. He would be comfortable; he would take his time.

And I would take mine.

The air was perfectly still and very cold. Sounds would carry clearly when they came. There'd be no change in the light value unless traffic passed along the street behind me or the street on the far side; the glow of the Wall was constant and so was the intensity of the rotating beam. I suppose it was cheaper than putting up a whole battery of spotlights; and there was a sinister aspect to this constantly moving finger that brought everything it touched into fierce relief. Its purpose was to deter.

Yasolev's going to ask you how you'll be planning your access to Volper. Will you tell him?

Cone.

No.

Do you know?

Yes.

Are you prepared to tell me?

You wouldn't like it.

How much protection are you going to need?

None.

My job is to get you through Quickstep *with a whole skin. I'd rather you didn't make it difficult for me.*

Look, it's out of our hands. Put it this way: they went for Scarsdale and they got him. They thought it'd warn me off but it didn't, so now they'll go for me. And that's the only access we've got, and I'm going to use it. Don't worry, they won't be long.

That had been four days ago, and this night would be the last.

Impact and I jerked my head and listened to the ricochet as the shell ripped through the metalwork of the vehicle in front of me and skated across the ground under dying momentum. It was a heavy projectile, I would say from a carbine or magnum with anything up to twelve shots in the magazine and fitted with a high-magnification night scope and a silencer. It wouldn't be expected to drive a hole in a human skull; it would blow it apart.

There was no smell of the gun. It could be a quarter of a mile away. I closed my eyes and let the scene come in as it would look from the sniper's position: a rectangular area of flat tarmacadam dotted with dominoes, regularly spaced, with the shadows of the swinging light shifting constantly at precise intervals. And within this circumscribed pattern, a man.

A man for the moment motionless. To lie here until dawn was a temptation, to lie here and use the dark hours to review my life so as to leave it with a feeling of something accomplished, not a lot but something. But I would also have to review the mistakes I'd made, the instances of gross incompetence incurred by pride or too much faith in the self's abilities, and the unwitting betrayals, the lapses in manners, in loyalty, in the concession to mercy when its need cried out. And that, my good friend, could not be countenanced; it would not look well in the reckoning. Besides which, I wasn't going to give up after the first two shots, or after the first two hundred if he'd got that many. One must be true to one's principles, so forth, but the terror was on me and I could smell it as the cold sweat broke out: *it's not the thought of death that makes us afraid, you know,* it's the thought of dying, of reaching the point of no return, of being too late; everything in life has always been reversible, hasn't it, or tolerable, manageable— there's always been time left in which to put one's house in order, to clean up the worst of the mess and say you're sorry; and then suddenly we're caught in the headlights, frozen in mid-stride, and there's nowhere to go any more except *there,* into the unknown.

Finis.

Exactly, my good friend.

Impact and the breath came out of my body as if the shell had blown it out. But it hadn't; it had crashed into the side window of the vehicle where I was sheltering, and the fragments fluted through the air in a dying chorus of notes as the vehicle moved on its springs by a degree and was still again.

Amusing himself.

The rotating light swung, sending the shadows of the vehicles shifting from left to right in a circling crossword puzzle. He was amusing himself: I hadn't moved and he knew where I was but he couldn't reach this side of the vehicle unless he changed his position and he didn't want to do that; he was too comfortable, too well placed. So he'd fired another shot to keep his eye in, to keep his eye in and to put the fear of Christ in me because the impact of a shell that size in the silence of the night is enough to shatter the nerves.

I lay flat, relaxing, trying to shift into alpha waves if only for a few seconds because the sound of the bullet was still reverberating through the system. It hadn't been loud but it had been sudden, and had expressed appalling power, enough power to fell an ox on the hoof. Relax, and let the body sink against the cold tarmac, the cheek resting on the back of the hand, the nose filling with the crude, heavy reek of engine oil. In a moment I would have to move; all through the night I would have to move and go on moving if I could, if one of those shells—the fifth or the tenth or the fifteenth—didn't blow apart the delicate array of intelligence inside the skull.

Alpha, and the sense of letting go, of the slackening of the nerves to the point of ephemeral euphoria, until confidence came back like a lost friend and touched my hand; and then I moved, crawling over the ground and underneath the vehicle, finding the crankcase and wiping my hands across the underside and smearing the blackened oil on my face and the back of my hands, doing it carefully, attending to the eyelids and the lobes of the ears. I couldn't tell if it was going to be enough and I wouldn't be taking it for granted: I'd use more oil from the next vehicle if I ever reached it.

My suit and sweater were dark and my shoes black, but I took off my watch and pushed it into a pocket. Then I began crawling again, pulling my body forward across the ground, flat as a lizard, until I was lying in front of the vehicle on the blind side to the sniper's eye.

And waited.

I couldn't try to go back to the street behind me because it'd mean moving straight into his line of fire. There were buildings on each side of the vehicle park and they offered no shelter because they were fully exposed. The only place I could try to reach was the street in front of me more than a hundred yards away, and the only hope I had of doing it was by moving from the shelter of one vehicle to the next and using their moving shadows for visual cover as the rotating light swept the area. It amounted to a suicide run but there was no choice.

I began counting.

The first move was going to be the most difficult to make; not difficult in terms of timing and distance because the vehicles were in orderly rows and equally spaced, but difficult in terms of will power. Later there'd be the factor of familiarity as an aid, on the principle that the more you do something the easier it gets, but as I lay waiting I couldn't be certain that I wouldn't get halfway to the next vehicle and lose faith and stumble and go down and offer a motionless target that he'd see the moment the light swung across my prone body.

Counting. Three, four.

The light swung, spreading the black-and-white cross-word in front of me.

The only sound was of traffic to the north-east along Treptower Park. To the west there was the deep silence of the Wall, where nothing moved but the guards, who made no sound.

Five, six.

It had taken the light six seconds to sweep from this vehicle to the next and that was the amount of time I had available to make the crossing and it would have to be done at a fast run so I pulled my shoes off, reverting to the primitive animal in order to deal with this primitive situation: the need to survive. Without shoes I could run faster and although they were black they were polished leather and could pick up light, barely a glimmer but possibly all he'd need, the sniper, to pick me out of the dark.

Waiting.

The next vehicle wasn't immediately in front; there was one each side of the gap between them and I chose the one to the left because the right leg is stronger in the right-handed and it would give me extra thrust as I pushed off, by however small a degree.

Waiting.

The light swung, brightening the zone in front of me and then leaving it dark and I hadn't been ready, hadn't wanted to be ready: I needed the rhythm of the light's movement to establish itself in my mind.

Waiting as it swept *and then I took a breath and blocked it and went for it,* going through the sprint starting position and driving with my feet and plunging through the dark with the bright beam swinging towards me from the left and the area becoming deadly with each passing second as I ran, feeling the touch of the terror I'd known I'd feel because of the inexorability of that moving light, because of the knowledge that whatever happened it wouldn't stop, if I stumbled or lost my speed or veered too far to the left or lost my nerve it wouldn't stop, it would find me, flooding across the ground and drowning me in its glare and reaching the retina of the eye of the man who would fire the gun, *shadow down,* the terror alone driving me now, *run run run* with the adrenaline alone keeping me mobile, keeping me alive *but the shot came* and I heard the shell striking the tarmac on my right side, *run run run* as if

nothing had happened but there were chips of tar and stone
flying up as the light swept nearer, nearer, *faster* than I'd
believed it would as I ran headlong *and he fired again* and
the impact was closer and I'd heard the windrush of the
shell as it had flashed past my head on the left side, the
side where the light was coming, strengthening as it came,
filling the receptors at the edge of the vision field as the
darkness in front of me grew to a lightening grey as I *ran
ran ran* with the terror still with me, with the scalp crawling as the nerves waited for the hit, for the bursting open
of the skull as the last thought sprang there—*over now*—
flashing across the synapses before it was blown into
oblivion.

Dive.

Dive as the light came flooding and my hands went
forward to break the fall and I dropped flat in the shadow
of the vehicle and the next shot smashed into the bodywork with a scream of metal against metal and I lay with
my face on my spread hands and my breath coming in
shock waves from the lungs, letting my eyes close and
feeling the inevitability of the next shot.

It didn't come.

Rest, rest now. It's over for a time.

Immediate plans?

Cone.

I'm going to see if I can get them interested.

The ground cold under my hot body, grit under my
hands, the smell of oil, the smell of rubber, nothing natural here in this civic hunting-ground, no tree, no leaf,
nothing but hard surfaces and the inhospitable furnishings
of stone and metal and concrete, the habitat of man.

Holding his fire.

I don't suppose for a moment he'd run short of ammu-
nition: there'd been planning done. They may not have

known I'd head in this direction, though I'd been moving
south from the cafe, east and then south; but they'd assumed I'd reach some area where I'd be trapped and
couldn't get out again. This site wasn't ideal because of
the light's movement but at least I was cut off from the
street behind me and on both sides by the buildings, and
the man with the gun could bring me down before I could
find effective cover and make an escape.

Light washing across the ground where I lay but unable
to reach me, the vehicle above my head and its shadow
shifting from right to left as the light swung left to right.

Get them interested, yes. Signal to London: *The executive has managed to get the interest of the opposition,
which was his intention.* Brief report on success; interim
objective achieved, so forth.

Not really.

More realistically: *Doubts as to the executive's survival
for more than another ten minutes are such that I advise
replacement if possible or termination of mission.*

Alas, poor Yasolev.

Move. Move now. We've got to do it again.

Silent night, unholy night, with only the faint sound of
the late traffic along Treptow and the harsh sawing of my
breath as the organism drew in oxygen for the muscles. I
wasn't ready yet. I would wait.

Or termination of mission, yes, with Holmes over there
in the signals room getting some more coffee with his eyes
on no one because the news wasn't good on the board for
Quickstep, not terribly good. *Where's Mr Shepley?* Pick
up a phone. *You think we should get him?* The last signal
on the board: *Executive attempting to trap opposition agent
and interrogate.* Or words to that effect; I couldn't be at
all sure, not knowing Cone enough to get into his mind.
He might have been talking to Yasolev the whole evening

for all I knew. *I'm sorry, but my agent has virtually gone to ground and thrown off my support people and at the moment I don't know where he is, though I do know he's in danger,* so forth. They could be in signals with London in the hope that somewhere they could find a shadow willing to work with Yasolev, someone Yasolev could approve of.

Or Cone might be tougher than I knew, with enough nervous stamina to go on working with an executive who had so far run wild at every turn and deliberately gone solo. Anything was possible; even that Shepley *knew* I'd have to work like this and had told Cone to put up token protests but let me run and put smoke out if I needed it or get me to a hospital if I needed it, just keep *Quickstep* running and by the millionth chance bring it home and bring me home with it.

Academic, yes: this is entirely academic, my good friend, you're absolutely right. Thing is to move on, isn't it, put up a show, go out with the blood hot and one small ray of hope shining in the night before the winds of chance blow it away.

Move, then. It is necessary.

Count-down: six, five, four as the light came sweeping from the left. I let its rhythm move into my mind again on the subconscious level while I reached up and wiped more oil from the crankcase and smeared it over my face and hands again, *this stuff stinks,* but only because the stomach is queasy, only because you'd rather smell roses, wouldn't you, in your last few minutes on earth.

Three, two, one.

Crawl forward, crouch in front of the vehicle, wait. Its shadow had begun darkening on the right as the searchlight flooded the buildings on the left of the car park and then reached the ground, sweeping towards me. *Wait.* Sweeping nearer, creating shadows to the right of the vehicles in front of me, brightening their bodywork, reflecting from the windows. Sweeping nearer—*starting position*—nearer, flooding over the vehicles and moving on—*go for it*.

Chasing the light, lost in the darkness it was leaving behind it—*flat out you've got three more seconds*—the scalp crawling on the right side, the side where the shell would come if I faltered, stumbled, fell—*run run run*—the light from the next beam coming behind me and catching up, catching up fast as I *ran ran ran* and pitched headlong into the shadow of the next vehicle in the row ahead, lie flat, lie flat, do nothing, a sheet of light spreading across the ground and then flooding the vehicle as I shut my eyes and rested, the heart-beat thudding inside the rib-cage and the breath sawing, the nerves sending a cascade of coloured light across the retinae until the tension slowly came off and the organism started returning to normal.

Light dying away.

Ten minutes. I would give it ten more minutes before I moved again. There was no hurry, though the dog might make a difference.

There'd been no shot this time; either he hadn't seen me or he was letting me run, toying with me, certain I could never make the next two rows of vehicles and reach the street. He could be giving me respite, giving me hope, playing on the nerves—a sniper would be liable to do that; they're a special breed, cold-blooded, subtle and meticulous, their egos geared to the intricate and finely-balanced mechanism of the guns they use.

"Aus mit dich!"

I hadn't seen it because my eyes were shut; I'd heard it snuffling, and when I'd looked up it had been coming through the gap between the next two vehicles ahead. I'd kept absolutely still but it had scented me: that was what it was doing here. It was a Doberman, big but not yet mature, and it was standing within three feet of me, watching.

"Weggehen!"

It didn't take much notice, just drew back a bit, the metal tag on its collar jingling. And went on watching me. I could feel the hairs on my arms and hands flattening again after the shock: when I'd seen that bloody thing I'd thought they were sending in dogs to flush me out of here, but this wasn't trained; it had broken its lead and was wandering.

The light came sweeping again and the dog turned its head and watched it, puzzled, because lights don't normally move; but it didn't look substantial enough for it to chase or try to catch. Its eyes became jewels as the light passed over them; then it was dark again.

"Aus mit dich!" I slapped the underside of the crankcase and this time it took some notice and when the next beam came past, the dog was halfway between this vehicle and the next, looking back at me and wondering why I'd told it to go away instead of being friends, and then it spun sideways and leapt once and hit the ground with blood spilling under the bright sweeping light and I thought *you bastard, oh you bastard*.

I knew him now. He was a sadist. There'd been a choice for him to make: the dog could have been useful to him; it had already shown him which vehicle I was using for cover and it could have gone on following me whenever I made a move, and that would have been tempting to a professional marksman, a technician—an ideal situation, with a dog to keep track of his quarry. But he'd made the other choice, of terrorising the quarry itself by showing me what it would be like when the last shot came and I spun and leapt and hit the ground with my blood spilling under the light, just like that.

Bastard.

Not because of what he'd done to me but because he'd taken a dog's life to do it: *that* was obscene.

Ten minutes, then, another ten minutes and I'd give him his chance, because there was no option. If I had to go then I'd go the way of the dog and at least have company.

Rest, relax, await the moment. It would be of my own choosing: I would move when I decided to move. If he took—

Voice.

It came from the left. I thought I'd heard it before but decided it had been someone in the street on the far side; this time it'd come more clearly from the left, and now there was the faint crackle of squelch. It was a man with a walkie-talkie and he was stationed over there and reporting his position—there couldn't be any other answer. The sniper had sent beaters in, at least one but more probably two, the other positioned on the right. They could be armed but I doubted it; East Berlin is efficiently policed and the penalty for bearing weapons is imprisonment.

It could be that the sniper hadn't expected me to make two moves and get away with it, and now he was worried because there were only two more rows of vehicles between here and the street, where there were lights and traffic and people, giving me ample cover and a first-class chance of escape. I suppose it should have encouraged me a bit but of course it didn't: he'd seen the danger and had dealt with it.

Five minutes.

But there was a new factor coming into play that I didn't want to think about. In front of me there were still two more rows of vehicles and I could reach the first row in darkness between the beams of light, unless the beaters caught a glimpse of me and signalled my run to the sniper; but if I reached cover alive there wouldn't be another move to make, because I knew approximately where the sniper was and from his position the front row of vehicles would be silhouetted against the lights of the street.

Two minutes.

And even if I could reach the front row it would be a dead end because beyond it was open ground and *I* would be a silhouette if I tried a final run.

One minute.

So there wasn't a great deal of point in going forward again. They'd set up an execution and there was only one man in the firing squad and he didn't have the dummy round in the gun. But the only alternative was to stay here and let them come for me sooner or later, taking their time, and I'd rather go the way of the dog, running flat out for dear life, than have them come and find me lying on my back underneath a bloody street-maintenance vehicle with nothing left to do but bare my neck.

Then go for it.

The light came sweeping and I waited till the dark came down and then got into motion with all the force I had in me and I was halfway there when a shell ripped the left sleeve at the shoulder and smashed into the rear window of the vehicle and shattered the glass as I kept running with the light nearing from the left and he fired again and the shell hit the rear of the same vehicle but lower down and pierced the fuel-tank and brought the reek of petrol into the air as I dived for cover. The third shot made impact at a flat angle and tore metal away from the side of the vehicle and I heard the shell ricochet and hit the ground and bounce and rattle against the vehicle ahead.

Lie flat and rest, let the shock expend itself in the

organism. Relax, let go, hands and face against the gritty tarmac, the heart thundering in the chest and the sunburst of colours fading from the nerves in the retinae, relax, we did well, we survived and here we are.

Here we are at last, at the dead end of the run.

Rest, relax, don't think about it. There must be something we can do; it can't be over.

Wrong. Because when I opened my eyes and studied the environment I saw the situation was exactly as I'd thought it would be when I reached here. From the sniper's viewpoint the last row of vehicles would be silhouetted against the lights of the street beyond and if I made a final run he'd take his time and check the aim and put the first shot into my spine.

A rose for Moira.

The light sweeping, flooding the ground and passing on, leaving the dark. Nothing has changed. You knew there was no real chance when you realised they'd trapped you here on this killing-ground. Nothing has changed, but when you feel ready then make your final run, just as a gesture, and die like a man.

Correction, yes.

Like a dog.

15

TRUMPETER

God knows what it was: something soft.

The only light in here was from the flames.

Soft and pliable, possibly a dead cat, though a dead cat would be stiffer than this. I raked lower, and found an empty box and some banana peel and a paper bag with something in it, though I didn't want to know what.

The light of the flames was coming across the top of the open bin and I tried to see things by it, but it wasn't easy, here among the rotting detritus of man. I was looking for rope, ideally, a piece of rope, or failing that, some wire, or even string if it were strong enough; it wouldn't have to last very long.

Be it known that the bearer is in the private service of Her Majesty the Queen, and shall be permitted free pas-

sage and certain privileges on demand, wherever her dominion shall extend.

Stink of fish as I dug deeper and found bones and a beer can, the bearer, being in the private service of Her Majesty, assiduously pursuing his duties, though it be in this bloody hole where *no one,* may they catch the pox, has left any rope. No point, you might well think, in flashing my *laissez-passer* and demanding certain privileges, since Her Majesty's dominion doesn't extend as far as the trash bins in the German Democratic Republic.

I reached for his throat and felt the pulse. I'd put my watch on again but I couldn't see it in this light and in any case you don't need a watch to tell you if a man's pulse is approximately normal. This one's was steady, perhaps a fraction slow. I'd put him out five minutes ago and he was probably still well under. He was one of the beaters.

Something long and thin and—bicycle tube, yes, and some rotten fruit by the feel of it, black market and an exchange of hard currency under the counter, and a wire coat-hanger—*that* would do. I hooked it over the edge of the bin and went on digging. It was ten or fifteen minutes before I found all I wanted, and the flames had died away. It had been a night for bonfires, you may have noticed.

There'd been quite a lot of petrol on the ground when I'd got my lighter out and it had made a sheet of flame before the whole tank went up and by that time I was diving for the vehicle in front and there'd been no shot: I think he was surprised by the explosion and couldn't bring the gun into the aim in time to drop me.

There were several bits of rope and I joined two or three and found another coat-hanger and untwisted the hook and got his wrists behind him and his feet together; then I forced his mouth open and stuffed some rag in and bound it with the rest of the rope.

I'd waited till the fire crews were milling around and then I'd gone for the buildings on the left and found him still there with his walkie-talkie and he wasn't carrying a gun. This stinking bin was farther along the wall and I'd had to drag him there because he'd tried to resist and that was when I'd put him under.

Got the worst of the oil off my face and then I took a look from the top of the bin. The fire crews were starting to roll their hoses but there were a lot of people in the area and I dropped onto the ground on the side facing the wall and kept in its shadow. His shoes were tight but better than bare feet; I didn't want anyone asking questions. From the sniper's viewpoint it must have looked as if I'd gone up in flames because there'd been a fifty-foot jet when the tank had burst and the two nearest vehicles had taken fire and their tanks had gone up too; but there could still be some of Volper's people in the environment and I wouldn't be taking any chances I could avoid.

The nearest phone-box was half a block away and I wanted to run there but it would have called attention.

"Gunter?"

"Yes."

"I want you to pick me up on the corner of Becker-strasse and the municipal vehicle park in Treptow. Do you know where that is?"

"I can find it." He asked me for the nearest cross-street and I told him and rang off and dialed again and Cone answered before the fifth ring.

"Look," I told him, "I'm bringing a prisoner in."

"Where are you?"

"Treptow. But I can't bring him into the hotel: we look too messy."

He told me there was a lock-up garage in Hausvogtei-platz and I noted the number.

"We should be there within the hour; it's the nearest I can say."

"I'll wait," he said.

It looked like a thieves' kitchen—concrete floor, bare brick walls, no window, a ceiling festooned with cobwebs, naked light-bulb hanging down from the middle, two drunken-looking chairs and a pile of cardboard boxes in the corner, stained from the rain that came in. But there was a phone rigged up, perched on a directory on the floor.

"You can have these back."

I threw them over to him but he didn't pick them up or even look at them. Cone had stuck him on one of the chairs and he was just sitting there with his head up and his eyes gazing at the wall like a bloody zombie.

Cone stood squinting at him for a minute, hands in his mac pockets, his scarecrow body hunched forward.

"We're going to leave him locked in here," he told me, "and then remote-control the bomb."

We were looking at the man in the chair. No reaction, so we went on speaking English; not that there was anything sensitive to say.

"I'll need some more clothes by the morning."

"I've brought some. You said you were messy. They're in the car."

"Thank God; these stink. And you'd better tell London they owe the municipal authorities of East Berlin three of their street-maintenance vehicles." The Bureau was punctilious about damage compensation during a mission.

"Are they total write-offs?"

"Burnt out."

"You've had a busy night."

"Been a long one. Started at lunch-time."

"What's your condition?"

"Active. But I'll have to look in at a hospital; someone stuck a knife in me, nothing dramatic."

"They ask too many questions," he said, "in the hospitals here. I'll get the doc along from the embassy when we get to the hotel. It'll wait till then?"

"The bleeding's stopped."

Cone nodded and looked at the man in the chair again and said in German: "Name?"

No reaction again. The man had come to in the cab but hadn't said anything. He looked fully conscious now but by the way he was holding his head up and staring straight in front of him he was the die-hard type, wouldn't even need a capsule, you'd have to break him and even then you'd get nothing.

Cone went closer to him and stood looking down for a minute; then without taking his hands out of his mac he went into a crouch and stared straight back into the man's eyes.

"What is your name?"

His tone quiet enough to chill. It reminded me that I didn't know much about Cone; he could have a reputation for strangling mice for kicks, like Ferris.

"Dietrich."

"I want you to tell me something, Dietrich. Where is Horst Volper?"

Nothing.

"The British government will guarantee your safety, Dietrich. We'll get you out of East Germany with official sanction from the Democratic Republic, and find a job for you. If you've got a family, you can take them with you. Now, where is Horst Volper?"

Nothing.

"Then give me a yes or no. Will you answer *any* questions?"

"No."

"All right, here's another 'yes or no' for you. Is there anything that would induce you to answer my questions? Money? Information that we wouldn't mind exchanging? Anything at all?"

"No."

"When I say money, I'm talking about one million pounds sterling."

"No."

"I see." Cone straightened up and took a turn and came back to the man in the chair. "The East German secret police snatched another of your people tonight. He didn't want to answer questions either. He's in an intensive care unit at the moment, and everything's being done for him, but he's not expected to live."

I didn't know if it was true, but if Yasolev had ordered that snatch he would have done it through Karl Bruger. *It is essential,* he'd told me at our meeting in the woods, *that the HUA is not informed that my department is operating in East Berlin on this particular case.* Bruger alone had his trust.

"We need you to answer questions," Cone was saying, "just as we needed the other man to answer questions. If you won't do it for me, I'm not going to hand you over to the HUA. I'm going to put you into an interrogation room with an officer of the KGB."

Got a flinch. Just a slight one. It's always like that over here: you can threaten a man with an intensive care unit and he won't necessarily break, but mention the KGB and you'll make an impression.

Understandable.

"So will you answer my questions," Cone said, "or his?"

He waited.

God it was cold in here.

"Yes or no?" Cone asked him.

"No."

"I see."

Cone went over to the phone, then turned to me before he picked it up. "This might take a little time. Do you want running to the hotel right away?" Squinting steadily; I suppose I looked tired.

"No." I might be able to help.

He picked up the phone and dialled.

I thought of going out to the car and getting into some clothes that didn't stink of fish but I didn't want to miss anything; I'd been to a lot of trouble getting Dietrich here and Cone might get just *one* clue out of him that could push *Quickstep* forward. Time was running out.

"Good evening," Cone said in Russian; he didn't give the parole because Dietrich was listening. "We've got one of Volper's people here and he doesn't want to say anything. I've told him you're ready to interrogate him, so I think you'd better come and pick him up. You know where we are."

I was watching Dietrich. He must have known a bit of Russian because the blood was leaving his face. Cone wasn't messing about, I knew that. We needed answers.

The Bureau's ruling on interrogation is perfectly clear: no director or executive in the field is to force any opponent to talk, other than by verbal means. With Skidder it had been different, a case of dog eat dog. I've been inside Lubyanka, locked in an interrogation room with a major of the KGB, and it wasn't nice; but as I watched the man in the chair I didn't feel any compassion for him. He'd tried to get me killed tonight, and if you think I was taking things too personally I don't give a damn, it was my life on the line, not yours.

When we heard a car stopping outside, Cone went over to the man in the chair again. "Before he comes in here, Dietrich, I'm going to tell you that he's a colonel in the KGB, highly experienced and effective as an interrogator, and with a reputation for being completely ruthless when people don't want to talk. I happen to be a different type myself and I'd like to save you a lot of misery, so if you want to answer questions now, I'm listening."

For a second or two there was nothing but fear in the man's eyes; then they changed, as he got the better of it. "I appreciate your offer, but this time he will not succeed."

Cone gave a brief nod. "It's your life," he said, and went to unlock the door.

Yasolev came in alone, and took in the scene immediately, staring at the man in the chair for a moment and then giving us a nod.

"He still refuses to speak?"

"Yes."

"You have searched him?"

"Yes."

"There was no capsule?"

"Just a knife."

"Where is the knife?"

Cone gave it to him.

"Thank you." He looked at me and asked formally, "Will you place your prisoner in my hands?"

"I will."

"Then you may leave him with me. Stay if you wish, of course, but—" he left it.

"I think we'll be off now," Cone said, and we went out to the car, and as I heard Yasolev locking the door of the garage the shivering began, partly because man's inhumanity to man during the interrogation process always worries me and partly because of delayed shock after the car-park thing: I'd been expecting it.

"Are you all right?" Cone asked me.

"It's so bloody cold."

"We'll get you into a nice hot bath."

"There's no need to be personal." Little joke, to take my mind off the garage.

"It's the *fish*," he said, and started the engine. "You fall in a rubbish dump or something?"

"You must be psychic." Shivering like a leaf. "Do you think he'll make that man tell him anything?"

"Cross our fingers." He turned left towards Spittelmarkt. "Meanwhile I took a call from Renata."

Lena Pabst.

"When?"

"Just after three this afternoon. She asked for you and I said you weren't available and gave her the parole. She's been doing some work. There's some kind of operation being set up at Werneuchen Airforce Base with the code-name of *Trumpeter*. Three of the bomber crews are involved but she hasn't been able to identify them. The best thing she gave me was that the whole operation's on file, if we can only get to it. She—"

"Where?"

"It's in Room 60 in the new Airforce Administration building in Brüder-strasse. She thinks the man behind

Trumpeter works there as an administrator. Room 60's his office.''

"This is very good."

"As far as it goes. She said she'd got some documents for us, but—"

"Did she ask for a rendezvous?"

"Yes, but our luck's run out, I'm afraid. She's been found shot dead.''

16

ROCK

"That's bullshit. I don't lay down some kind of kinky funk-jazz hybrid like Billy Kid—I blow free, see, I give it a rush, a lot of pressure along the vertical and a *lot* of thrust on the level, you know what I mean? And I let them solo if they want to, guitar, sax, drums, whatever they want to do, you know? Musically I'm democratic."

Thin, small-faced, made up like a cat with the corners of her eyes drawn out across the skin, a white leather coat thrown open, tiny hands on tiny hips, a silver sweater and skirt, the skirt a thin tube stopping short just above the knees, the knees bare, alabaster, knobbly, the feet in silver boots, a thick belt made of her own plaited hair—Cone's briefing—caught by a silver snake's-head buckle, the hair on her head exploding like a mane, the colour of ocean surf. Cat Baxter.

The reporter was making notes but stopped when she turned away—"Wiz, get out of here will you, you're stoned—" and turned back. "*Drum*-mers . . . I work with hieroglyphs, see, and that's where the song takes me, wherever it wants me to go—it's free-wheeling, ethereal, a kind of unstructured take-off into the heights I haven't flown before, and this happens *every* time, it's not just Top-Rock Jingle sentimentality and it's got nothing to do with the Protestant Work Ethic—that really makes my boil bleed. No, change that—it really offends my sense of the political, it's so *bourgeois*, I mean you can't have a message in *everything*, talk about the Sound of Mucus."

Pollock came over.

"Well, well. Come here to get her autograph?" Quick white smile.

"Something I've been meaning to ask you," I said. "Isn't it a coincidence that Mikhail Gorbachev is flying in here at the same time that Miss Baxter's giving her concert?"

"Goodness. It never struck me. But we only knew he was coming the day before yesterday. I started fixing up her concert last month."

Cone walked in and looked around the room and came across.

"Last month," I said, "she did a concert in Moscow."

In a moment, scratching his head, Pollock said: "That's right. That's absolutely right." Quick smile. "I never thought about it. I mean, any connection. After all, there's quite a lot going on in Berlin when important visitors fly in. Excuse me, I'm just making sure they're looking after her." He went over to the phone.

"I couldn't come earlier," Cone said. "I was talking to Yasolev."

I felt the scrotum tightening.

"Did he get anything?"

"We're trying to put it together in London. It's a bit disjointed."

"Where's Dietrich now?" I didn't really mean where.

"It looks as if he had a weak heart."

"*Shit.*"

Scarsdale, Lena Pabst, Dietrich. Every time we looked like we were getting some information it got cut off.

"I don't try any of that street-wise visionary stuff and I don't try and get the fans screaming—that's camp. I don't use my pelvis, Christ, I haven't got one—no, change that—I don't use body language, I use my throat."

Pollock came away from the telephone and Cone said something to him and he shook his head. When I went closer he was saying—"and she earns something like a million pounds a year. I can't just break up the interview."

Cone went across and spoke to Cat Baxter and in a minute the reporter put her notes into a briefcase and went out of the room and Pollock left just afterwards, giving me a wave. That left the man in the blue serge suit and dark tie.

"Miss Baxter, we'd like a word with you," Cone said, "just by ourselves."

"It's okay for Boris to stay. He's my bodyguard."

"Is he KGB?"

I'd thought so too.

"Yes."

Cone went over to him. Colonel Yasolev of Department V would like you to leave us for a moment, so forth.

"You've done well," I said to Cat Baxter.

She presented herself to me, and that's the only way of putting it that I can think of: she turned her diminutive body in its hair and silverware and thrust it towards me no more than half an inch, but the air seemed to vibrate. Her eyes were wide and innocent, and I could even believe she thought it was the truth when she said she didn't use body language.

"Done well?"

"You haven't let it all go to your head."

"Meaning fame?"

"That's right." I heard the door shut, and then Cone joined us and Cat took a step back and looked at each of us in turn.

"My manager said you were from the Foreign Office."

"Yes," Cone said.

"You look so *official*."

"I suppose that can't be avoided. Now this is Mr Ash, and I'm going to leave you to do your talking alone. Nothing goes onto the record, don't worry."

He nodded and went out. It had been agreed: we didn't want her to feel outnumbered.

"He looks as if he's had a bad time," the girl said.

"He's in a difficult job." She didn't ask me to sit down so I leaned against the wall alongside one of the windows. "I'm not going to keep you long. What gave you the idea of coming out here?"

"I thought it was about time. Bill Collins brought Genesis right up to the Berlin Wall on the west side, and so did Dave Bowie with his Eurythmics, and the East Berliners practically rioted. The police wouldn't let them get nearer than four hundred yards to the Wall. It was the most serious outbreak of public anger for years." She turned and took three crisp steps, turned again and threw her mane of hair back. "I don't have to tell you that—you people keep tabs."

"We read the papers. Of course you wouldn't have been allowed to come here before Gorbachev's time."

"I wouldn't have thought so. He's fantastic."

"When the East Germans said you could come here, was there any Soviet connection?"

She looked down. Step, step, step, turn, the hair.

"Why?"

"You've performed in Moscow."

"I don't know what you're getting at."

"We're just interested in the way things are changing, over here."

"Let's keep it straight, Mr Ash. You were talking about a Soviet connection."

"I was simply asking. It's interesting for instance that the KGB offered you protection."

"People like me get mobbed. We'd be skinned alive if—"

"The KGB, I mean, rather than the HUA—the East German police."

Turn, step, step, a sudden fast turn back. "What *exactly* do you want to know?"

Getting somewhere.

"Anything you can tell me about your relations with the Soviet government."

Threw her head back, force of habit, meant nothing. "Are you really Foreign Office, or Secret Service?"

"You catch on quickly." Though I'd expected it earlier, because I'd been trying for it.

"Look, I'm a rock star, okay? But I also went for a B.A. and got it, before I started singing."

"Pretty good."

"For a rock star."

"Pretty good anyway, at your age. What in?"

"Political science."

"That explains a lot. The things you've said about human rights."

"You don't have to be political to want people to be

free." Looked away, looked back. "Are you here to jam up the works for me, Mr Ash? I just want to know."

"I didn't know there were any works to jam up."

She was halfway through a step and she faltered and threw out a hand and it was the first time I'd seen her make this particular gesture.

"I mean the concert."

She didn't.

"Of course."

"I think I'd better ask you something," she said. "Have you got any right to question me like this?"

"No."

Threw out a hand again. "When my manager told me a couple of men from the Foreign Office wanted to talk to me, he said it was to help smooth out any problems for me over here. That's what he *said*."

"That's what we told him. D'you mind if I sit down?"

"Feel free, but you haven't got long."

"Just for a minute." I dropped into one of the chrome-and-velour chairs. It hadn't been a good night; the knife-wound had festered and I was on antibiotics.

"If you've any problems," I told her, "we'll smooth them out for you. It was a genuine offer."

"That's very nice of you, but I'm doing fine."

"It hasn't crossed your mind that someone could be using you as a tool?" Long shot.

Step, step, step, turn, the hair. "You know you really have got a bloody nerve."

But she looked shaken, deep inside all the mascara.

"I'll put it this way," I said. "Although I've no right to ask you any questions, the government feels that you'd want to avoid doing anything against your own country. Unwittingly."

"I do a great deal *for* my country, thanks. I'm quite a

valuable British export, and wherever I take my group I get a lot of reaction. In Israel a month ago the fans broke through the police cordon and nearly overturned the limo. I might add that I donated twenty-five per cent of the proceeds to the survivors of the Holocaust. That's bad for Britain?''

"I'm sure we're all very pleased."

"So what's the gripe, Mr Ash?"

The phone rang but she didn't move.

"I believe you were a cultural exchange student in Moscow about three years ago, or am I wrong?"

"Christ, I do wish you'd stick to the point."

The phone went on ringing.

"The point is that if you have any communist leanings we don't want them to lead a very talented, charming and popular international artiste into any kind of deep water."

"*Communist?* Me?"

"What do you think, for instance, of Mr Gorbachev?"

"I've never met him."

"Don't you think it's a coincidence that you'll be performing here during his visit?"

"Maybe he planned it like that."

"Let's try it the other way round," I said, "shall we?"

The phone stopped ringing.

"Look, I didn't plan anything. I was *invited* here."

"By the City of East Berlin?"

"Not straight off."

"Wouldn't you like to sit down too?"

"I'm fine like I am."

And angry, and beginning to be scared.

"Where did the invitation come from, then, initially?"

"It wasn't exactly an invitation. I got a letter from the British Embassy saying that if it'd interest me to bring The Cats here, they'd ask the authorities."

"The authorities in East Berlin?"

"Well of course."

"I just want to be sure I understand you. And who was it at the British Embassy who wrote to you?"

"Mr Pollock."

"Of course. He's the cultural attaché, that's right." I got up, and one of the stitches pulled. "That's all I wanted to ask you, Miss Baxter."

"What have I said?"

Very scared now.

"You've been very cooperative, and you've set my mind at rest."

"You people are so bloody *smooth*, aren't you?"

I thought if I offered my hand she might have spat in it. "Let me wish you a very successful concert. The East Berliners are lucky to have you here." I went to the door, and she followed, step, step, step in that tiny silver skirt, her eyes bright.

"Okay, Mr Ash, I'm taking a risk, out here. But it's going to be worth it."

I'd leave that one to Cone.

"Then look after yourself. I mean that."

I opened the door and found the KGB bodyguard outside.

"Mr Ash."

I looked back at her.

"Will you be at the concert?"

"I hope so."

"Try and make it." Eyes shining. "It'll blow your mind."

"He knew very little."

Yasolev's eyes were sunk deep under the brows and he was pouring himself another shot of vodka.

"He knew very little, or only said very little?" I wasn't

on vodka but it wouldn't have needed much for me to blow up in his face. It'd taken me close to ten hours to snatch whatever I could off the streets and it had been that man Dietrich and I'd handed him over to a KGB colonel with a reputation for squeezing blood out of a stone in an interrogation cell and all he'd come up with was close to zero.

"He *said* very little, but I believe he would have said more if he had known it."

Bloody assumption, that was all.

"What about the other man you searched, the one on the bridge?"

Those nicotine-stained eyes of his had never looked at me with this much animosity before and I was warned. I'd come out here to run *Quickstep* for the KGB and Shepley would quite rightly blast me into Christendom if I provoked Yasolev into calling the whole thing off.

"We had no better fortune."

A tone of icy control.

"Interrogation," Cone said, looking at no one, "doesn't carry a guarantee."

Pouring oil, so forth, perfectly right. Bureau One would blast him into Christendom too if we lost control.

"Point taken."

"Thank you," he said.

I liked his manners. "All right, Viktor, give us what you got."

It was the first time I'd used his Christian name, waving a flag of truce.

"Mr Cone has sent it for analysis to London, and I have of course sent it to Moscow." I think some of the edge had come off his voice. "For what it's worth." He knocked back the shot and absorbed its force. "He obliged me to use pressure. There was no time for sophisticated procedures." Hooding, love-hate, psychiatry.

"The General-Secretary," Cone said, "arrives here in forty-eight hours, yes."

"Would you care for some vodka?"

"Thanks, I'll stick to tea."

A tilt of his head. "It was also clear that Dietrich didn't have the confidence of Horst Volper. He said that he had only ever spoken to his master on the telephone, and that he spoke German with an English accent. Dietrich has no English. He was no more than a minion, like the man you questioned that night in the river, with as little success."

Touché.

Cone stepped in. "How long did it take, with Dietrich?"

"I think perhaps half an hour."

Mystery of dead man discovered in garage. Signs he may have been tortured.

"The rest of what I have to tell you," Yasolev said, "is patched together from the scraps of information Dietrich was willing to part with. My feeling was that the little he gave me was true, that he has never met Horst Volper nor heard of *Trumpeter,* and that Volper's operation is aimed at the General-Secretary—as we already knew."

Cone put his tea-cup back on the tray. "You think he was talking about assassination?"

"Whether he was talking about assassination or not, I am assuming an attempt will be made. From the information you have given me, it is Volper's speciality. But you can imagine how I feel. I have reported to my department on the inherent risk to Comrade Gorbachev, and that would normally evoke immediate and urgent concern." A bitter shrug. "But the visit is not to be cancelled. The General-Secretary's meeting with President Honecker is apparently considered vital. What more can I do?"

"But they'll strengthen the guard."

His eyes flicked to mine. "But of course. And we shall

request the HUA to do the same. But this is *Gorbachev*. We must not lose him. He is . . . precious.''

It was extraordinary how much charisma this new man of theirs possessed. People had gone crazy about him in London and Washington and here was a KGB man getting emotional. Of course he was right: *no* one could afford to lose this totally different breed of Soviet leader.

''We'll have to do what we can,'' I said.

''Do you think—'' he took a step nearer—''do *you* think that the man Volper has *any* chance of succeeding?''

Oh God what a question. The answer was even worse.

''Yes.''

''A chance,'' Cone said. ''Let's not put it at much more than that.''

''You are not optimistic.'' Yasolev looked as if we'd thrust a knife in him.

''Look,'' I said. ''We know that Horst Volper specialises in assassination and we know that he's here in Berlin and we know who the target is. He hasn't got a reputation for failing. All I'm saying is that we shouldn't rely on doubling the guard round the General-Secretary. We've *got* to pick up someone much closer to Volper than these minions. They've been given the job of wiping me out because he thinks I'm a risk and he's damned right—but they don't *know* anything. We still need *information*.''

''How do we get it?''

''Tonight,'' I told him, ''I'm going to have a look round Room 60 in the Airforce Administration Building.'' I turned to Cone—''You filled him in?''

''Yes.''

''I will give you support,'' Yasolev said and I swung on him.

''Viktor, if I see *one* of your people in the field again I'm going to pack my bags—now is that clear?''

"I gave no instructions to have you followed last night. My agents were following only the tags, in the hope of seizing one. Which we did. We—"

"Oh for God's sake, I really don't know how to convince you." In English—"Cone, I'm going to leave you to work on him. I do *not* want the field cluttered tonight and he's *got* to understand that."

"Do what I can."

"All right. And listen—" I switched back to Russian—"I'd put someone reliable on Cat Baxter, if I were you, in fact two or three people. Talk to her yourself if she'll see you."

"What did you get out of her?"

I checked the time. "I'll have to report on it later because I've got to get into the Airforce building before they close the doors at five. But in brief I think she's playing with fire and it could be some kind of demonstration she's thinking of putting on because Gorbachev's going to be here. We're sitting on dynamite and we can do without some little jumped-up Joan of Arc throwing matches around."

This was at 4:13 in the afternoon and at 4:46 I walked into the Airforce Administration Building in Brüder-strasse and showed my police card to the man at the desk and went across to the elevators and started work.

17

MIRRORS

He was watching me.

The ideal scenario when you go into a building to search one of the offices is that everyone leaves by five o'clock and the doors are shut and there's only the janitor in the basement and you come out of the cleaners' cupboard and start work, but on this particular night there were still some people in the building at six o'clock and it occurred to me that since this was a military administration headquarters they might run a night shift.

Or at least he seemed to be watching me—it wasn't easy to tell. The whole place was a honeycomb of glass and brushed aluminium panels and wherever you looked there were reflections.

I didn't move.

I was sitting in Room 60 and the name of the man who

worked here was on the plate outside the door: A. V. Melnichenko, Soviet Adviser to the Directorate. I didn't know what he looked like. If he looked anything like me at a distance of fifty feet through a series of windows and their angled reflections it might go well: here was Comrade Melnichenko, Soviet Adviser to the Directorate, still sitting at his desk and catching up on his work. But if he didn't look like me, and I started moving about and opening drawers and going through the filing-cabinets it wouldn't go well at all: that man at the desk in the office across the corner would be in here to ask who I was and what I was doing, and a captain of the HUA had no right in this place because the military took precedence, and even if I said I was here on some kind of liaison work I'd have to name the officer in the Luftwaffe Administration who'd allowed me in here.

In addition to which, this was the office of the Soviet Adviser, and he would be no lightweight: he would be a member of the GRU, Soviet Military Intelligence.

The man across the corridor wasn't in uniform; nor were the others I could see in the more distant offices. My camouflage was thus in order: I'd put on a dark suit and tie, and this at least gave me a chance. And he was on the telephone, the man who seemed to be watching me, and when we're on the telephone we tend to stare at things without really seeing them. On the other hand he might have noticed me after he'd started talking, and might have decided to wait until he'd finished before he came across the corridor to find out who I was.

I suppose it sounds like a harmless intellectual exercise but if that's what you think then you're dead wrong. I'd only been in here five minutes when that man had walked out of the elevator and gone into his office and switched the lights on and sat down at his desk; and when he'd looked up he'd seen me through the glass panels and there hadn't been time for me to drop out of sight and in any case that might have been a mistake because once out of sight I couldn't suddenly appear from nowhere.

The thing is that if *anyone* came in here and asked who I was it wouldn't be easy, because the military don't get on with the civilian intelligence departments or the secret police and the least they'd do would be to ask me to show my identity card and they'd check on it by phone and find it was false.

The HUA are on no account to know that you are liaising with the KGB.

Yasolev.

Someone came out of an office halfway along the corridor and went into the one where the man was at the phone and he looked up and shielded the mouthpiece and *this* was when he would ask his visitor to go across and check on that man sitting at Comrade Melnichenko's desk, if he was interested.

I waited.

The only man I could call on in the HUA was Captain Karl Bruger, if I had to get out of a sticky situation, and he might not be available or he might have had instructions to deny knowledge of me and I couldn't even call the Soviet ambassador because that would expose the KGB connection and if I blew Yasolev I could blow *Quickstep*.

Waited.

It wasn't cold in here but I felt the chill. I could possibly get away from the police escort if they tried to take me along for interrogation but they'd know my face again and there'd be an all-points bulletin put out immediately and I'd have to go to ground *and stay there,* and I had a very definite intuition that even if Yasolev panicked his chief directorate into sending the KGB into East Berlin en masse to escort General-Secretary Gorbachev when he arrived in less than forty-eight hours *they wouldn't be able to protect him.*

Horst Volper was a professional and he was a specialist and he was believed to be here in this city with the single intention of assassinating Gorbachev and he would expect his target to be heavily escorted and protected, as at all times on foreign soil, and he would make his plans accordingly. The *only* way to protect the General-Secretary was by finding Volper and incapacitating him.

Incapacitating, Jesus, I was as bad as those snotty-nosed scribes stuck up there in their stuffy little offices in London— *killing,* yes, we have to *kill* Volper, get him out of society's way.

The man at the telephone was still talking to the other one who'd gone into his office and his hand was still blocking the mouthpiece and I still didn't move and it had started to be a test of the nerves, and the sweat was making my scalp itch and I couldn't scratch it, the immobility of my right leg was bringing on cramp and I couldn't move it, *well either tell him to come and see who I am or don't.*

It was as if he'd heard. He nodded and took his hand away from the mouthpiece and started talking into the telephone again and the other man went out of his office and shut the door and came along the passage with two of his ghostlike reflections moving together across the windows and merging as he got to the corner and turned in this direction, looking down at something in his hand, looking up again and not stopping, not going into any of the other rooms, coming straight on and turning his head to look at me through the glass until he reached the door and opened it.

"Where's Melnichenko?"

"He said he'd be back shortly."

Looked at the folder in his hand. "I'd like a word with him."

"I'll tell him that."

A nod, turning to go, turning back. "Have I seen you before?"

"Not unless you've ever visited the Commandant at GRU Headquarters in Moscow."

Head went back an inch and he opened his mouth but didn't seem to know quite what to say, went out.

I'd spoken German with a Russian accent to make the whole thing plausible but it had been *very* close and if anyone else came in here they might not be so impressed.

Sitting here like a fish in a bowl and I hadn't expected it, wasn't ready for it. Question of choice at this stage: get out of here and don't stop moving until I was in the street, or stay where I was and ransack this room and risk exposure at any next minute. Question of urgency, too: Lena Pabst had said there was a file on *Trumpeter* in this room, so I was infinitely closer than I'd ever been to finding Volper or blowing his operation. Urgent, then, that I should stay here and take the risk of blowing *Quickstep* first.

There was also the temptation of picking up the phone and calling Cone.

I'm in a red sector and if I can't get out of it you should be informed that the man who works in Room 60 is A. V. Melnichenko, Soviet Adviser to the Directorate, presumably GRU.

It would then be up to Cone to work out why the file on *Trumpeter* was in the safekeeping of an officer of the GRU. Two possibilities: the GRU was simply *watching* the operation and waiting to blow it up, or *Trumpeter* had nothing to do with Horst Volper.

I opened the top left drawer while the last thought went through the processing stage; then it came back very fast indeed. Play it again: Trumpeter *had nothing to do with Horst Volper*.

Nothing to do with the assassination.

Then what *was* it to do with? Something of major importance, because soon after Lena Pabst had started infiltrating it she'd been found shot dead.

No question now: pick up the phone.

While I waited for the ringing tone I watched one of the reflections of the man in the office over there; he wasn't interested in me: he'd put the phone down and was writing.

Five rings.

Eight.

Someone came into reflection from the direction of the elevator and his images merged and then split apart again. I watched him.

At the tenth ring I pressed the contact down and waited and let it up again. Dialling tone.

He was coming in this direction and I closed the top left drawer.

Ringing.

Where did Cat Baxter come in?

Four rings.

I know I'm taking a risk. What had she meant? A risk of what?

He came past the door without turning his head, a young man, uniformed, lower rank. You do not, if you are lower rank, glance in at the offices of the directorate.

"Yes?"

Yasolev.

"Liaison."

"Well?"

"For your information, Room 60 is the office of A. V.

Melnichenko, Soviet Adviser to the Airforce Directorate. I assume he's GRU, not KGB, this being a military headquarters. It—''

''Wait.''

Making notes.

''Yes?''

''It could be possible that the *Trumpeter* operation is *not* being run by Horst Volper, and has nothing to do with our main concern.'' A KGB officer with a room in an East Berlin hotel uses a telephone that is totally free of bugs, but I shied at mentioning the name of Gorbachev as the target of an assassination project.

''Perhaps Melnichenko has acquired the file and is observing the operation.''

''Giving it rope, yes, that's possible. But I phoned you because if the other possibility is fact, there's got to be a major switch in our thinking. We've got to infiltrate *two* operations.''

In a moment: ''We already suspected this.''

Because Dietrich, under the intense pressure of interrogation, had known nothing about *Trumpeter*.

''Yes. This seems to confirm it. I'll leave it to you, all right?''

''Yes. I shall go to work on it immediately. But I am concerned about your position. If you are found in that building—''

''I've been in hazard before. You'll hear from me as soon as I'm clear.''

''Very well. I hope—'' I could see him shrug.

''Over and out.''

I rang off.

He wouldn't waste any time. Immediate signal to Moscow: *Require all possible information on A. V. Melnichenko, believed to be a member of the GRU. Also try the person-*

nel files of the KGB. Request immediate and most urgent attention.

My hand went to the drawer again but I froze on another thought. I'd just told Yasolev that it was possible that *Trumpter* had nothing to do with "our main concern," simply because it was nothing to do with Horst Volper. That could be dangerous thinking. Crows are black but all black birds are not crows.

Were there *two* independent operations with Gorbachev as the target for *both* of them?

Mother of God.

You must understand that inside the Kremlin there are factions opposed to the Comrade General-Secretary's policy of perestroika. Yasolev, in that chill dawn among the trees. *Inside the KGB there are factions similarly opposed.*

Hand on the drawer.

And inside the GRU?

I would have liked to talk to Cone. He'd said that if I couldn't reach him at the hotel I should try the Soviet Embassy but he might not be there either and I didn't want to spend any more time on the phone; I wanted to rip this office apart and find the *Trumpeter* file and get clear before someone else came in here and asked if he'd seen me before and refused to be put off by the Russian accent.

There came to me, my good friend, as I sat here at Comrade Melnichenko's desk in this hall of mirrors, in the centre of this critically red sector, the feeling that I had also arrived at the centre of *Quickstep,* at the point where the entire mission had become focussed, its components coalescing into a gem-hard reality. It was a good feeling. The wounds I'd received out here in the field, the underlying grief for those who had met their death—Scarsdale, Skidder, Dietrich, the man on the bridge, the smouldering distrust I felt for Yasolev, even Cone, even Shepley, the paranoid suspicion that they were setting me up, all of them, and running me through this city like a rat in a maze—all these things were leaving my mind, so that my attention could become focussed, like the mission itself, on the immediate and paramount objective. The *Trumpeter* file.

I've had this feeling before, and I've learned to trust it. It's a good feeling, yes. But do not be quick, my friend, with your congratulations. The centre of any mission is like the eye of the hurricane, and there was the warning in the blood, in the atavistic brain-stem, that if I didn't leave this treacherous hall of mirrors while I had the chance I would lose the day, and all I would know would be the dying echoes of the explosion as *Quickstep* blew apart.

Bang of a door and the nerves jerked and I watched the man going along the passage to the elevator, the man who had been in the office across the corner. His room was dark now.

Only two others were still lit, but the passage itself was bright under the argon tubes. They would be left going all night, for the janitors.

I could see six faces from where I sat, two of them substantial except for the filming of the glass, four of them reflections. From where they sat they could see three faces, all of them mine.

Movement attracts the eye at the periphery of the vision-field; nothing is actually seen, only movement; but it brings attention, and turns the head. It took time, therefore, to reach the filing-cabinet in the corner, perhaps fifteen minutes; it wasn't important; but I'd had to move in the chair, lowering my body behind the desk, by imperceptible degrees, and by the time I was at the filing-cabinet in the corner of the room the muscles were trembling from the strain. But there were no faces in the windows now. Visually I was alone.

There wouldn't be anything on *Trumpeter* here in the cabinet; even if the drawers were locked it'd be dangerously accessible: there'd be a wall-safe somewhere and I would look for it. But this was the only corner of the room where I was invisible, so I could do some work here to pass the time. The man who had left his office wouldn't be the last; the other two would follow—there wasn't, after all, a night shift here. If I were wrong then I'd have to rethink.

The drawers were locked but I'd brought the keys I'd been looking for in the desk and I used them now.

Aircraft Deployment—State of Readiness—Estimated Scramble Delay.

The second drawer held personnel statistics, the third drawer an inventory of ordnance and specialised weaponry, the fourth a breakdown of the fighter units and their strategical disposition throughout the Democratic Republic. The bottom drawer was more interesting: *Werneuchen Bomber Base: Deployment of Aircraft—Availability of Optimum Strength—Personnel*.

It didn't surprise me that Werneuchen was featured and had an entire drawer to itself. *My air base, Werneuchen, is in the front line of the war*. Lena Pabst, her dark eyes shimmering. *I am in the front line of the last war on earth, and when it's over I shall still be here to see the dawn of the new world*.

But for a bullet.

Werneuchen: the focus of *Trumpeter* was on Werneuchen, and I left the bottom drawer unlocked in case there were a chance of taking anything with me when I left here. The whole cabinet was stuffed with the type of classified product worth mounting a specific documentation snatch on its

own, but if I took away everything I came across tonight
I'd need a truck outside.

I moved to the next corner, where there were three more
files, and I had the keys in my hand when a panel of light
in the environment went out and I froze. Sound of voices,
footsteps. I watched the six reflections and saw them come
together and part again where the panels of glass formed a
corner. The footsteps were fainter now. Sound of the
elevator doors thumping open, thumping shut.

Totally alone, and I got going in earnest, opening the
three files and ransacking them for any material in code,
because there'd be nothing on *Trumpeter* in plaintext. I
still believed there was a safe somewhere, in a wall or in
the floor, and I slammed the last drawer of the third
cabinet shut and began looking for it, and within the next
half an hour I'd sounded every inch of the walls and the
panels of the desk and the base of the carved ottoman that
was the only decorative piece of furnishing in the room.

Sound.

Freeze.

Elevators. Not the doors, just the machinery, the low
whine of the motors.

Doors now.

This floor.

I'd worked thoroughly but I'd covered my tracks and
there was nothing in sight that hadn't been there when I'd
first come into the office. From where I was standing now
I could see two reflections of the elevator and the three
figures in the corridor.

Steady the breathing, stabilise the nerves.

They weren't janitors: I couldn't see clearly through the
reflecting panels but their peaked caps were distinct.

Walking steadily, keeping in step, talking; I could hear
their voices now.

Didn't move. Watched. It would be ten or twelve seconds before they reached the corner and came into full sight of Room 60 and if one of them raised his head and looked straight in front of him he would see me clearly. One of two things was going to happen. When they reached the corner they would keep straight on and move out of sight, or they would turn and come in this direction and either pass Room 60 or come in.

A gleam of brass on their caps: two of them were high ranking. A civilian in the middle—he could be Melnichenko.

I waited. Tidal breathing, the itch of sweat as it gathered in the scalp. They were still talking. Then they reached the corner and turned in this direction and came on without stopping.

Rat in a trap.

18

VERTIGO

"I would have liked to be presented to him."

"Of course. But it's my understanding that—Hans, will you sit here?—it's my understanding that the chiefs of service haven't been invited to the press luncheon. They're playing down the military side of things during this particular visit."

"I shall be over at Werneuchen that day, in any case. The—"

"On the Pabst matter?"

"Yes. It's unsettling—she was highly respected and devoted to the Party. Does anyone feel a draught?"

"Draught?"

"Yes, this window's not quite shut."

A bus halted at the lights.

The window was shut now; the latch had clicked home.

Traffic was slowing behind the bus: two or three cars and a taxi.

I could still hear voices but they weren't intelligible now that the window was shut.

Cold. It was very cold here.

The lights went to green and the traffic moved off, the bus leaving a cloud of diesel smoke drifting across the street. I couldn't smell it from here.

The ledge was less than a foot wide. I had to angle my feet.

He would be Melnichenko, the man who said he was going over to Werneuchen. He was the only one with a Russian accent, and the others wouldn't be interested in whether Lena Pabst was devoted to the Party or not. So it would have been strictly no go if I'd stayed in the room— Melnichenko's own office. But this might not be any better: I was seventy feet above the street and I could only shuffle sideways and if I put any pressure at all against the concrete behind me I would lose my balance, *finis*.

The windows of Room 60 had plastic blinds but they weren't totally opaque so I'd crabbed my way along the ledge until there was a wall behind me. I suppose if I felt the onset of fatigue or vertigo I could shuffle back to the windows and knock on them and think up an acceptable reason for being out here and look for a chance of getting clear while the military police were taking me along for questioning, but I didn't like throwing in the towel without trying to find a better way out—an unfortunate metaphor, yes—if you threw a towel from here it would go floating and curling and dipping lower and lower until it met the street. A body would go straight down.

So Melnichenko was reported to have a file on *Trumpeter* in Room 60 and Lena Pabst had been got out of the way because she'd been infiltrating *Trumpeter* and Melnichenko himself would be at Werneuchen making enquiries. I was glad I'd phoned Yasolev. If I came unstuck from the side of this building at least I'd reported on Melnichenko and it might give them a clue, even provide a breakthrough.

Bitterly cold. I didn't put my gloves on because I wanted to feel things with my fingertips: the rough concrete and the next window-frame when I worked my way along there. The only chance I'd got was to keep moving and hope to find a handhold somewhere before the tension brought on fatigue and I tipped forward. That could happen at any time, minutes from now, an hour from now.

Nothing below me but the street: no balconies, canopies, guttering, nothing to break a fall. This was a new building with a flat modern facade and only a single ledge jutting at each storey.

The cold alone could finish me, inducing torpor. In still-air conditions it would have been more tolerable, but there was a wind that came in sharp gusts, tugging at my coat.

Move, keep moving. And don't look down. I could hear the traffic and that was all; the wind was taking the exhaust gas away before it reached this height, and bringing in the river smell from the west.

There's a difference between a tight-rope and a ledge along a wall: on the rope you can swing from one side to the other to keep your balance; on a ledge you can only keep still, and even though this one was wider than a rope the wall itself was the danger because when you feel yourself losing your footing you instantly reach out for support but if I let my hand touch the concrete with more than the slightest pressure it'd pitch me into the void.

I don't like heights. I'd seen a man go down, once, from the twenty-first floor of a construction site. They say you scream but you don't. They call it going down the hole, the construction workers, and when one of them does it the rest of them are told to go home for the day because it's unnerving and therefore dangerous.

One foot, then the other. The ankles had started aching and I wanted to angle the feet the other way but it would mean shifting the body's equilibrium and the nerves were already under stress; I was beginning to feel that the wall had started leaning towards the street, and the ledge tilting. This was normal: fear begets illusion; but it would have to be dealt with, combatted.

Like a crab. Moving like a crab along the wall. A dull ache had started at the top of the spine. I was keeping my head to one side, to the left, the way I was moving, because when I turned it to the right the building across the street swung across the vision-field and affected the sense of balance.

A captain of the HUA?

I was now certain that it would have been safer to stay in the room and face it out.

What department are you, Captain?

It would have been dangerous to let them put me under interrogation but less dangerous than this dizzying height in this killing cold.

This is Commandant Melnichenko, Adviser to the Airforce Directorate. I have a Captain Kurt Heidecker here, with the HUA service number D/435-05. Is he known in your department?

A gust of wind came and my shoulders met the wall and I froze and contracted the leg muscles and waited, for a moment sickened. If the wind got stronger in the night there wouldn't be a hope in hell: it'd blow me off the building.

He's not known in your department?

And there would have been *no* explanation he would

have accepted when he asked what I was doing in his office; compared with a commandant of Soviet Military Intelligence a captain of the HUA had no authority.

But there would have at least been a chance, even in the hands of the GRU. I couldn't have given them Yasolev's name because Yasolev was using me to infiltrate *Trumpeter* and Melnichenko had a file on that operation in his office and he would have had me shot, just as someone had had Lena Pabst shot. The situation here in East Berlin forty-eight hours before the arrival of the General-Secretary of the USSR was ultra-sensitive. Yasolev was here on a secret assignment known only to his immediate cell within his department; he'd made it a condition of our liaison that I didn't expose either him or his assignment to East German Intelligence; and the GRU had an adviser buried in Airforce HQ with a file on *Trumpeter* in his care.

In addition there was the London connection, and if I ever got close to blowing my own cover the Bureau would expect me to use the capsule and I would do that.

Window.

I'd been watching it for minutes now, trying to see if there was any chance of using it. When I'd got out of Room 60 I'd left the window open an inch so that I could have climbed back inside after they'd gone, and it was conceivable that another window somewhere had been left open by mistake and I could—*watch it, you're losing rationality*. It was *not* conceivable that *any* window of this building had been left open in winter conditions with the heating system going full blast.

Glass. Perfectly smooth glass and a frame less than an inch proud of the wall, drawing blank so move on, keep moving. Given a wider ledge, wider by only a few inches, I might have jabbed an elbow against the glass and smashed it and gone through. On this ledge there wasn't enough room for leverage.

Wind gust and it tugged at me and I froze and waited and longed to shut my eyes but without a visual reference the balance would have gone. The gust had rocked me sideways a little before I'd had a chance to contract the muscles, and the buildings opposite took on a tilt and tilted back and that was when the vertigo began, the real thing, and for the first time I realised there wasn't necessarily a chance of reaching the corner and making the turn and finding some kind of purchase on the next face of the building.

Keep still.

The street steadied and held and then shifted again, and all I could do was try to keep still, but vertigo is not just a sensation, not just a fear of heights: it's the primitive fear of falling, of dying, of taking time to die, of being cut off from the safety we have known since we crawled across that solid floor and began to know on the subconscious level that it would always be like this; there would always be the safety of solidity beneath us, the arms of the Earth Mother.

Keep still.

But it was here to stay, now, the vertigo, and I was keeping still because I couldn't move any more, unless I could deal with the enemy within the gates, within the mind.

Breathe deeply, slowly, call upon prana.

The consciousness of known values was diminishing, slipping away, and soon there was no mission to be accomplished, no action to be accounted for; London was the shred of a thought, a name for a place where a man called Shepley lived, had once lived, in the past. Another man, with the name of Melnichenko, floated through my mind as a figment, a ghost seen moving through a hall of mirrors, of reflections, as reality seeped away and took with it the demands of normal life, that I should somehow make my way along this ledge and find a place where I could be safe, and pick up a telephone and say, I am safe now, I am safe.

Life had become refined and narrowed down, with the trivia of earlier ambitions stripped away and leaving the stark immediacy of the present. The world had shrunk to a few square inches of concrete where I stood, where this organism stood with its feet at the precise angle at which they could best sustain life, with its splayed fingers touching the mass of concrete behind its body for the purpose of tactile orientation but with the knowledge that any slight pressure on the wall would begin the mechanical process that would eventually extinguish life, as the body was tilted forward and was poised at an angle above the void, an angle from which it could not now return, but from which it must tilt progressively forward until the feet lost the security of the ledge beneath them and followed the body as it began curving over with the weight of the head turning it in the air as it gathered speed and plunged directly to the earth below as the mind played out the drama of the occasion, first experiencing the swift access of terror as the windrush moved through the hair and pressed against the eyes, the terror of annihilation, of obliteration as the details of the street grew larger and more defined as if seen through the zoom lens of a camera, and then, following the terror, the experience of rage, of rage against the gods, against the fates, bringing to the organism a semblance of identity after its loss in the helplessness of the terror, and then, following the rage, euphoria, easing all travail away and leaving in its place

the onset of spiritual peace, of acceptance, of an understanding that would know nothing of the body's gross
concerns of physical death as the head hit the ground and
the brains were smashed from the skull and the arms were
flung out and the stillness came, the inertness, the muta-
tion from creature to object, to chemicals, while—

Gust of wind—

Oh God—

Stay . . . stay . . . hold still . . .

Hold still, and fix the eyes on the window there, on the
window across the street, so as to keep stillness in the
mind through the eyes' reference, *hold still* and wait it out,
with the feet braced and pressing forward by infinite degrees until the shoulders feel the presence of the wall and
all movement ceases and the wind's sudden tugging dies
away, dies away.

Cold sweat drenching the skin beneath the clothes, the
eyes fixed on the building opposite, the ears picking up
sound in the environment, a voice.

Somewhere below.

Below in the street. Look down.

A group of people on the pavement, one of them pointing upwards as others came, lifting their heads to stare.

One of them shouting, but I couldn't make out the
words. I looked upwards again, because they were so
small, so far away, so far *below*.

Move, move again, we have to reach safety.

The feet shuffling, angled on the narrow ledge—we
must make haste before they upset everything I've got
to do, the people down there, they'll call—yes, they
have already called, I can hear the siren voicing in the
night.

There's a man trying to commit suicide.

Not really.

All patrols vicinity Brüder-strasse . . . man reported on ledge, seventh floor, the Airforce Administration Building.

But this is not convenient, good citizens.

I have plans, you see, and I don't need help with them, *so why don't you mind your own bloody business and let me—*

Steady.

There's nothing you can do about it now, so—

But I wouldn't have fallen, for Christ's sake—

Possibly not. By no means certainly not, but possibly not.

Move—keep moving—

Not terribly wise, to hurry. You get another wind-gust like the last one and—

Move, get going, there's still time to find a safe place before they—

Actually no.

A fire engine, immense, with its sirens and bull-horns cutting out as it came to a halt below. That was all I saw because the movement and the colour were disturbing the visual equilibrium and that was dangerous. I heard men running and the moan of a winch-engine.

What were you doing on the ledge?

I was contemplating suicide, so forth, because there was nothing else I could say.

What's your department, Captain?

Not known, not known there.

Interrogation.

Finis.

I went on moving because I wasn't far now from the corner of the building and there was a million-to-one chance of reaching the next wall if I could manage the right-angle turn, of reaching it and finding some kind of escape, a roof below where I could drop and break the fall and run, a million-to-one.

Oh, bullshit, you haven't got a chance in hell.

Perfectly right.

Movement at the edge of the vision-field and I looked down as far as the next window below me on the building opposite and saw the reflection of the ladder.

The whole street was filled with noise by now and I suppose there was a crowd down there. The police radios would be busy: I could hear a chorus of three sirens loudening from the distance.

In a workers' state, Captain, attempted suicide is seen as anti-social and irresponsible. We—

All right, I'll take over—he's not known in that department. There's more to this than attempted suicide. I'm taking him in for questioning.

Window behind me: I'd got almost as far as the corner, *Gott straffe* their bloody workers' state and social expectations.

Wind-gust and I braced against it, the nerves shocked again and the sweat coming chill on the skin, *don't move,* hold still, *you are not safe yet,* you are not in safety.

I took in what I could without disturbing the equilibrium: the top of the ladder was still rising and from the reflections in the windows opposite I could see that a fireman had started climbing as the winch-motor moaned below. The sirens had neared and died short, cut off as the vehicles reached the scene; voices floated upwards as the crowd grew bigger—this was better than television, better even than the Western stations, though not so colourful of course—one man on a wall could hardly qualify for casting in *Lifestyles of the Rich and Famous*, nothing so fancy.

No, sir, we're taking him along for questioning; for one thing his police papers are false, so there's a great deal we want to know. He was also found on the Airforce Administration Building.

The winch crew on the fire engine were very good—the top of the ladder was now leaning on the wall beside me and the fireman was only a few rungs below.

"You all right?"

"Yes," I said, but at last I'd got leverage and I grabbed the top rung and arched my spine and lowered my head and smashed my way backwards through the window behind me and pitched into the room.

19

CHECKPOINT

Three rings.

"Yes?"

Cone.

"*Liaison*. I think I can get clear of the red sector, but I'm not sure. I'm phoning you to confirm Soviet Adviser A. V. Melnichenko's involvement in *Trumpeter*. Listen carefully: *he will be at Werneuchen Airforce Base when the target arrives*. That clear?"

"Yes. Where—"

"Yasolev will obviously recommend the target lands at Schönefeldt instead. I think we should treat Melnichenko as highly suspect and get London to put his name into the computer for background. Clear?"

"Clear. Where are you now?"

Police car.

"In the streets." I did *not* want support.

"Then you'll have to be careful. I had a call from Karl Bruger an hour ago and it looks as if Volper or someone else has blown you to the HUA."

I think I flinched.

"I'm listening."

"Bruger told me there's an all-points bulletin out for your arrest for questioning, and they've got a photograph."

It was probably one of the police cars that had been protecting the scene below the Airforce building. I watched it cross the intersection, heading away from the phone-box.

"How did they get the photograph?"

I have never felt so cold.

"It could have been taken at any time with a telescopic lens. When you arrived in Berlin, or when you left the club at lunch-time yesterday. Bruger says there's hardly any grain and the light was sharp."

"I see."

I was sorry for him, for Cone. The director in the field is meant to support, advise and succour the executive; to keep him in signals with London and to observe his progress through the mission and report on it and monitor feedback from the Bureau and pass on what he feels to be necessary; to love, cherish and act as nursemaid if the executive is beyond the ability to help himself, to survive alone; and to respond to an emergency by calling in whatever help he can from sleepers, agents-in-place and in extreme cases the intelligence chief-of-station at the British Embassy.

The director in the field is not expected to inform the executive that he has been exposed to the host-country's police forces and intelligence services, but that is what Cone had just had to do and I felt sorry for him.

The streets had been dangerous for me since I'd arrived

in Berlin but only because of the opposition's limited surveillance and hit teams. The streets were now the more dangerous to an infinite degree: the whole city had become a red sector.

Mr Shepley?

Speaking.

We've just had to revise the signals board. The DIF reports the executive has become the subject of an APB and the Berlin police have been ordered to arrest him on sight for questioning.

On the board it would be expressed more briefly than that, with a red-and-white-striped line underneath my name and the time the information came in. For an executive behind the Curtain it's not uncommon to be the subject of an arrest-on-sight order during the last phases of the mission. It is not uncommon, but it is none-the-less hazardous in the extreme.

"Is there anything," Cone asked me, "I can do?"

"Yes. I'd feel easier if you could man that phone constantly until I can stabilise things."

"I'll have my food sent in."

"If you've *got* to leave the phone, get Yasolev in. But he can't signal London and we might need to do that, anytime now. I don't—"

"I'll be standing by without a break. Is there anything else?"

"No. I'm going to ground and I'll phone you when I'm there."

Another police car, cruising slowly. I turned my back to the street.

"I'd like," Cone said quietly, "to send you some support. I've got six men."

"Offer them my respects."

I rang off and waited until the police car had crossed the

intersection and then I walked into the alley and reached the next street and got into the BMW and for a moment sat doing nothing, thinking of nothing, letting the muscles go limp and feeling the mood deepening towards the alpha state and the benison of not caring, not knowing, not being afraid.

Then after a little time I began thinking again, going over things carefully, assessing the damage, trying to plan the future. I didn't know how many people there'd been in the Airforce building when I'd gone through the window. I'd heard shouting on the seventh floor and that had probably been Melnichenko and the other two as I ran for the emergency stairs and hit the walls at the corners on the way down and went through the door on the sixth floor and pressed the elevator button to delay pursuit and took the stairs again to the ground floor.

There were police lights flashing outside the front entrance and some people in the lobby and I went back into the stairwell and opened the door to the street and found it clear. There was a window and I twisted round and took a look at my back; the leather coat had been slashed by the breaking glass up there but there was no blood and in East Berlin you can get by on the streets with worn clothing and not attract attention. I could feel some blood that had started from cuts on the nape of the neck but it was already clotting and I left it alone and pulled up the collar and started looking for a phone kiosk on the way back to the car.

I'd left the BMW the prescribed distance from the work-scene—the Airforce building—three or four blocks. It's dangerous to leave a car closer than that because if you think there's going to be any problem about getting clear you're going to do it on foot because the sound of a vehicle starting up will bring them running and if you leave the car

near the scene without using it you won't get back to it
that easily: the police will normally set up a watch in the
area and check any vehicle standing unattended.

The street was clear and I switched on the parking lights
and got out and checked them front and rear. It wasn't far
to the safe-house but I could be stopped anywhere along
the way by police for a dead bulb and that could be fatal.

The lights were all right and I got back in and started up
and moved off and stopped again at the intersection until
the lights went green but there was a police car standing in
the middle of the road with its lights flashing when I tried
to turn right, so I kept straight on and tried the next street
but there was a barricade with an officer manning it and I
kept on again and tried the next left and got through until
the next intersection. Two Vopos and another barricade to
the right and straight ahead, the officers waving their
batons to show me the way I had to go.

By now the BMW was one of a dozen vehicles working
through a maze—Brüder-strasse, Unterwasser-strasse,
Spittelmarkt, Gertrauden-strasse—with the Airforce building as its centre.

The centre of the trap.

The night had been quiet; now it was loud with the
sound of running engines and the shouts of the Vopos as
they directed the swell of traffic into the net. I checked
two alleys as I passed them but they both had a guard; the
whole area was being sealed off and I stayed where I was,
rolling the BMW forward a yard at a time between halts as
the police PA system started up.

*You will switch off your engines. Switch off your en-
gines, please, and stay inside your vehicle.*

I'd come full-circle and the Airforce building was
directly ahead at the next intersection. Lights were flashing
in front and behind me and green-uniformed police were

taking up positions wherever there was an exit from the
street.

Switch off your engines, please.

Yes indeed, comrades, petrol is expensive at twenty
marks a gallon and we don't want to sit here in a cloud of
asphyxiating bloody exhaust gas until you're ready to check
our papers and flash a torch in our face, do we, *this is a
trap,* we don't want to sit here choking on carbon-bloody-
monoxide while you take your time turning over all the
little minnows in the net to find the one you want, do we,
this is a trap—

I know.

We can't get out.

I know.

You can't show your papers—

Shuddup. Leave me alone.

Panicky little bastard, the rotten little harbinger of doom,
won't let you alone, *this is a trap,* I know it's a trap so
shuddup.

Stay where you are. Do not leave your vehicle.

I wouldn't dream of it. Get out of this car and take one
step and there'll be a Vopo closing in, two or three of
them closing in like sharks that've seen something in the
water; I'm going to stay exactly where I am, comrades,
sitting in my sweat.

Coloured lights flashing wherever you looked, lights
reflected in the windscreens and the windows and the
metalwork of the 280 SE in front of me, in the rearview
mirror and the chrome strips along the dashboard, lights
wherever you looked, but no sound now except for the
movement of boots as the police deployed themselves and
the trap was finally shut.

"What are they doing?"

Girl with light hair and green eye shadow and a red

mouth, a cigarette in her small white fingers as she leaned in the window of her Lancia alongside the BMW. I couldn't see who was at the wheel.

"It's a police block."

A look of surprise, "Well yes, but I mean—"

It's a trap.

Shuddup.

Fireman.

A door opened somewhere behind me and a man got out and a Vopo moved in from the building—"You will stay in your vehicle, didn't you hear?"

"But what are you stopping us for?"

"You are to stay in your vehicle."

And you'd better get the message, Fritz my good friend, where the hell are you from, West Berlin or somewhere, you don't question the police on this side of the Wall: they question you.

Fireman, yes. This was an identification parade and every one of us would have to be cleared by the fireman somewhere up there at the end of the street, the only man who knew my face.

This is the one?

I think so.

Take a good look. Make sure.

Staring at me from the top of a ladder one minute, seventy feet in the air, staring at me in the street the next minute, in the middle of a horde of police. Life is a game, my friend, life is a cabaret.

And this is the man with no papers?

Yes, Captain.

Then bring him along, two of you.

Thirty minutes, at an approximate estimation. Thirty minutes from now.

You will now leave your vehicles and form a single line.
Please leave your vehicles.

Doors opening and slamming shut like a fusillade of
shots along the street, the echoes bouncing from the buildings. The lights still flashing in the eerie silence that came
down now, except for the shuffling of feet.

"Are they searching them?"

A small man beside me suddenly, keeping his voice
low; he was on his toes, trying to see the front of the line.

"I don't know," I said. "Why not leave it in the car?"

He flicked a look at me. "If they're searching us,
they'll search the cars too."

Not the first time he'd been caught in a drug bust.

But that wasn't what it was.

It's a trap.

I don't need telling.

It had probably been Melnichenko who had started this.
As a high-level member of the GRU he'd carry a lot of
clout and he'd use it. He would have put two and two
together when he'd found the window open and seen the
fuss in the street: the man he'd seen later, running for the
stairs, might have been in his office earlier and been
surprised there. He would think immediately of the
Trumpeter file and pick up a telephone very fast indeed.
The file would still be there—he'd check on that—but he
would want to know who'd been in his office and what
they were looking for.

I want police blocks set up immediately and the area
contained. I want everyone searched and questioned.

I shall remain in my office in the Airforce building and
you will please report to me there.

Thy will be done.

Move along, please. Keep the line moving.

It wasn't, at this end. We were a stationary herd, twenty

or thirty of us in the immediate group, standing around the cars. The police kept well back against the buildings, hands behind them, guns on their hips, their peaked caps turning slowly as they watched the crowd.

"I think they're going to search us."

"Try dropping it between your feet."

I moved away from him; he might try something cute, and I didn't want them to find a bag of cocaine in my pocket.

It wouldn't matter.

You're perfectly right.

There was another man.

"You'll be late for the party."

The girl with the red mouth.

"Yes," I said.

"You want to take us along?"

This was the other girl, the one who'd been at the wheel, a mane of black hair, gold earrings, hips tilted, one leg dipped at the knee.

"If I ever get there," I said.

The other man was looking around him, though not obviously, not obviously at all, just taking a quick glance as he shrugged deeper into his coat, as he brushed ash off his sleeve.

"If you're too late for the party, would you like to come home with us?"

"Very much."

And you cannot, my good friend, say that I was lying.

He'd been standing close to the pagoda-top Mercedes until a few minutes ago, but now he was deeper into the crowd, not so isolated.

"We'll give you a good time." The hips tilting the other way. "I'm Lili, and this is Marie."

"Delighted."

He was worried, the man in the crowd. The police weren't likely to notice it because they had to keep so many of us under observation, whereas I could watch the man with more concentration.

"What's *your* name?"

"Mickey Mouse," I said and they both laughed.

When I'd got out of the car I'd done the same as the man, taking some quick glances around the environment; I'd no need to check it again. Behind us there was the intersection and a police car was stationed there and a barricade set up. In front of us was the group of police and the head of the line. There were doorways along the street but none of them offering cover. The only exit was a narrow gap between two of the buildings, not wide enough to call an alley; perhaps only a passage where trash bins were kept. Two Vopos were stationed there.

"Are you married?"

The man had a belted coat on; he was middle-aged, medium height, with a fur hat and a good pair of gloves. He wasn't a businessman, because of the soft rubber shoes; he wasn't, had never been, an official, despite the belted coat: he carried no air of authority, nor even a semblance. The car he'd got out of was the black pagoda-top Mercedes, an old model but light and fast; it suited him.

"Yes," I said. Married.

He could conceivably be an agent of some kind; not necessarily a spook but an entrepreneur in one of the intelligence services; or free-lance.

"What's your wife's name?"

But he didn't have nervous stamina.

"Minnie Mouse."

Got another laugh. By nervous stamina I mean that he was visibly beginning to break down. His head was turning more often now as he looked for a way out, and the colour was leaving his face. This is the way a trap will work on you, bringing the onset of panic by infinite degrees; and every time you look around for some way of escape and don't see one, the nerves go through another little death. I could see what was happening to the man over there because it was also happening to me.

Movement, near the Lancia.

"If I were you," I said, "I'd shut the windows of your car."

Marie turned her head. "What?"

"That chap's trying to get rid of some stuff."

"What stuff?" Then she saw him, the short man; he was standing right against the Lancia and she took straight off like a good gal and clobbered him with her handbag and I turned away because one of the policemen had caught on and was coming across from the buildings and with the all-points bulletin out for me I couldn't afford to let them come too close.

"What's going on there?"

The poor little bastard had dropped the package he'd been trying to shove through the Lancia's window and stood there with one arm up as a shield against the handbag.

Everyone turning to look, except the man with the belted coat, and he was using the chance to move nearer the gap between the bank and the library and I decided to head him off but it took a good ten minutes, stamping my feet quietly to keep them warm, shifting them backwards an inch at a time, watching the comedy going on near the Lancia—a cop, two tarts and a drug-pusher, what a cast— and finally I made the distance and got between the man in the coat and the alleyway and stood there with my back to it blowing into my hands slapping my shoulders.

Keep the line moving. Keep moving.

You must be joking, we haven't budged for the last fifteen minutes.

He looked at me now, just once, his glance passing across me and away again, and by now his face was bloodless. I would have said he'd got more on his mind than a packet of snort, though God knew what it might be. Both his hands were in the pockets of his coat and I noticed that the right one seemed a little larger, as if he were holding something.

Keep the line moving. Keep moving now!

The PA horn wasn't close but its sound hit his nerves and he flinched. And then we were off at last, shuffling towards the checkpoint, and he broke and swung round and started his run and I got in his way and he tried to dodge round me and I let out a shout and he pulled his gun as the nearest policemen came away from the buildings very fast in a crouching run with their own guns out and I moved backwards out of their way and got to the alley as the first shot sounded and then a fusillade so I suppose he'd fired first and they'd just wiped him out before he could hurt anyone, they're very efficient in East Berlin.

20

BLIND

Staring at his face.

Mission status: *The executive is clear of his red sector and has gone to ground. He is maintaining contact with his DIF.*

The face in the photographs.

Clear of his red sector, so forth, yes, but it didn't get us very far did it, just saved our skin, all that work and all I'd got was the Melnichenko-*Trumpeter* connection because the file was in his personal office.

Volper's. Volper's face.

Smooth, flat-looking, featureless except for the eyes, their being farther apart than the norm, and the nose, dead straight and with almost no bridge.

He was somewhere in this city and within the next twenty-four hours I would have to find him, and there was only one way and it was deadly because it meant taking to the streets and that was where the police patrols would be.

I telephoned Cone at eight o'clock in the morning, with the hydrogen peroxide stinging in the cuts at the back of my neck.

"I'm at the safe-house."

"What's your condition?"

"Active. There wasn't a lot of trouble. Few cuts. I got some sleep."

"What do I report for the board?"

I told him, gone to ground, so forth.

"Do you need anything?"

"Yes. I need funds placed at the Ost-Deutschebanke in Dimitroff-strasse in the name of Gunter Heinrich Blüm and made available to him on demand. The amount should be the replacement cost of a Mercedes 280 SE." I gave him time to make notes.

"How old?"

"Last year's."

That'd get the dust out of their bustles in the Accounts department.

"Is there a rush?"

"Make it within two days."

He didn't ask for any explanation because if I wanted to give him one I would do that. We'd got twenty-four hours left to bring home *Quickstep* and if I could do it for the price of a second-hand 280 SE they'd call it pocket-money in London.

"More?"

"I want official freedom of passage from East Germany to the West in the name of Frau Hilda Marlene Blüm. Her identity number is 325-A-467-10, date of birth July 9, 1937, place of birth, Berlin. Ask—"

"East or—" then something like oh, *come* on. He was feeling the strain.

"Ask Yasolev to see to it. There's no immediate rush, but before this time tomorrow the shit's going to hit the fan and I'd like things in order as soon as possible."

Making notes.

"The pass should be left at the bank together with the funds, in an envelope with the KGB seal on it."

"One or two?"

Not Cone. Gunter, in the doorway.

"Two."

"What?"

"I was talking to someone."

Eggs.

"Am I going to be able to reach you?"

"Only by phone." I gave him the number and he sounded relieved. "I commend your fortitude," I said.

"You know you can get me thrown out, don't you?"

"Yes."

He wasn't joking. The director in the field is expected to keep control of the executive in terms of his whereabouts in every phase of the mission providing the executive can remain in signals with him. I was going to remain in signals but I wasn't going to tell him where I'd gone to ground and that left him way out on a limb and Bureau One could cut off his career the moment he got back to London for final debriefing.

Hiss from the kitchen as the eggs went into the pan. "Look," I said carefully, "I think you know that when any given DIF runs me through a mission he's likely to lose track if that's how I want things to go. Shepley knows it too. I don't think he'll come down on you if I can't bring this one home. And if I can, you'll be an overnight saint."

He didn't say anything for a bit. "You could be pushing your luck. And mine. But I wish you well."

I liked his manners. We were moving very fast now into the end-phase of the mission because Gorbachev's scheduled arrival was tomorrow morning and I'd have to do a lot of work and take a lot of calculated risks and if I went down with a shot in the spine or ran afoul of East German Intelligence and had to pop the capsule or got washed up on a garbage heap for the want of a better grave he was leaving me with a last signal I could take comfort in as the dark came down, *I wish you well.*

"I'll remember that."

"When you're not there to answer the phone, will anyone else?"

"Yes. Gunter Blüm."

"Is he a professional?"

"No, but he's totally reliable and he'll do anything to get that pass."

"For his wife?"

"That's right. Use German; he hasn't any English."

"More?"

"Just one thing—I had to abandon the BMW. It's red hot and the police will be keeping a long-distance watch on it for a while and then they'll impound it and inform the rental company. I assume they can't trace it back to you."

"I used a sleeper with false papers. How soon do you want another car?"

"Not yet, but have one standing by and I'll tell you where to leave it for me."

"Any specific model?"

"Something fast."

"Anything else?"

"No. I'll keep in contact, don't worry."

Over and out.

Gunter put the tray on the kitchen table for me and I told him to sit down while I was eating. "Listen to me. Today and perhaps tonight I'm going to ask you to drive me wherever I want to go. I shan't ask you to follow anyone or break the speed limit or the law in any way, but I might want to take over the cab and leave you behind in the street."

He sat scratching the blister on his huge hand, watching me with his head lowered and his eyes lifted. "I don't know that I—"

"If you'll let me do that, you can tell the police later, if necessary, that I took your cab at gun-point and threw you out. That will leave you in the clear. Is that frying-pan still hot?"

He took a second to switch his thoughts.

"Yes."

"Drop this one back for a minute, will you?"

I can't stand them runny.

He lumbered away and I did some thinking and when he came back with the egg I told him: "I've made arrangements for you to pick up the cost of a replacement cab in case I do in fact take over and write it off. The funds will be in your name at the Ost-Deutschebanke in Dimitroff-strasse and all you need to do is show them your ID card. If I don't damage the cab, then take enough from the funds to cover my bill, and be generous. The balance can stay there and it'll be picked up."

"I don't like it." Scratching his blister. "You can lose your licence easily in this city. They get you for the slightest—"

"I will look after that too, but you'll have to trust me. If you can't, then forget it." I wanted to use the cab because I was going to try making a switch in the streets and it's a terribly difficult thing to pull off, but quite a bit easier if you can sit in the back of a taxi and check the environment the whole time without having to drive; you can also get out and do some work on foot and have it follow you around as a mobile base. "Whether you decide to trust me or not," I told him, "there'll be an envelope at the bank for you with an official Emigration Office pass for your wife in it, sealed by the KGB."

In a moment, "By the KGB?"

"I'm not a member of their organisation, but I've got useful connections." With emphasis—"The pass will *not* be a forgery."

He took time again before he answered. "I'll do whatever you say."

Cone made contact soon after four in the afternoon when the early-winter gloom was settling over the city. I'd spent the day working on the mechanics of the switch I'd have to do and testing them out. It would need darkness, and Cone caught me within an hour of leaving the safe-house.

"I've just had a call," he said. "It was for you, but when I said you were unavailable he agreed to give me the message."

"Did he use a parole?"

"No. He said his name was Geissler, and that he's got something for you from Lena."

"He just said Lena? Not Lena Pabst?"

"That's right."

"Anything else?"

"He left a number for you to call."

I wrote it down.

"This was minutes ago?"

"I phoned you right away. Does the name mean anything?"

"No."

"When she phoned yesterday," Cone said, "she said she'd got some documents for you, remember?"

"Yes."

A shrug in his tone. "It could be that."

"Or it could be someone in *Trumpeter*."

After a bit he said, "Yes in which case you'll have to step gingerly."

"I'll work on it and report back."

I rang off and gave it some thought. Lena Pabst could have had someone with her when she'd started infiltrating *Trumpeter*, and he could be Geissler. Or someone in *Trumpeter* itself could have gone through her papers after she'd been shot dead, and found my number at the hotel and decided it was worth trying. They would have been desperate to know how much she'd found out and what she'd passed on.

Pick up the phone.

"Speaking."

He had a quiet voice, though not passive; quiet in the same way as Shepley's.

"I'm told you've got something for me."

I was listening very hard, particularly for the sound of aircraft in the background, or an office PA system. I was probably speaking to Werneuchen Airforce Base.

"Yes," he said.

I hadn't turned the light on in the room, and the distant glow from the Wall was coming through the window.

"How do I obtain it?"

The brief, circumspect language of caution. I might even be speaking to the chief of the *Trumpeter* operation.

"We would agree on a rendezvous."

She hadn't mentioned anyone. She hadn't said, *I know someone who can help me*.

"I'm willing to do that."

"You would have to be alone."

"I agree."

I might even be speaking to Volper.

"Then we shall rendezvous at six o'clock this evening, in Karl Liebknecht-strasse. Is that convenient for you?"

"It is."

"What car will you be driving?"

I was trying hard to detect an accent. In a blind rendezvous it can help if you can establish the other party's voice in the memory. This man's accent was educated and I thought Jewish.

"I'll take a taxi," I said.

"Very well. Tell the driver to go east along Karl Liebknecht-strasse and pass the church and cross Liebknecht Bridge. Tell him to put you down between there and Spandauer-strasse. Do you understand?"

Said I did.

"When you get out of the taxi, forget to tip the driver. Walk a short distance and go back and give him the tip."

I liked his style.

"Understood."

"Then walk towards Spandauer-strasse. You will be met."

"What do I look for?"

"Just keep walking. I will meet you."

Captain Friebourg . . . Will Captain Friebourg report immediately to Wing Command . . .

Faint, but clear, metallic, a woman's voice.

Werneuchen.

"All right," I said.

"I repeat. You will come alone. If I see anyone who might be with you, I shall not meet you, and of course you will receive nothing."

"Understood."

The line went dead.

A slight tingling along the nerves, but this was normal. Russian roulette is like that; it worries the primitive brain; and this was Russian roulette, though the odds were shorter: they were even. Either the man had been a friend of Lena Pabst's and had been working for me alongside her, or he was in the *Trumpeter* cell, and it might be fun to put it a little differently: tonight, if I kept the rendezvous, I could obtain valuable, even vital information on their operation that might advance *Quickstep* like a slingshot and send me straight to the objective. Or I could walk into a trap.

Ask for support.

You're not—

Ask Cone. Call him now.

You're not thinking. He could put six people into the field—he said he'd got six standing by—or Yasolev could put fifty into the field and I wouldn't be taking any risk, but this man Geissler sounded professional and he would put his own people into the field to make sure I went to the rendezvous alone, and they would report to him and he wouldn't even show up.

If I were going to the rendezvous it wouldn't be to waste time.

They could finish you off, don't you—

Of course I see.

Call Cone and get support. You can't—

Oh for Christ's sake shuddup.

All right then there wouldn't be a chance of seeing the trap in time and doing anything about it, if this was a move by *Trumpeter*. But the rendezvous was set up in a lighted street at a busy time in the evening and there'd be people around and police patrols on routine duty in the area and this made a difference, gave me an edge.

Bullshit.

Well yes, if you want to put it that way, I agree. I'd go to this rendezvous even if it were at midnight in a deserted wharf on the riverside with not a soul in sight, because I wanted to reach the objective for *Quickstep* and that might be the only way to do it.

So I told Gunter I wanted the cab at 5:30 this evening and he said he'd stand by.

"What time do you eat?"

His eyes in the mirror. "Any time I can make it."

North on Friedrich-strasse towards Unter den Linden.

5:42.

"Take a loop or two. We're a bit early."

He used Behren-strasse.

At thirteen minutes to six we were back on Friedrich-strasse and turned east along Unter den Linden. There was rush-hour traffic, but less heavy than it would have been on the other side of the Wall, where there were more private cars.

At five minutes to six we crossed Marx Engels Bridge and I saw the church coming up on the left.

"Gunter. I want you to drop me in Karl Liebknecht-strasse, halfway between the church and Spandauer-strasse. When I get out, make a circuit of the block and cruise past the place where you left me."

"Very good."

"Cruise past there twice. If you don't see me, park at the church and wait for one hour. If I don't show up, go and find a cafe and have your meal. After that you're free."

"Very good."

Not really, but he didn't know that.

The adrenaline was already starting to flow: I was feeling high. The organism was going through the process of trying to survive, stopping digestion, diverting blood to the muscles, tightening the nerves. Fight or flight, so forth, but there might not be a chance to do either.

We don't like a blind rendezvous, even with support in the field, even with an overkill response mapped out, because the timing can be critical and the other party can make his strike and get clear before we can do a single thing about it. Some bright spark at Norfolk did a survey of the past ten years' history of intelligence and terrorist operations and came out with the figures: in the total number of a hundred and seven blind rendezvous actions, nineteen were carried out safely and in sixty-three cases the agent was kidnapped and in twenty-five cases he was killed, in fourteen cases by a long-distance shot.

Three minutes to six, the blood singing.

Two minutes, the mouth dry.

One minute, and the thought quick as a bullet—*You shouldn't have come*.

"All right, drop me just here."

21
STEPS

I walked six paces, turned and walked back.

"Supper's on me."

Be generous. 250 marks. Placate the gods.

Thanked me, surprised.

I started walking again. A woman with two little girls, one of them swinging on her arm; three businessmen, visitors from the West, look at their suits—one of them waved at Gunter but he didn't stop. Walking steadily. A priest of some sort, holding a woman by the shoulders, offering his handkerchief; a man eating bread from a paper bag, hopeless with age; four or five girls half-running, laughing towards the bus stop; chimes from the church, six o'clock, *in fourteen cases by a long-distance shot*.

Squeal of brakes and the sound of an engine quite close and I turned round.

"Good evening."

He was out of the van and gesturing for me to get in, a man with a thick body in a black padded ski-jacket, no expression on his compact face, the eyes nowhere, the whole attitude totally impersonal.

I got in and sat down on the bench-type seat and he came in after me so that I was between the two of them and the driver botched the gears in and got moving as the two men prodded me in the sides with standard service revolvers and I didn't work out any kind of action because the finger has to move less than two centimetres on the trigger to produce the effect and a double elbow strike would have to move across a much greater distance than that and it'd never make impact in time.

Handcuffs, the old-fashioned kind, steel, possibly military police issue at Werneuchen; a black bag over the head, smelling of oil, perhaps gun oil.

No one spoke.

What would anyone have said, *One move and we'll blow you away?* They weren't the kind of people to state the obvious. *Don't worry, I'm not going to try anything*, and nor was I.

We took a left off Karl Liebknecht-strasse into Spandauer —it must have been Spandauer because we'd turned within half a minute; then a right and two lefts and I stopped trying to work out the track we were leaving because I didn't know the topography too well on this side of the Wall. I'd have to rely on the time, if I could get a look at my watch or theirs or a clock when we arrived: given an approximate estimate of the speed of the van including stops, I could use a map and more or less establish the destination as being one of a dozen points according to which streets we'd used, and a dozen would be better than none.

I'd only seen the side of the van when I'd got in but it had the look of a small military transport with five bench seats and a rack for cases or kit bags along each side. None of these men were in uniform but that didn't mean anything. I didn't think the man who'd ushered me in was the one I'd spoken to on the phone, but he could be; he'd only said two words just now, *Good evening*. He could have been the man who'd shot Lena Pabst.

I had to raise both hands when I tried to ease the neck of the cloth bag they'd pulled down over my head, but I didn't get far before the man on my right dug the muzzle of his gun into my side, bruising a rib.

"Keep still. Keep your hands on your knees."

"I can't breathe."

He just dug the gun in again and said nothing.

I could in fact breathe adequately but I wanted very much to take in more oxygen for the muscles. I didn't think there'd be a chance of doing anything until they got me out of the van but I didn't know what they were going to do after that and I wanted to be ready to make a break if I could, because this was a strictly shut-ended situation and if I left it too late they'd do the Lena Pabst thing, *finis*.

Executive reported to be in opposition hands awaiting probable terminal incident.

Shepley wouldn't be pleased. *I chose him because to date he's proved himself capable of dealing with very unfavourable conditions in the field, and if he survives I shall expect an explanation as to why he allowed himself to be compromised, together with the entire mission.*

The explanation, sir, is that I took a calculated risk, and there's an odd misconception going around that a calculated risk isn't in fact a risk at all, but you of all people, your eminence, should know better than that. You should also know that the executive must sometimes stick his

neck out and invite flak because there's simply no other
way to get close to the opposition, and if you think I was
overdoing it in this particular instance it just means, with
respect, that you're not thinking straight.

Very nervous indeed and getting worse, he'd understand, Shepley, he'd been there himself and he'd taken the
same kind of risk, plenty of times, if he'd been in the
SAS.

Hot under the bag, very little oxygen, they could as-
phyxiate me like this. But then they wouldn't be terribly
concerned because when they finally put the bullet in the
brain it wouldn't make any difference whether there was a
condition of oxygen deprivation at the time: the skull
would be blown open like a coconut just the same.

Flying-boots.

We turned left again and then right, waiting at the lights
and botching the gears in; either the driver wasn't all that
conversant with the box or there was wear on the shafts, it
was getting on my nerves, I tell you it was getting on my
nerves.

Fur-lined flying-boots: it was about all I could see below
the neck of the bag. Pilot. Pilot or bombardier, air-crew.
They probably both were.

Slowing.

"Close as you can get."

"Sir."

Slowing and turning, bumping over rough ground, turning tightly now, the vehicle heeling on the springs, then
pulling up, the sound of the engine louder, confined on
one side by a wall.

"Raus! Raus!"

One of them hit the door open and dropped to the
ground and the other one pushed his gun into my back and
I clambered down, the handcuffs a real handicap because

we were in the open and if I couldn't do anything now the last chance would be gone; but I couldn't see anything except the split tarmac under my feet and a cigarette-end. One of them had a grip on my arm and pushed me forward and I heard a door opening.

Steps, down, and I lost my footing because I didn't know they were there, hit my shoulder on a wall or a doorpost and someone caught me and pulled me straight, smell of cooking from somewhere and a car starting up outside, not the van we'd come in, *dampness,* a smell of dampness now, still going down with a gun bruising my spine, I suppose they thought I wasn't getting the message; I would have liked, I would very much have liked to swing round fast and make at least one strike and use the handcuffs as a weapon, but it was just a feeling of spite, I didn't like these bastards, they weren't professionals, all this bloody prodding, I *knew* they had guns out, for Christ's sake.

"Put him there—"

Chair, seat of a chair behind my legs and I let them buckle, sat down, very bright light as they dragged the bag off my head.

"Can I have some water?"

Simply to make them talk, do something, show some kind of reaction so that I could learn what they were like, get to know them, get to know useful things that might help me find a way out. But they didn't take any notice.

"Go and fetch him."

The taller one nodded and went back up the steps; the thick-bodied one stayed behind with me, standing with his legs astride and the revolver aimed at the diaphragm, not terribly good at his anatomy, the heart is where you aim a gun if you're serious; for a professional it's a learned habit. They weren't professionals and that could give me an edge: one has, you see, to clutch at straws, lacking a boat.

This place was quite well furnished, compared with the standard interrogation cell: telephone, three or four antique chairs with the veneer chipped and the brocade worn thin, an *art déco* chest of drawers and a lamp with a chrome post and a red plush shade—they'd raided a junk shop and taken the first things they could lay hands on, I suppose, not that I'm fussy as a guest when I've got a gun aimed at my guts.

"This is just for your information," I said. "I'm an officer of the HUA with captain's rank, and it will go better for you if you and your colleague agree to release me at this stage with no harm done. I'm sure you'll see the logic of that."

There was no point in telling him that my department knew I was making the rendezvous and would be initiating an immediate search, because if the HUA had known about the rendezvous they would have filled the streets with patrol cars before we'd even got as far as Spandauer-strasse.

I think he'd understood what I'd said, though he didn't take any immediate interest; he was still looking at nothing in particular, his eyes blank, his entire presence imper-sonal, very like a customs officer who spends his day chewing people and spitting them out again without really enjoying the taste.

But now he was taking an interest; he'd been turning things over in his mind.

"Give me your wallet."

I reached for my hip pocket, both hands together, and got the wallet and held it out for him so that he could look at my papers to see if I was telling the truth, but he wasn't a professional and his mood was perfectly calm because he'd got a gun on me and I was in handcuffs and there was nothing I could do and in this he was in error because my survival was threatened and the system was full of adrenaline and the nerves were singing with tension and the muscles taut as a bowstring and I raked the edge of my shoe down his shin with force enough to strip the flesh off the bone and bring a scream of agony as my foot impacted on the angle of his flying-boot with the whole weight of my body bearing down and the hips spinning and the hands driving against his gun-wrist and the links between the handcuffs snapping it at the joint as the gun fired and I heard the bullet hit the wall behind me.

I think he was already unconscious before he hit the ground; with most people the degree of pain I'd induced will be enough to cross the threshold and demand relief and the only relief available is the cessation of awareness and the brain will look after things.

He shattered the leg of an antique chair as he went down with his face white and his neck twisting as his head rolled against the concrete floor and I left him there and crouched and picked up the gun and had it in my right hand with my left forearm across the small of my back to give me an adequate position for the aim as the door opened at the top of the steps and Pollock came down, no bright smile.

22

POLLOCK

"God," he said quietly, "what a mess."

The pilot had vomited when he'd regained consciousness and the pain had started up again, but I don't think Pollock meant that; he meant the whole situation.

"Move over there," I said, "behind him. And don't let him get up."

"I doubt if he can. But I've got to get him to a hospital."

"Pollock," I said, "this isn't a fucking cricket club. *Get over there.*"

He moved now, but not because the gun worried him. That was my impression.

"If the other man comes down the steps," I said, "and you give him any kind of warning, I'm going to put a bullet straight into your head. *Parlez-vous* English?"

He gave a slow blink, as if keeping patience. "Look, if I take the handcuffs off, will you put down the gun?"

"In that order, yes. But first we've got to wait for the other man to come back. I want his gun too."

"His name's Schwarz," he said with a formality that would have amused me if I hadn't been so enraged. On the trip from the rendezvous I'd been certain they were going to shoot me as they'd shot Lena Pabst, and there was all that adrenaline still hanging around the blood and going sour. "We need to talk," Pollock said, and then a door opened and someone came down the steps and Pollock looked up. "Jürgen, put your revolver on the floor, will you?"

The man took a look at things and began pulling his gun out of the holster and I said, "Do it *very* carefully," and he just used his finger and thumb on the butt as if it were something smelly, and laid it on the bottom step. Then he looked at the man on the floor.

"We'll get him to a doctor," Pollock said.

I was still holding the gun with my left arm twisted behind my back and it was tiring. "Pollock, come over here and stand with your back to me."

The man on the floor was crooning over his broken wrist, his face still bloodless. He was the one who'd kept digging his gun into me on the way here.

"Closer," I told Pollock, and he went on backing towards me until the muzzle of my revolver was touching his spine. Then I told the pilot in German, "Unlock these things." I didn't need to tell him what would happen to Pollock's spine if anyone played about. Schwarz, Pollock had said his name was.

When the handcuffs were off my wrists I told them both to move into the corner behind the man on the floor.

"Schwarz, is that driver still up there in the van?"

"Yes."

"Get him down here. If you're longer than two minutes I'm going to put your friend out of his misery."

"Look—" Pollock said.

"*Shuddup*." I was in a rotten mood and it was their bloody fault.

Schwarz went and got the driver, a young low-ranker in a windcheater and boots, his movements sharp and circumspect in the presence of the pilots.

I looked at Pollock. "Where is this place?"

"The cellar underneath the club."

I told the driver, "Go upstairs and get a bucket of water and a cloth and come back and clear up that mess on the floor. Then you'll take the officer to the nearest medical centre. Now *move*."

"Sir!"

"Pollock, you can light a cigarette. Schwarz too."

It'd help cover the smell. I watched their hands as a matter of caution, but Pollock hadn't got anything on him or he'd have reached for it when he'd come down the steps and seen the mess.

I went over to the phone and dialled the hotel.

Second ring: Cone was nursing it.

"The rendezvous," I told him, "was set up to make a snatch. I've restored order and I'm now in the *Trumpeter* operations room, though it looks more like a junk shop: we're not dealing with a very sophisticated cell. I'm—"

"Where is it?"

"I don't want you sending people around. Listen, I'm going to get all the information I can, and I'll phone you again in an hour, at 7:45. If I don't, call the British Ambassador and tell him that Pollock, his cultural attaché, is in the *Trumpeter* cell, and by the look of it I'd say he's running things. But do *not* give that information to *anyone* unless I fail to call you. I don't want to blow this operation until I know what's happening, and there's an awful lot of stuff hitting the fan. With this man Pollock involved we've got a *second* UK connection, so we don't want to make any waves.''

Cigarette smoke drifting on the air. The driver came down the steps with a red plastic bucket with the Kronnenburg logo on it and started to clean up, making a lot of haste.

"You can't do this."

Cone.

"What are you talking about?"

"I've got to signal London. You must realise that."

"I'm not stopping you."

"But I've got to tell them you've successfully penetrated *Trumpeter*, and—" on a thought—"you *are* in charge there, aren't you?"

"Yes."

"That's very nice, but I can't tell Bureau One that you're in contact with me but you're totally alone in the centre of the opposition cell and refuse to let me know where it is."

"Oh for Christ's sake, I've had a long day. I'm—"

"I know, but you're not listening. What sort of director will I look like?"

I thought about it while the driver took the bucket up the steps, boots banging. I suppose it was the only way Cone knew he could break me down, by appealing to my respect for him.

"It's not your fault if I don't do things by the book."

I heard him let out a breath. "You are in—" no contraction, articulating carefully—"the centre of an opposition cell and may at any time find yourself compromised, and when questions are asked later I shan't be able to explain why my executive lost all trust in me and refused all confidence." His voice went very quiet. "It's not a question of not doing things by the book. It's a question of *manners*."

Oh Jesus Christ, he was as bad as Ferris: we were only ten days into the mission but he'd learned *exactly* how to manipulate me.

In a minute I said, "You go straight for the groin, don't you?"

"That's better," he said.

The driver came down again and went over to the man on the floor.

"Hold on a minute," I told Cone, and put the phone down and got the gun from the bottom step and swung the chamber out and dropped the bullets into my hand and threw the gun into the corner of the room; then I did the same thing with the one I'd borrowed and picked up the handcuffs and gave everything to the driver. "You'll drop these bullets down the nearest drain in the car park and put the handcuffs into the van." The man took them but looked across at Schwarz and I told Schwarz: "Order him."

"Do as he says."

"Sir."

He got hold of the other man and helped him onto his feet. He was fully conscious now and in a great deal of pain.

I looked at the driver. "Can you manage the steps?"

"Yes, sir."

"Quick as you can, then." The movement wasn't going to help the pain and I didn't want any more mess in here.

I picked up the phone again. "Something I had to see to. All right, but you'd have to give me your word that you'll send *no one* into this area unless I fail to make that call."

It took him a few seconds. "I will send no one."

"Fair enough. I'm in the cellar underneath Charlie's Club. Got that? If I don't make the call, you can send in a

whole platoon of the KGB and blow the place open.''
Watching Pollock as I said that, and he looked *very* surprised, though he kept most of it blanked off. I was
beginning to think he was a spook of some sort, running
his own thing. "Look," I told Cone, "I don't want to
handle this on my own for the moment just for kicks. The
thing is it's so bloody sensitive that I want a clear field to
work in until I know which way we're facing. But I'll give
you everything I've got as soon as I'm ready. I hope you
can accept that.''

A question of manners.

In a moment, "Yes, I can live with it for now.''

"I'll phone at 7:45.''

Rang off.

Pollock hadn't moved; he was standing on one leg with
his back and his other foot against the wall, his cigarette
half through. Schwarz was moving up and down, less tall
than he'd seemed before: it had been in comparison with
the other pilot; but he was much thinner and his face was
hollowed and his eyes strained, his mouth tight, a nervy
man, his own cigarette-end already in the tin ashtray on
the floor by one of the chairs.

"I think we could use a drink, couldn't we?''

Pollock.

With care I asked him: "Where is Horst Volper?''

"I've no idea.''

"Look, I can play it two ways. I can pick up the phone
and get the KGB here and give you over to them for
exhaustive interrogation under a very bright light or I can
get all the information I want out of you here and now and
in relative comfort, if that's your choice. But if that's your
choice, don't think you can piss me about.''

Pulling in smoke, blowing it out. "We really have no
idea where Horst Volper is. He's nothing to do with us,

but I know he's in East Berlin on an operation of his own, and I personally know that you're working his case."

Secret Service idiom, not Bureau. Meant Volper was my objective.

"Who's your chief of station at the Embassy?"

"Technically, Saunders."

"D.I.6?"

"Yes."

"But they're not running *Trumpeter*."

"No, that's mine." The back of his head was against the wall too, and he was sighting me along his nose. He looked relaxed. He wasn't. "When I say mine, I mean I'm just coordinating it all from this centre."

D.I.6 idiom again. "As a free-lance?"

"Of course." Sudden bright smile. "They wouldn't do anything like this."

I knew that. "Lena Pabst," I said. "Whose orders?"

It brought him off the wall and he went over to the ashtray, not looking at me. "No one's orders, and certainly not mine." I heard anger in the tone.

"Who shot her, then?"

"Bader."

"Who's he?"

"The man you messed up."

"The pilot who's just left here?"

"Yes. I pitched into him over that." Putting his hands into his pockets, pushing his fists out, the old school habit. "In fact I said I was going to drop the whole thing."

"Why didn't you?"

He took a deep breath. "Melnichenko said I'd have to stay in and see it through. He said it was too important." In a moment: "It is."

"Too important to let a little thing like killing a woman bother you."

Self-righteous bastard, I was as guilty as anyone, sending her into an infiltration exercise that I should have
known might be lethally dangerous.

"I'm sorry about that part of things," Pollock said
quietly. "Very sorry." He switched to German and looked
at the pilot. "What happened when I heard about Lena
Pabst?"

A shrug. "You hit the roof."

"What else? Be more specific." I heard the edge to his
tone and the authority in it. That clean white smile of his
was just something he flashed on and off when he was
being cultural attaché to the British Embassy.

"You said you were finished with us," Schwarz said.

Pollock looked back at me. "Make up your own mind."

"She must have been doing very well. Getting very
close."

"That's why Bader panicked."

"Is he anything more than a bomber pilot?"

"He's not in intelligence, if that's what you mean."

"I mean precisely what I said. Is he anything more than
a pilot? I want straight answers, Pollock, so don't fuck me
about."

Not keeping my cool terribly well, no, but in the last
hour I'd been in handcuffs with a hood over my head and
absolutely sure I'd taken the final calculated risk and then
I'd found I was right in the nerve-centre of *Trumpeter*, and
there was a *lot* of work to do before I could move into the
end-phase and find Volper and put him away before the
General-Secretary of the USSR landed in East Berlin with
a massive protection screen that would *still* be penetrated
by Volper's operation unless we could stop him, so I wasn't
in the mood to put up with less than straight answers.

"Bader's no more than a bomber pilot," Pollock said
evenly. "Except for his involvement in *Trumpeter*."

"What about this bloody fool here?"

I was watching Schwarz and his eyes didn't change. I wasn't being rude: I wanted to know if he understood English, to know that when he said that Pollock was "finished with them" he hadn't just been picking up from what Pollock had said earlier, that he'd been going to "drop the whole thing."

No reaction from Pollock either; he knew what I was doing. "It's the same with him. He's just in the mission with us."

"And what is the mission?"

Dead silence while the tension in the room hit infinity, and this was understandable. Of the hundred or two questions I was going to ask tonight, *that* was the ringer.

I waited. Everything depended on this. I could blow *Trumpeter* and they knew it, but I wasn't ready to do that until I had a lot more answers. One thing stuck out from the rest: I couldn't see this man Pollock involved in an operation *against* Mikhail Gorbachev.

In a moment: "Difficult to say."

"Then get Melnichenko here."

"Right-o." He sounded almost relieved.

As he went to the telephone I said, "Pollock, this is exactly what you'll say. *Can you come here immediately? It's urgent.* Repeat that."

He did, and got it right.

"If you slip in any other word, I'm going to tell the KGB to take over, and God help you."

"Point taken." He picked up the phone and dialled.

I listened carefully and he got it right again and rang off before Melnichenko could put any questions.

"Is this an extension line?"

"No," he said. "It's separate."

"Then you can ask the people upstairs to send down whatever you want to drink. It's going to be a long night."

"I rather think it is." He was trying to relax, but wasn't managing; the quick clean smile didn't work any more. "What'll you have?"

"Black Russian tea, no lemon."

"Jürgen?"

"Beer," Schwarz said, and dropped into a chair. He was worried about Bader; I assumed they were close friends.

When Pollock put the phone down I asked him: "You're still officially in D.I.6?"

"I suppose so. I mean yes, I am, but if they knew what I was doing they'd throw me straight out."

"What have you been doing officially?"

"Oh—" he sat down too, leaning forward, playing with his hands—"mostly I've been feeding stuff from some of the agents-in-place here to the desk. Then I did a special for them, last year. The Ericson exchange."

"You supervised that one?"

"I initiated it. We—"

"From which end?"

"Moscow." He sounded quietly pleased. He should be. "I asked them outright who they'd take in exchange."

And they'd said Komoroff and Bulgin, who weren't all that much of a catch anyway. We knew about that one—everybody did.

"Nice work," I said.

"Thank you. It wasn't that difficult."

"You've got some good friends in Moscow."

"They're all right. They want watching." Quick smile.

I made a mental note to ask Cone to hit the computers in London with a question: Who handled the Ericson swap? Pollock could be lying through his teeth. But from what he was telling me and the idiom he was using I knew at least that he was either in D.I.6 or liaising with them from some other official department.

"So what made you go off the rails?"

His hands stopped playing. "I wouldn't quite put it like that, if you're talking about *Trumpeter*."

"How would you put it?"

He didn't answer for a second or two and I knew why. I'd told him I was going to open up this operation of his and look at it very hard, and I'd told him that if he didn't cooperate I'd throw them all to the KGB to do it for me. The only thing he could do now was to appear to tell me everything and at the same time try to tell me nothing.

And the very best of luck.

"*Trumpeter*," he said, "is an operation that's going to change Europe, and—" he gave a little apologetic smile— "I hope this doesn't sound too dramatic—and change the geopolitical world, overnight." He must have remembered what I'd just told Cone over the phone, because he said, "You can't judge the size of an operation by the furniture."

"Touché."

"There's only one thing wrong with *Trumpeter*." His voice had gone terribly quiet, and I noticed his hands were shaking.

"I've blown it."

"That's right."

23

MORNING

A big man, big-bodied, not overweight, his head totally bald and pear-shaped, widening downwards to a heavy face, his eyes very alert indeed, especially now, his mouth fleshy and pink, his ears flattened against his balloon-smooth head, his neck thick, with a double chin, his flushed skin shining from the top of his head to his collar, washed, polished, giving him a baby's glow.

He came down the steps quickly.

Melnichenko.

And stopped. Wrinkles developed across his forehead as his eyes moved to take in the scene. To me, in German with a Russian accent—"That was you, wasn't it, in the building?"

He got an A for that: he could only have caught a glimpse of me as I'd run for the elevator. I didn't answer.

"You were in my office?"

I didn't say anything. Pollock had got out of his chair and the pilot, Schwarz, was on his feet too.

"Aleksy," Pollock said, "this is Mr Ash." To me: "Commandant Melnichenko, GRU."

I said good evening. He inclined his head, his pale blue eyes engaged. Then a glance to Pollock.

"I was in the middle of dinner."

I didn't know whether he resented the interruption or was excusing himself for not getting here sooner.

Pollock ignored it anyway. "Mr Ash wants to ask us some questions." He glanced at Schwarz. "Ludwig, would you mind getting another chair down here?"

"Make it two," I told him.

Then someone else came down the steps with a big pewter tray, and Pollock told him to get a bottle of Smirnov too and a shot glass. It was very busy for a bit and I noticed Melnichenko trying to pick up whatever he could from Pollock's expression, which was strictly non-committal, the spook's language for extreme caution, his eyes deliberately not meeting the Russian's but just looking casually all over the room.

The two extra chairs and the bottle of vodka arrived and Pollock was nice enough to pour me a cup of tea and I held my hands round it because it was so bloody cold in here.

"Commandant," I said, "I'm in British intelligence and I'm out here to assist the KGB, at their request. I want to know everything about *Trumpeter*. If you won't answer me, you'll have to answer the KGB."

Lovely hot tea.

"What is the exact position?" he asked Pollock in Russian.

Jesus Christ, that wasn't very clever.

"The exact position," I said in Russian, "is that you've got to do what I tell you, because I've blown *Trumpeter* and you might as well face up to it and cooperate."

But I was only feeling my way. In this situation anything was possible: Pollock was running a rogue operation, but the GRU could be working with him unofficially but with direct orders from someone extremely high in the Kremlin.

"I feel it is a little too early." He'd switched back to German.

"Too early to cooperate?"

"Well yes. I would require official assurances, for instance, as to your bona fides." His chubby smile was like Pollock's, an automatic reflex.

"You're not in a position to require things," I told him. "Your only hope is to assist me—and my government— to the point where you might save yourself from the high displeasure of the Kremlin."

I waited. Pollock's hands were restless again; he couldn't keep them still, because when he stopped playing with them I could see they were shaking.

"Aleksy," he said quietly, "I can vouch for what Mr Ash has said. He is in fact an agent in British intelligence."

"Then we can conduct discussions on an official level."

I decided to give him five more minutes, because in those five minutes I might get him to fall with his pink polished face flat in the doo-doo, which would give me a real kick because these people had handled me as if I'd been a bloody amateur, guns in my guts and all that.

"If you were in a position to conduct discussions on an official level, Commandant, what are you doing in a freezing cellar underneath a club run mostly for the top brass in the black market?"

I suppose Pollock had thought I hadn't noticed, when

we'd had lunch together; but he wasn't worried about that now. I'd got Melnichenko into a corner and he knew it and he was smart enough to try another gambit.

"The thing is, we don't see why you should be taking an interest in *Trumpeter* at all. It's basically a Soviet operation."

"I'm taking an interest because it's patently clandestine and there's an Englishman 'coordinating things'—as you put it—from this centre and that man Bader will shortly be up on a murder charge because I'm going to see that he is, and the objective of my own mission is the protection of General-Secretary Gorbachev and I haven't got the slightest assurance that *Trumpeter* is not in point of fact aimed at him. And if what you're doing is liable to change Europe and the geopolitical world then my department is going to inform the Prime Minister very quickly indeed." I took another swig at the tea. "And you know what she's going to do? She's going to get Mr Gorbachev on his private line and make absolutely certain he's informed."

Melnichenko was very good; he could keep his eyes blanked off and he could keep his hands perfectly still but he hadn't got any control over his parasympathetic nervous system and the beads of sweat were gathering on his naked head and glistening under the light, and it was cold enough in here to immasculate a brass monkey.

But he made an attempt. "I was called here at short notice, as you know. Perhaps if you'd give me a day or two before we meet again? I can then confer with my contacts in Moscow."

Couldn't learn.

Pollock came in at me fast—"Look, you've talked about getting the KGB in on this, but we're not at all sure you can do that. I mean frankly, both sides need assurances, don't you agree?"

They'd had their five minutes and I finished the tea in my cup and poured some more and got up and went across to the telephone.

Cone picked up on the first ring.

I asked him: "Is Yasolev with you?"

"No. He's at the embassy."

"His own?"

"Yes. What's the position?"

"They're being uncooperative, so I'm going to throw them to the dogs. I'll keep you well informed."

I think he was going to ask something else but I rang off.

"Commandant Melnichenko, how long have you been here in East Berlin?"

"Almost three years." He was looking particularly bland, but his head was glistening.

"Then you see quite a bit of the Soviet Ambassador."

"I do, yes."

"And you're familiar with his private telephone number."

"Yes."

He was sitting near enough to the phone to be able to see what I was dialling, and that was all I wanted.

"Chancery."

"I'd like to speak to Ambassador Polyakov."

"I'm sorry, but he is dining now. May I take a message?"

"Tell him Liaison is on the line."

He asked me to repeat it and I did; he was confused because it wasn't a name.

Pollock got up and started mooching about. I was sorry for him: he'd had his mission blown from under him, but it was his own fault. He shouldn't have given these pilots such a free hand; they weren't in intelligence and didn't know how to operate.

"Polyakov."

"Your Excellency, let me apologize for disturbing you at dinner."

"It doesn't matter, because in any case the duck was a disaster. I requested *flambé*, not *incinéré*. What can I do for you?"

"Do you know a Commandant A. V. Melnichenko?"

"I do."

"Is he here in an official capacity as a member of the GRU?"

"As far as I know. He's an adviser to the Airforce."

"Thank you. Is Colonel Yasolev there this evening?"

"I'll call him to the phone."

Pollock was still on the move, hands dug into his pockets, fists pushed out. I put a hand over the mouthpiece.

"Colonel Yasolev is KGB. He'll be your chief interrogator; it's his speciality."

I'd spoken in German so that Melnichenko and Schwarz could pick it up.

Laughter broke out faintly from the rooms above, an odd sound, surrealistic in this context.

"Yasolev."

"Good evening. Let me ask a question. Would you be ready to put two people under intensive interrogation immediately?"

"But of course."

Pollock had stopped walking about, and was staring at the floor. Melnichenko was wiping his face. I was speaking in Russian, and Schwarz wasn't getting anything, but he was watching the other two, and that was good enough.

"As you know," I told Yasolev, "we haven't got much time left. You may have to be very persuasive."

"These people are with you now?"

"Yes. But they're refusing to talk. I know you'll be more successful."

"Is it a suitable place?"

"It's a cellar, but it's not really sound-proof. You can do it at KGB Headquarters, can't you?"

"Of course."

"Then I'll have them available for you to pick up. I'd suggest four men and a van. I don't—"

I broke off because Pollock was looking up at me.

"No KGB," he said. "Full disclosure. Deal?"

"If you don't change your mind."

"It wouldn't make sense, would it?"

"Yasolev," I said into the phone, "go and finish your dinner and I'll call on you again when everything's ready."

"But I insist on knowing what's happening. Are these two of Volper's people?"

"No. You can ask Cone about it: I've got my hands rather full."

I told him I'd keep in close touch and rang off and dialled extension 525 at the hotel.

Second ring.

"It's time you came down here," I told Cone. "Bring the tape-recorder and five sixty-minute tapes, plus the mains charger." I looked at Pollock. "Where exactly is the door to this cellar?" I'd had the bag over my head when I'd been brought here.

"It's on the east side of the building at the end of the car park. Green door, next to some railings."

I told Cone. "And listen, this location is strictly covert. *Strictly.*"

I didn't want to mention Yasolev's name again and let Pollock know that I was keeping him uninformed. It was simply that it wasn't the time to let the KGB loose on *Trumpeter;* it sounded much too sensitive.

"Understood," Cone said. "Shall I tell Jones?"

"No. It's not his concern."

He was just making sure I wasn't in fact a captive and phoning him under duress to bring him into a trap: I'd told him earlier that I was in the *Trumpeter* operations room. If I'd said yes—tell Jones—he would have had this place surrounded straight away and put under siege conditions.

"I won't be long," he said.

"Can somebody open that door?"

Place was stinking of cigarette smoke, getting on the eyes. There'd been a bit of hope a couple of hours ago when Pollock had thrown his empty packet of Players onto the table, but he'd called the barman upstairs to bring another one. I hadn't stopped him because I'd wanted his nerves kept sedated.

Schwarz went up the steps to open the door.

It was gone three o'clock and the place was littered with plastic plates and the remains of bread and blood-sausage and sauerkraut and hard-boiled eggs and everything looked in a real mess but we'd got *Trumpeter* nailed down, the whole thing.

And Pollock was perfectly right: if we let this one go forward to completion it could change Europe, and the world.

"I shall have to inform London," Cone said at last.

He'd been edifying to watch, sitting there for hours in the seedy plush chair with his thin chilblained hands folded on his lap and his eyes squinting from one to the other as Pollock and Melnichenko had answered the questions, listening with great care and sometimes asking for repetitions, sometimes trying to trap them into conceding they were holding something back, once or twice succeeding and leading them on again, bringing in a whole string of questions about Cat Baxter and her critical role in the operation, cornering Pollock once or twice and carefully bringing out the relationship between him and Melnichenko. Pollock answered most of the questions, using fluent German, but now the Russian got out of his chair and loomed over us, wiping his face the whole time.

"But why must you 'inform London,' as you put it? Who is 'London'?"

"My department," Cone said.

"Your department of what intelligence agency?"

Cone looked at me and said, "I think we've got all we want here. Unless you've got any questions?"

He'd been hitting the pause button on the recorder a dozen times a minute for hours on end, editing out inconsequential material as he went along. His finger was on it now.

"It's out of my field," I told him, "at this stage." I'd blown *Trumpeter* and it was for Cone to give a brief outline to Bureau One and let him take it from there. "You might want to question Bader sometime. He's the second pilot."

"Where is he?"

"In the hospital."

"What's his problem?"

"He got injured."

"Very well." This was Melnichenko, having another go. "Very well, it is for you to ask the questions. But I fail to understand why you should inform your government. This operation is strictly to do with the USSR and Germany, as you must surely realise."

Cone said nothing, sat watching him.

"We've done our best," Pollock told Cone. "This has been a very thorough debriefing. I think you owe us consideration."

"I'll give you five minutes," Cone said, and looked at his watch.

"It might take a bit—"

"This is a *Soviet* enterprise." Melnichenko was standing over Cone, his pink hands flat with the fingers spread, orchestrating what he was saying. "The Soviets alone are responsible for the consequences." Thumping his chest—"*I* am responsible for the consequences, not Pollock, not you, not your government. The action will take place on East German soil, the soil of a country under *Soviet* protection. Our intention is to *advance* General-Secretary Gorbachev's efforts to bring the USSR into the open, into the world community; our intention is not to *harm* the General-Secretary, and we have made that plain enough. You say your mission is to protect him. So, indirectly, is ours." Spreading his hands, holding the crescendo—"Now, come, let each of us get on with our own business."

Cone sat thinking. Pollock lit another cigarette. I finished the tea in the pot; it was cold by now, and bitter, just what I wanted, an astringent for the tongue.

"If this is a Soviet operation," Cone said at last, "who's running it?"

The pink brow wrinkled in surprise. "We are."

"Look," Cone said, "if you want my help, don't give me any bullshit. It's late and I'm tired. I want the name of the man in Moscow who's holding the reins."

Melnichenko glanced at Pollock.

"We've got to," Pollock said.

"Very well. His name is Gregor Talyzin. He is a deputy chairman of the Politburo."

"Well well," Cone said, and looked at me. "And a close friend of Gorbachev's." Back to the Russian. "Give me his phone number—his direct private line."

Melnichenko brought out a card and Cone took his finger off the pause button and noted the number and shut the machine off and got up and gave the card back and went over to the telephone and dialled, waiting.

"If your operation," he told Pollock, "weren't such a whizz-bang, I'd probably leave you to it. But there's going to be an awful lot of fallout, and I don't want to be in it." Into the phone: "Viktor, you can take these people now. Yes. Did he? Yes, a van would do nicely." He told Yasolev how to get here and put the phone down.

Melnichenko said without much conviction, "But you have no *authority*."

"I know. You'll be the guests of the KGB."

Cone stood in the car park watching the van turning onto the street, arms folded across his chest against the cold.

"If they can do it," he said, "it's going to shake a lot of things up."

"If the KGB lets them."

"It won't be up to them. Ask me, Thatcher's going to get on the phone to Gorbachev just as soon as Mr Shepley's told her the score. It'll be decided at that level."

"You think they'll let *Trumpeter* go ahead?"

"God, how do I know? I'm just half-hoping they will and half-hoping they won't." He got the keys of the car. "It scares me to think how close we are to making history. I prefer a good game of darts, actually, down at the Whistle."

We got in and he fished in the glove pocket and gave me a hotel envelope and I opened it.

"Just in from London. The one marked B is the latest, taken three months ago."

Two photographs, 10 by 8, of Horst Volper, one without any grain at all, or at least not much. From this one alone I could recognize him, or perhaps it was because I'd looked at the others so often that his face had become familiar.

"These'll help," I said, and put them away.

"Good show." He didn't start the engine.

"All I can do," I told him, "is whatever I can."

"I know."

The conversation was Pinteresque, loaded with all the things that couldn't be said. He'd been worrying the whole time we'd been down there in the cellar.

The clock on the dashboard showed 3:57.

"Four hours," I said, "is quite a long time."

"It is?"

Mikhail Gorbachev's Tupolev was due in at 8:05.

"It won't take me any time to start things."

"No?"

Just letting me talk.

"They'll start themselves. It's a fast-burn fuse."

"What makes you think," he said, "you're going to have any better luck this time?"

"It won't be a question of luck. Volper knows he's only got four hours, too, and he's going to throw the whole thing at me. He's got to, or I'll get in his way."

The windscreen was starting to mist over because of our breath. The engine ticked sometimes, cooling down. Cone still had the keys in his hand, as if when he started the engine he was going to blow something up. I sat with my hands inside the chest-pockets of my padded jacket, not wanting to move.

"And there's nothing you need from me?"

"No," I said. He meant support. "Nothing."

"How big," he asked in a moment, "is the risk?"

Shepley had asked me the same thing, in the underground garage in West Berlin, and now I gave Cone much the same answer. "If I measured the risks, I'd never take them. Go back and sleep. But sleep by the phone."

He started the engine then, and drove out of the car park. "Where d'you want to go?"

"Find a cab station, will you? I'll need this car."

"All right. She's three-quarters full."

I'd already checked the gauge. "I don't suppose I'll be going far."

"I got you a BMW," he said. "It's at the hotel. You said you wanted something fast."

"This'll do me."

There were three taxis outside the S-Bahn on Unter den Linden and Cone pulled up and left the engine running and got out and I shifted behind the wheel. He leaned in at the window.

"What shall I say, exactly?"

I thought about it, not wanting to give a false impression. In a moment I said, "Tell them the odds are fair."

"They'll want something more precise than that."

I gave it some more thought. "Tell them to keep the board clear. If Shepley can be there for the next few hours, I think it'd be wise, in case you need to flash anything that could help us. I'm in active condition, good morale, ready to go."

"No actual plan?"

"I'm going to try doing a switch."

He was looking at the ground, or maybe the door-handle or whatever; I mean he was looking down, not at me. "All right," he said. "That's what I'll tell them." Then he looked up quickly before he turned away. "Take care."

24

TRUCKS

The car was quiet. I'd watched his cab into the distance, and turned off the engine, and since then I hadn't moved.

It was like being frozen in glass, in a heavy glass paperweight, the way they do it with coins and things. It was as if the billionfold nerve impulses investing the system had reached the synapses and couldn't make the leap and had shut down, leaving the organism in a state of suspended animation.

I just needed a minute, that was all, perhaps a few minutes. It was a form of meditation, of seeking the self within the self and consulting with levels of wisdom beyond the norm. It was necessary because when I started the engine again, a minute from now, or perhaps a few minutes from now, I would be breaking through into the end-phase for *Quickstep* and nothing could stop it until they put one of two things on the signals board, *Mission accomplished* or *Shadow down.*

They were busy now, in London, burning the midnight oil.

I really can't say, sir. He sounded, I don't know, depressed.

That's not like Cone.

Shepley, his washed-out eyes looking quietly into infinity while his brain went through a hundred scenarios, a thousand, trying to take an intuitive leap and find the best thing to do, the best way of guiding *Quickstep* through the end-phase with a shadow executive who had requested him to stand by the board "for the next few hours," who had reported that "the odds were fair," whose morale was good and so on but who had no actual plan in mind to bring the mission home between now and eight o'clock, Berlin time.

Cone has plenty of support for him?

Yes, sir. He said he didn't need any.

Holmes, going to get himself another cup of coffee and then not drink it, let it get cold.

The other voices at other boards, quiet under the focussed glow of the lamps, with people drifting in to take a look at the one for *Quickstep,* because the Chairman of the Presidium of the Supreme Soviet was involved.

And finally one of them would take the bit of chalk and scrape it across the board. *Executive at point of initiating end-phase, no details.*

Executive, actually, sitting in a black and rather dirty 230 SE—it's very difficult to get a car washed this side of the Wall—and looking along a deserted stretch of Unter den Linden with three quarters of a tankful of petrol and his nerves shut down because he was staring at the brink;

and even though he'd seen it before it still had the power
to make him afraid, afraid to go forward.

Is that really what's happening?

Probably.

You're not just trying to get your nerve back?

Well yes, that too. Give me a break, for Christ's sake.

Not often you ask for charity. You—

Shuddup and leave me alone.

I could actually feel everything shutting down again and
giving me a kind of peace as the brainwaves slowed into
alpha, touched theta perhaps, lulling the mind into the
green and gentle domain of not-knowing, not-fearing, until
with brilliant clarity I understood the process and my
desperate need for it, for these few minutes of oblivion and
surrender before I let consciousness take over again and
calculate the needs of the moment and tell me to switch on
the engine.

Awareness, as if at a great distance, of the hum of the
digital clock on the dashboard, of the creak of the uphol-
stery as the muscles went into deep relaxation, of a man's
voice from the taxi-rank behind me, of a jet lifting from
Tegel on the far side of the Wall, awareness of all these
things and then, by infinite degrees, the surfacing of consciousness and the return to the beta rhythm and the sharp-
ness of what we are conditioned to believe is reality, with
the harsh and angular perspective of the street under its
garish lights and the hard plastic and glass and metal
surfaces of the interior of the car and the small black-
covered ignition key jutting from the lock.

Switch on and go.

4:07.

I drove to the British Embassy, two miles distant. This
had to be the initial step: to make contact.

He would be arriving, the General-Secretary of the USSR, in almost exactly four hours from now, direct from Moscow. I didn't know how long Horst Volper would need—had apportioned—for the final stage of his project to remove the General-Secretary from the world scene, but the incident might be scheduled for any time from his arrival on German soil, and I would assume that the assault would be made at the earliest moment, from the moment when the target came down the steps from his plane.

West along Unter den Linden, past the Palace of the Republic.

But I didn't believe that Volper would attempt the kind of shot that had succeeded in Dallas; it was too chancy. Oswald had had luck, at that distance and with that rifle. Volper would use a superior weapon if he had it in mind to use one at all; but the visitor would be arriving under very close protection and no one would even get near any building where a sniper could set up his post.

The Hotel Unter den Linden on the right, with lights burning in the foyer.

There was the chance that if I gave it enough thought, and if I could put myself in Volper's position with effective enough verisimilitude, I could find out the exact method he would use. I would try to do that, in the next four hours, if there was time; but the possibilities were countless, from a close shot into the motorcade to a black olive laced with cyanide at this evening's reception.

Crossing Friedrich-strasse with the red just flicking to green.

The moon was at three-quarters and I noted it as a matter of routine. We would be working within the close confines of the city, where there would be bright artificial light; but even if this weren't so, I couldn't predict at this stage whether moonlight would help me find my way or render me fatally discernible as I crawled from cover to cover. Nothing, in these few imminent hours, was predictable.

Grand Hotel on the left.

I felt quite good, now, quite contained. The brief period of meditation had calmed the nerves, and besides, I was in control of the moment as I took my foot off the throttle and moved it to the brake. I was to precipitate the action, and that gave me the advantage. Later, things would be different, but it didn't come into the reckoning as I slowed the car and stopped outside the furrier's next door to the British Embassy.

Above the street lights the sky was black, its stars lost in the city's albedo. There was no movement in the street: these were the dead hours before the dawn.

There were reflections in the windows of the shops on each side, the street's facade repeating itself in mirror images. In the show window of the Embassy, photographs of Stratford-upon-Avon, Kevin Brannagh as Hamlet, Anthony Cher as Richard III. Beyond it, a clothing store, and in the distance the massive Soviet Embassy and the Brandenburg Gate, with a taxi crossing the intersection at Otto Grotewohl-strasse. The French Cultural Centre was dark, and so were the headquarters of the Party Youth Movement opposite the British Embassy, but there was a car standing on the far side of Neustädtische Glinka-strasse, a dark-coloured Audi.

At that distance I couldn't be sure whether there was anyone sitting in it or not, but I believed there would be. In my rearview mirror there was another car, a Mercedes 280 SE, standing not far from the Komische Oper building. It was closer, and there was a man sitting at the wheel.

I didn't turn my head to look at the car directly; that

would have been hamming it, and Brannagh would have been appalled. Scenario: I'd come here to visit the Embassy or leave something there, but I'd noticed the two cars and decided not to get out of my own. I wasn't to regard it as a trap; I had simply moved into a surveillance operation that I hadn't expected, and the only thing to do was get out if I could.

04:15. Executive has made contact with opposition surveillance and is moving away.

It would have been interesting for them to make periodic changes to the board during these last hours of the night, if I could have signalled progress to Cone. Perhaps, an hour from now, two hours, I would in fact be able to call him from some phone-box or other, to tell him I'd got a fix on Volper or had dealt with him and in time or was trapped and totally unable to get clear, my apologies to Bureau One, so forth, as the blood pooled at my feet or they came for me at a run or their headlights swung suddenly and caught me in the glare and the first shots centred in the rib cage and Cone flinched, hearing them over the phone.

But one mustn't be anxious; one must not, my good friend, anticipate the worst; let it come, if it should, unheralded, like a thief in the night, to pluck away dear life.

I got into gear and drove as far as the second intersection at Otto Grotewohl-strasse and turned north, and after half a block I'd got the Audi in the mirror. At the next street I'd got the Mercedes and a Fiat within view, taking up stations at a distance and moving at my own pace. I had expected this much attention from the moment I'd entered the surveillance area, because at this stage Volper would have given orders to make a certain kill. There would be other cars standing on other streets in the hope of seeing me, especially near the hotel: they hadn't specifically expected me to visit the Embassy; it was simply a place where I might appear at any time and they'd staked it out as a routine.

Now that I'd been sighted and was under permanent observation they wouldn't waste any time and it was going to be very difficult to do what I wanted to do: make a switch. But it was all that was left to me and I now had the material I needed to work with.

A switch is an operation easy to describe and in many cases impossible to bring off. When followed, one has to vanish and then follow one of the opposition to his base. I have only done it twice, in Istanbul and Prague, and in each case it had taken me half a day; tonight I had less than four hours, and if I chose the wrong man I might not be led to his base, to Volper, but to any one of a dozen stations in the network. But when there is *nothing* else to do, the impossible seems less difficult.

Two blocks, three, going north-west and crossing Spandauer-strasse and Karl Marx Allee with two more cars making strategic loops as the others kept mobile watch and we began meeting the first of the trucks coming in with produce for the markets and police cars became more in evidence as early traffic started moving from the suburbs into the city's centre.

Then they began making rushes, first the Audi and then the Mercedes, one of them bumping the rear end and swinging me against the kerb, the other coming from in front and cutting across and forcing me into a swerve because its headlights were on full beam and I was blinded. A truck loomed at a cross-street and the Fiat behind me made impact and pushed me forward against the brakes with the wheels locked and the tyres shrilling over the surface and the truck grazing across the front end and taking away a headlamp, the driver shouting and his voice snatched away as his vehicle thundered on.

I don't think they were hoping to smash me up in the car because it's not that easy if the driver knows what he's doing; I think they were trying to get me out of the car and on the run and *that* was when they would close right in and get me into the centre of a concerted rush and make the kill with their guns or their hands or however they chose, once having me trapped.

I hadn't thought it would be easy to make the switch. I had thought it would be like this, and I settled down to the business of keeping them off and staying alive and trying to manoeuvre the Merc I was driving into a last-ditch crash that could give me room to run before they were ready, and by now the pace was so fast that a lot of the driving had become instinctive as the images flashed across the retinae and clamoured for attention, the streets merging into a lurching continuum, a brick and concrete channel cut through the city between earth and sky and flowing past and behind me in a dizzying stream of lights, vehicles, intersections and trucks—always the huge and monolithic shapes of the trucks with their horns blaring as someone cut across their path, one of them lurching past me with its wheel wrenched over and ripping away the doors, while the mind began shifting focus under the stress of the constant demands on the intellect to base its judgement on the torrential rush of feedback coming in from the environment.

I no longer knew which streets we were running through or which direction I was going but the object of the operation was to let them hound me until I could leave the car and get to cover and vanish and hope to sight them, one of them or more than one, and wait until they believed I was clear and went back to their base.

A long shot, oh yes indeed it was a very long shot and for the first time I wondered if this had been the only way to shift *Quickstep* into the end-phase and get to the target in time, but the left brain was almost shut down by now and my hands moved the wheel of their own accord as the eyes sighted and the brain interpreted and instinct triggered the motor nerves and we hit a wall and bounced and ran on with torn metal screaming against a tyre while headlights swung in from their vectors and blinded me time after time and I drove unseeing, with memory trapping the last image and the brain taking me through an opening and getting me to the far side where vision came in again and the kaleidoscope of the street's perspective was broken into a semblance of order and I hit the throttle and braked and swung the wheel and used the kerb to kick me straight and the corners to get me clear until the police sirens began and the flashing of lights coloured the night.

Then they came for me and I wasn't ready for it but there was nothing I could have done as a Mercedes came up very fast in the mirror and swung out and drew alongside and I felt the impact of something against my leg and heard it thud to the floor *and knew what it was* and hit the brakes and wrenched at the wheel to roll the car over and use its underside for a shield as the explosion came and its force blew glass and metal in a hot wind through the air and I was pitched headlong across the pavement as the fuel tank went up in a burst of orange light and the heat came against my back like a blowtorch and I got up and tripped and pitched down and got to my feet again and ran, ran anywhere, just away from the inferno in the street behind me with the sirens coming in, wailing and dying as the first patrol car slammed on its brakes and backed off as the black smoke billowed between the buildings.

A truck halted at the intersection as the driver saw the blaze and I dropped and slid underneath it and reached the other side and clambered onto whatever I could find that gave a handgrip and lay flat across the top of the huge fuel tank as the truck backed, bumping with its twin rear wheels across the kerb and then moving forward again, swinging full-circle away from the heat, so that I had to drop and crawl underneath again to the other side because there'd be Volper's people in the area watching for me: if they were professionals they wouldn't assume the grenade had finished me before the Merc rolled over.

A Fiat went past the truck on the other side and I saw its reflection in a store window as it reached the street where the Merc was burning and hit the brakes and slewed sideways as a Vopo patrol waved it back. They'd be moving in, all of them, the whole of the opposition hit team, and they'd be looking for me. Nothing could have survived in that inferno and there was no question of the police or fire crews trying to pull a body out, dead or alive, and none of the hit team could get close enough to find out if I was still inside the Merc or not.

Black Audi going very fast towards the blaze, underestimating its closeness and braking hard and slamming against a sandbin and bouncing off and spinning and getting control and coming back past the other side of the truck. I twisted on top of the fuel tank until I was lying with my back to the street, a black polyethylene and fabric bundle in the half-dark as the truck lumbered through its forced detour and another came up alongside, one of the drivers shouting something to the other.

A police car neared from the intersection with its lights splashing against the buildings and I waited until the truck was moving close to a wall and pulling up and then I dropped and rolled underneath, reaching for a handhold on the cruciform chassis beams, heaving myself up and hanging on as a wash of light flowed across the road surface and the wheels of a private car rolled past at a walking pace and then halted and turned as one of the Vopos shouted.

I shifted over as the big propeller-shaft of the truck began brushing my arm but the handhold was too smooth and I had to cling on to a brake cable, swinging with both feet lodged against a cross-member. The truck slowed again and turned between two rows of wooden platforms, coming to a halt as a man dropped from the cab; all I could see were his legs. The wheels of another truck were rolling to a halt behind us and I hung there taking slow shallow breaths as the diesel gas clouded from the exhausts.

Dropped, crawled under the platform and lay there among a litter of crates, pulling the nearest ones around me for cover.

Take stock. I was in a freight yard and the trucks were coming in to unload for the markets that would open for shopkeepers, probably at first light. There would be Volper's people moving through the area, checking everywhere before they assumed one of two things: either the grenade had finished me or I'd managed to get clear. Then they would leave, moving in larger circles with the truck depot as their centre.

There was still a chance of making the switch: of keeping one of them in sight and waiting until he moved away and moving after him and staying on his track until he led me to base, to the objective for *Quickstep*, to Horst Volper.

Must've been a drunk!

Or a stolen car, going that speed!

Truckers calling to each other as they came alongside

and began work on the ropes and the tarpaulins, big men in big coats, in from the country, mud on their boots.

Makes you sick, with him still in the car.

A woman, maybe.

Worse, then. Hans! Gimme a hand with this rope, the knot's frozen!

I began checking the environment. There must be ten or fifteen platforms in the yard, a hundred feet long, with twenty or thirty trucks crawling between them and pulling up, the rattle of their diesels dying one after another and leaving only the shouts of the men and the banging of their boots as they moved about, stowing the tarpaulins and pulling the crates on their backs, the crates, baskets, sacks and bundles, dropping them onto the platforms—

What's he coming here for?

Give us a talk about bloody Lenin, what else?

He's all right, Otto, he's shaking things up over there!

Pity he doesn't knock the Wall down, now that'd be something!

Below the platforms, a backdrop of red brick walls and store fronts, doors, windows, sandbins, street lamps, two cars standing within fifty yards of where I was lying in cover, a man moving away from a BMW and coming into the depot, looking at no one, talking to no one, hands shoved into the vertical chest-pockets of his black polyethylene parka, his head turning left, turning right. I wasn't in hazard: this was good cover among the debris of broken crates and cardboard boxes, with the light factor so low as to be shadowless. I could lie easy, letting the body go through its healing processes and the nerves relax—I'd skinned a hand when I'd hit the door of the Merc open and pitched out, and my back had twisted as I'd started my run, falling and getting up and falling again and finding my feet and lurching towards cover; I didn't know what I looked like from the back, whether the rush of flame had actually seared the plastic jacket, how much attention I'd attract when I finally walked out of here. There was a lingering degree of shock from the instant when I'd known what they must have thrown into the car, worse than when the thing had blown up because I'd been expecting that.

Relax, then, relax and observe.

The scents of damp earth and greenstuff came on the air, sweet after the man-made reek of exhaust-gas, the smell of the country drifting in to the stone and steel and concrete milieu of the man-made city. The smell of black tobacco as the truckers lit up again as they worked.

Within the next ten minutes I'd counted four men moving about in the area, the one from the BMW and three coming in from the street that ran at right angles, their figures silhouetted against the last of the blaze as the fire crews worked with their hoses and extinguishers. Black smoke drifted as thick as black water from the mouth of the street, coloured by the lights of the police cars and the fire trucks, and one of the men coming across here was coughing the whole time, probably because he'd stayed close to the burning car, trying to see if the driver was still inside.

A rat ran close to my face as I lay perfectly still, a huge rat, a city rat here for the feasting, and another followed, scampering across my leg and stopping, its feet splayed as it sniffed; and I moved slightly and felt it leap in alarm and heard it scuttle away; it had felt flesh underfoot and suspected I was carrion. Feast, my good friend, but not on me.

Ten minutes more and two of the men had passed along the row of trucks behind me: I could watch both rows by turning my head at intervals. It may have been a subcon-

scious concession to social convention that stopped them
going through the debris under the platforms; the truckers
would hardly notice them as they walked past, but they
would have attracted attention if they'd started scavenging.
And they were looking for a man on foot, the silhouette or
the shadow of a man loping in the distance from cover to
cover, someone they could give chase to and run down and
kill. If this yard had been deserted, I think they might have
made a thorough search, taking their time, taking an hour,
two hours, before they were satisfied.

Get it, Heiner!

Don't move!

Clang of a metal bar, maybe a tyre-iron, as one of the
rats leapt and vanished in the half-dark.

Another ten minutes and a truck started up at the front
of the row and moved off, the sound of its diesel drum-
ming within the walls of the yard, the gas from its exhaust
creeping across the ground.

There was only one man now, the one from the BMW
that stood fifty feet away near a fire hydrant. He was
moving towards the area where I was lying, checking the
trucks for the second time. He would be my last chance for
making the switch, and it worried me.

There was no other vehicle in sight and even if there had
been it'd be locked and I could smash a window and get in
but the key would almost certainly not be there and I
wouldn't have time to hot-wire the ignition and take up
station behind the BMW.

The BMW was the only car I could use, and if this man
was the last of the hit team left in the area I wouldn't have
to follow him anyway. I would have to take him with me.

He was coming along the nearest row between the trucks
and the platform and was within thirty feet of me. I got a
glimpse of him now and then between the slats but his face

was strange; he wasn't one of the tags who'd been with me
through the streets the day before. A blunt face with short
black hair, worn leather jacket, not a big man but strong,
wide-shouldered, thick at the wrist. He was ducking to
look under the trucks now, then turning and looking under
the platform.

There was deep shadow here, the flat white light of the
street lamps blanked off by the trucks; but he would see
me if he looked under the platform and was close enough.

If I couldn't do the switch there was only one option left
to me. It was something I have never done before in any
mission, on principle and because the Bureau disallows it,
but I believed as I lay there among the mess of broken
crates and beer-cans that I would have to do it now.

Not now: later. But prepare it now.

Paul, can you shift up a couple o' metres?

What for?

I've got to let the tailboard down.

Half a jiff.

Another truck was moving off at the end of the row
behind me and a crate dropped off the platform and split
open, spilling green apples. Paul's truck started up, and
the huge twin wheels rolled as the man, the man with the
blunt face, stood back. Small flat-beds and vans had started
coming in from the street as the shopkeepers arrived to
load up. Engines were running everywhere in the crowded
yard, and the air was thick with carbon monoxide.

All right, that'll do it!

A tailboard slammed down against the rubber stops.

The man was close now, two or three metres away.

Heinrich! Where's Veidt?

Haven't seen him.

I've got his quota!

The door of a cab clanged shut and boots hit the ground.

The section of platform above my head took the weight of potato sacks as they were swung from the truck. The man ducked and looked under the platform, closer still now, but didn't see me yet among the debris.

Veidt's not coming!

Why not?

He's off sick.

Shit!

The engines rumbled. The big wheels rolled. The truckers shouted.

The man looked under the platform again and saw me.

25

END-PHASE

It was a long way.

A minute ago a police car had gone past the entrance to the freight yard with its lights flashing. I suppose it was one of the patrols who'd gone to the scene of the bombed-out Mercedes. I didn't want any police near me.

A long way, maybe fifty metres, dragging him behind me through the litter, through the mess.

It had been an easy enough strike because he hadn't been ready for it and couldn't reach his gun. He'd given a shout as I'd pulled him down but there were shouts going on all over the place and no one took any notice. It was a 9mm Mauser and I'd emptied the magazine and scattered the bullets and wrapped the gun in some newspaper and dropped it into a crate. They're dangerous, and can hurt people.

I'd put the keys in my pocket.

He must have caught his leg on something, one of the platform supports or a splintered crate, when I'd brought him under here with me, because sometimes when I looked back I caught the glint of blood across the ground. So I turned him over and went on dragging him to the end of the row.

He was valuable. I prized him. He was the custodian of my enterprise, *Quickstep*. I didn't at this time dwell on the future, on what I would have to do.

Against your precious principles.

Yes.

It's nothing to do with principles. It frightens you.

If you say so.

You know it's true.

Shuddup.

I was dragging him by the wrists and it wasn't easy because I was having to move in a crouch below the platform and it was a strain on the lumbar muscles. But to get him from here to the end of the row wouldn't be the worst of it.

I felt his wrists jerk suddenly as he came to and tried to get free, and dropped him and did some minor work on the left side of the neck and then started pulling him along again.

A wrecking truck went past the gates, its lights dappling the dark with colour. They would haul the burnt-out wreck of the Mercedes away, like a dead elephant. It had been a nice motor-car: I like that particular model.

And then we reached the end of the platform and I stopped work and rested a little, lying flat on my back, keeping one of his wrists in my hand so that I'd know if he tried to do anything.

Just gone five, 05:03 to be exact. Less than three hours,

then, to the deadline. It wasn't long. It depended on how things went, how effective I could prove, and what kind of man he was, how strong, how weak. Three hours wouldn't be long, because I also had to locate Horst Volper and deal with him, and in time.

Back off, there! Get in the next line!

Green uniform. Green uniform and a holstered revolver and polished boots, peaked cap. He was directing the trucks.

Until he moved I couldn't bring my prisoner into the open. It was going to be bad enough with the other people around.

Get in behind that one—come on!

An engine gunning up.

I watched his boots. I watched them for ten minutes, fifteen, and listened to him shouting, telling them where to bring their vans and their pickups and flat-beds. Then a bit of trouble started in the next row, a scraping of metal, and a lot more shouting than usual. I think one of them had buckled someone else's wing and they were arguing the toss. The policeman went over there.

I got the man's wrists again and dragged him clear of the platform and began walking him to the gates with his arm round my shoulders and my own round his waist but his feet were dragging and it would have been easier to give him a fireman's lift but I couldn't do that because it would have looked very odd, something serious.

Headlights sweeping across the yard as the shopkeepers kept coming in. If they saw me they wouldn't do anything; this was a narrow time-gap for them—they had to get the produce off the platforms and through the checkers and into their shops and on display before they opened.

"What's the trouble, then?"

"He fell and banged his head."

One of the truckers, sweating in the chill morning, his breath steaming as he stood fishing for his pack of cigarettes.

"Tell the cop, he'll get an ambulance."

"He's not that bad," dragging him faster, swinging him along. "I'm getting him to the car—"

"You ought to tell the—"

"He's a friend of mine, had too much to drink—I don't want to get him in trouble."

"That's different," grunt of a laugh as he lit up and clicked his lighter shut, turning away.

Swinging him along, a dead weight, one of his feet getting in the way of my own, sweat on the back of my neck as I felt the cop's eyes on us—*you there, what's the trouble?*—don't let him turn, don't let him see us, swinging the bastard along, he would've shot me between the eyes if I hadn't been so fast, those were his instructions, his instructions from Horst Volper, come on you *bastard* lift your bloody feet up, *come on*.

"Had a skinful?"

"How did you guess?"

Face in a window of the van going by, laughing.

Crossing the street and I got the keys and let him slump against the BMW while I opened the passenger door and pushed him in, his eyes coming open but with no understanding in them. Coloured light flashing as a police patrol crawled past, pulling in to the kerb as the wrecking truck turned in from the next street, hauling the blackened shell of the Mercedes.

05:37 on the dashboard clock, the fuel gauge at half. I started up and waited until the wrecker had gone by and the police car swung in a U-turn and followed it and then I took the opposite direction, turning left at the intersection to keep clear of the police crew throwing sand on the road where the fire had been.

Heard his breath coming in a jerk as he recovered enough to realise the situation and instinctively tried to do something, lifting his foot and bringing it down as I used the edge of my hand on the knee-cap—I suppose he was trying to break the gear-lever or smash my ankle and hit the brake-pedal, something like that.

His breath was hissing now and he was holding his knee.

"Give me your name."

Didn't answer.

Later would do, but the name is important, the key to the psyche. Our name is the most personal thing about us, a cipher for all that we are, our claim to identity. It is the first thing you do, when you begin the matter: you get their name, so that you can turn it as a weapon against them.

I drove circumspectly, slowing in good time for the lights when they changed to amber, keeping five kph below the speed limit, driving west and south and reaching the safe-house at 05:52.

Before we got out of the car I said: "You are in my hands, as you realise, but you have a choice."

I told him what it was.

Gunter Blüm, looking down, his face white.

"Don't stand there," I said. "Don't just stand there like that."

I wanted to be angry with him, for showing me what I had done, for holding up a mirror to me, to the picture of Dorian Gray.

That was how it felt, how I thought of it.

"What happened?" he asked me.

I didn't answer. The light was still very bright: I'd taken

the shade off and put some aluminium foil round it to intensify the glare. That too is important, another tool of this most hideous of all trades. There were smells in the room, too, none of them strong but none of them pleasant. There was no sound, except for his breathing. Dollinger's, Helmut Dollinger's breathing. It was all, one might say, that he had left: the ability to breathe.

Gunter was watching me now, his mouth open a little, his eyes naked and appalled under the fierce glare of the lamp.

I'd called him in here.

"I want you to take him somewhere and leave him, and phone for an ambulance, tell them where to find him."

I was very tired. This business had drained me, and I hadn't expected it to be so bad. But if I had expected it, I would still have had to do it.

Against your principles.

Indeed yes, against my principles, against the tenets of human conduct that alone can keep some sort of brotherhood alive in this angry world. These I had transgressed— and this is not, my good friend, my friend, I am sure, no longer, this is not to purge myself in an outpouring of spurious confession. I shall remember the name of Dollinger. I shall remember it.

"Take him where?"

Gunter.

"What? Anywhere. In a doorway, where you won't be seen." It occurred to me, either because I was finding it difficult to regain my focus on reality or because he looked so stunned, Gunter, so removed from ordinary understanding—it occurred to me that I should spell it out for him, for his own sake. "That's the important thing, of course, that no one sees you. Then phone for an ambulance, without giving your name."

I began taking off my gloves, the thin nylon driving-gloves they'd told Cone I preferred, when they'd briefed him as my director in the field. I'd put them on in a grotesque attempt to distance myself, my hands, from the other man's body while I worked on it, on its nervous system, its most sensitive sites of pain. They'd been meant to anaesthetise my hands, to separate them from what they were doing. Don't you think that's the most appalling part of it?

"Is he still alive?"

"Of *course*." Said with anger, the first murmuring of self-rage, like distant thunder. "But he needs hospitalising. For God's sake switch off that *light*."

He seemed not to know where the switch was, though our apartments were identical. Then he found it and the glare was cut off, to leave the reflected glow of that bloody Wall in the room.

He came towards the man in the chair, tied to the chair with torn cloth, towelling, I forget what I'd used. "What do I do if he dies, while I'm taking him there?"

"You'll leave him there just the same, you clod, and call an ambulance, for Christ's sake, *now is that clear?*"

He said it was, and got Dollinger across his shoulder and went out with him and I soaked a towel in the bathroom and held it against my face and stood there a long time with the nerve-light spangling the dark behind my lids and my heart's beat hammering. The worst of it, with things like this, as you know, is that you can't have your time over again, and not do whatever you've done, and I can't think of two other words in the whole of the language that carry the weight of such infinite despair as these: *too late*.

Went over to the telephone.

"Just reporting in."

Brief pause. "What happened?" Cone.

His tone was wary, apprehensive, because, I suppose, of what he'd heard in my voice.

"I know where the target is."

Volper.

Another pause. That had been telling him rather a lot. It had been telling him that we had a hope of completing the mission, of bringing *Quickstep* home. In a moment he asked, "Can you reach him?"

"Yes."

"How long will it take?"

"Not long."

"I'd feel more comfortable," he said, "in the end-phase, if you had some support. Not close. Just in the field."

"It won't be necessary. He'll be alone."

Another pause. "All right. I've been in signals with London. They're prepared to let *Trumpeter* go ahead."

"That should be interesting."

"They also told me that the only danger to our protégé is from the target. No one else."

Not from *Trumpeter*.

"Do what I can," I said. "I'll report when I'm through."

I put the phone down and went into the bathroom and drank a glass of water with its rank taste of chlorine; then I got my Lufthansa bag and went out of the room and down the stairs and across to the car.

07:04.

Over the past minutes the sky had been lightening.

I shifted on the seat, leaning my shoulder against the door, one hand hooked across the wheel-rim.

There were no clouds, only a thin haze from the city softening the lights across the airport. I'd seen three planes come in since I'd got here, their landing lights coming on as they settled into final approach, directly in line with the street where I was waiting in the car.

The hotel was less than a hundred yards away. I'd chosen this location because it was near enough to see Volper clearly when he came out of the hotel and got into the car that was standing there, and far enough to give me a certain amount of cover. There were no lights in the hotel, and almost no windows: a wrecking gang had started demolition work on it a month ago, Dollinger had told me, and stopped again because of some bureaucratic holdup.

Dollinger.

His name still tolled like a death-knell in my mind.

But you had to do it. Give yourself a break.

No excuses.

It was that, or risking Gorbachev's life.

There should have been some other way.

It was for the mission.

Do *that* to a man, for a mission?

There's no quarter, in this trade. You know that.

Yes of course I've always known it and I've done a lot of things I couldn't live with and then lived with them but don't expect me to do them and then go whistling on my way, damn you.

Steady, lad.

07:42.

I didn't like this. I was beginning to worry.

I still didn't know where Volper had planned to intercept his target but it was obviously going to be soon after the General-Secretary had landed, at some time between his leaving the plane and leaving the airport, or just afterwards, soon after his leaving the airport; and that wasn't illogical because although the protection around him would be at its most concentrated, Volper was a man to strike where it'd be least expected.

He should be leaving his temporary base at any time now; the main route from the airport was eleven minutes from here, from the hotel: I'd timed the run at legal speed when I'd got here.

He would have to leave here, then, within seven minutes from now.

I could only wait. But he was running it close and it worried me.

Cone would be worried too. He hadn't expected me to get so close to the target so fast. I hadn't kept in touch, and he knew nothing about a bombed-out Mercedes burning in the streets, or about the man sagging in the chair buying his life with betrayal.

London knew nothing either, except for the last signal Cone had just sent in through Cheltenham for the board.

Executive has initiated end-phase, reports within reach of target.

Theirs not to do or die, theirs but to stand and wait, so forth. I didn't envy them. But *Trumpeter* was to go ahead, and *that* was a surprise. On whose decision? Not Shepley's. The Prime Minister's, possibly after consultation with the Chairman of the Presidium on the private line.

Pollock would be delighted.

"No. I'm just a kind of coordinator."

"But it was your idea?"

"Yes."

The tape-recorder turning, Cone sitting there shrunk into his raincoat, Melnichenko sweating hard, Schwarz saying nothing, the smoke thick in the cellar.

"How did it begin?"

"With Schwarz, actually. He and Bader used to come into the club, and we got talking. A lot of it was political, like most of the talk. There was a feeling in the air that Miki was coming to East Berlin to open the Wall, you know—an official ceremony and all that; but I knew he couldn't do it. They'd sling him out of power.''

''That was your impression?''

Cone.

''Most of us felt that way. With a man as charismatic as Gorbachev, there's always the risk of his opponents feeling jealous, and scared of his getting too powerful—look what happened to Khrushchev. Then it was something Schwarz said that put things together for me.''

''What did Schwarz say?''

Pollock looked across at him. ''I think this is your bit.''

The pilot got up and walked about, hands tucked into his belt. ''Listen, I am Jewish, like Hans.'' Bader. ''And these people won't let us go over there to see our families. They gave us the high privilege of taking us into the bloody Airforce but won't trust us on the other side of the Wall for a couple of days. They—''

''But they'd be afraid you'd give away military information.''

''Others have been allowed across—people with classified information in their heads. So we hate the Wall, more than most people do. So one day I told Dickie—'' Pollock—''that it was getting to be an obsession with me, and with Hans. Every time we flew on training and exercise missions there was the Wall down there, and we were flying bombers . . .''

Cone leaned over to check the recorder, see that it was running. Everyone had gone very still.

''So I talked discreetly to someone else.'' Pollock again. ''He was someone at the Soviet Embassy and he was close to Talyzin, in the Kremlin.'' Quick clean smile. ''From that point it all built up into *Trumpeter*.''

Walls of Jericho.

''It was Talyzin who took charge, then?''

''That's right.'' He got out of his chair too. ''You see,

he knows Miki very well; he's his right-hand man, behind the scenes. Of course in the Kremlin *most* things happen behind the scenes. Politically, it was felt that if Miki tried to get the Wall down officially it would cost him his career, but if someone could breach it *for* him, he could make the grand Marxist gesture of yielding to the will of the people and leaving it open—and in fact ordering a new street to be driven through it in the name of peace and the brotherhood of nations—you know the line.''

"My God," Cone said. He was hunched forward now, squinting up at Pollock. "You'll never get away with it."

"Talyzin says we could."

"You mean he's talked about this to Gorbachev?"

Pollock stopped pacing. "Put it this way. Talyzin is a staunch ally of the General-Secretary's politically, and a close friend on a personal level. I don't think for a moment he could master-mind *Trumpeter* from the wings *without* sounding Gorbachev out first.''

Cone turned a glance on me and looked back at Pollock again. I didn't know what he meant. I think he was wondering if I could accept *Trumpeter* for what it was, for what it could do in Europe, with global repercussions.

"Look," Pollock said, "Miki's brilliant at PR work and he's a showman. He's also got a great deal of savvy and a great deal of courage. I think he might have told Talyzin to go ahead.''

"Whose idea was Cat Baxter?"

"That was mine." Pollock looked rather pleased. "Just making a gap in the Wall wouldn't do it. We had to get world-wide attention and we needed a symbol, in a big way. Like ten thousand East German rock fans climbing over the rubble and crowding through the Wall and dancing in the streets with the West Berliners. They—''

"Not *escaping*," Cone said.

"Oh no—that wasn't the thing at all. Germany reunited—*that* was going to be the message. Cat Baxter jumped at it, as you can imagine. What a role to play . . . Joan of Arc at the barricades with banners waving, leading the faithful through. Talk about promotion . . ."

Mr Ash, she'd said to me, will you be at the concert?

I hope so.

Try and make it. It'll blow your mind.

Cone glanced at me again. He thought Pollock was mad. So did I. But I remembered Einstein. *No new idea will ever succeed unless at first it sounds crazy.*

"You'd be forewarning the media?"

"I'm ready to send the same message" Pollock said, "to every major TV news network and every newspaper and magazine world-wide: warn your camera crews and reporters in East Berlin to stand by for a major story. There'd be instant replay."

"What about the police? Casualties?"

"The HUA would be willing to turn their backs on the scene when Cat goes through the Wall, with a request from Moscow. They—"

"From Talyzin."

"Yes. They want a united Germany themselves. They'd be asked to evacuate the area around the projected breach on the excuse that toxic chemicals are escaping from a crashed truck. A warning would go to West Berlin, with the same story. I don't have to tell you the planning that's been necessary." A shrug, and no bright smile. "You've *got* to tell London? Now that you know the project?"

"They'd have my head," Cone said, "if I tried to keep this dark."

Another shrug. "Then I can only hope I'm right in thinking that Talyzin has sounded Gorbachev out. Then if Thatcher calls him, it won't change his mind."

He lit another cigarette, and I remember thinking it looked like a slow fuse burning.

"If we can't nail Horst Volper," Cone had said, "there won't be any point in bombing the Wall."

He'd shut the recorder down and got onto his feet.

Leaden light was seeping over the sky from the east, casting a metallic sheen across the landscape and the distant buildings. There was no sound in the area, no traffic; Dollinger had told me that a redevelopment scheme had been started and then become stalled, leaving two or three square miles of no-man's-land.

07:49.

Twice I thought I heard a sound from the derelict hotel, but it had been without identity—not the closing of a door or footsteps or a voice. It could have come from the airport.

He will be there alone. Dollinger.

Then he'd waited, forcing me to use more pressure, to drain the blood from his face and bring sweat springing.

But where will he attack the target?

Waited again, forcing me to induce a degree of pain that I had to share with him, to identify with, so that my own face was bloodless as I brought the nerve to breaking point.

I don't know. I don't know.

07:50.

Nothing moved inside the hotel. The car still stood there, half-concealed. There was no sound in the immediate area.

A spark came into the sky to the north and gradually broke into two as the landing lights of the plane grew brighter and it lowered towards the runway, passing directly overhead and landing within half a minute, reversing thrust as the brakes came on.

And then I knew that Volper was not going to leave the hotel at all and that I'd left it too late.

26

TUPOLEV

Smell of death.

I climbed to the next floor. The elevators were not working. The electric power had been cut off months ago.

On the next floor I waited again, listening.

The smell of the death that this building was going to die when the men came again with their demolition tools, the smell of damp plaster, mildew, decay along the corridors and on the stairs. The glass had gone from most of the windows, and some of the balconies were sagging. This was the sixth floor, below the roof-garden I'd seen from the car, with its collapsed trelliswork and dead plants and the remains of a flag shredded by the wind.

I had seen tracks on some of the floors below, but they might not be his; workers had been here, disturbing the thick patina of dust and grime along the passages. Some of the doors had been left wide open, and the strengthening light of the morning came into the windowless rooms, pooling along the corridors, innocent, shadowless.

I stood perfectly still, breathing tidally, projecting my sense of hearing across the environment, desperate now to pick up any sound that would give him away.

Silence.

I moved again, crossing the corridor and going into an open room, keeping clear of the window until I'd studied the components of the view: three windows in the other wing of the building and a section of the rubble-strewn courtyard below. Then I moved nearer, keeping to the side, looking across and down. I had made this survey on each floor from the second level upwards, and I suppose the angle of reflection in the broken pane of glass on the opposite wall hadn't been right, as it was now, because I hadn't seen movement before.

It was very slight: the broken pane was only a few inches across and it was dirty; but the movement was there, and I watched it, stilling the breath and listening to the blood coursing past the tympanic membranes. It still wasn't definable; it was still no more than movement, except that it didn't seem to be made by a rat or a bird, because there was a glint to it, like a watch would make on a moving wrist.

At this angle the source of the reflection must be on the floor below, the fifth floor, and from the room next to where I was standing. I could hear sounds now, small ones, some of them identifiable as metallic or hard wood, hard plastic, an object or objects not moved about by rats or birds.

When I looked at my watch it showed four minutes to eight o'clock and when I looked down at the balcony below and to the left I judged it to be five feet to the side and nine feet down, a total distance of ten feet. The balcony was sagging, like most of them, with the railings broken away. The one outside the room where I stood was in much the same state, with the railing on the left end rusted and buckled.

He was, then, ten or twelve feet away from me.

Volper.

07:57.

Yes indeed, when I'd been waiting in the car below and suddenly realised the truth, I could have driven as fast as possible to the nearest telephone and called the airport and told them to warn the General-Secretary's plane and divert it to an alternate but there would have been no point in it—*divert his plane? Who is speaking?—This is Colonel Heidecker of the HUA and I tell you it is imperative that you warn the pilot that—Wait a minute, please, where are you speaking from?*—so forth, and yes I could have driven as far as the airport itself but time would have been dangerously shorter and I would have met with the same suspicion because a hoax is a hoax and I was wearing a ripped coat and there was stubble on my face and after the bomb thing and the nightmare with Dollinger I didn't look like your standard respectable policeman so that was the choice I'd been faced with and this was the one I'd made because I'd known by the way Dollinger had given his information that he hadn't been lying and this was where Horst Volper had to be, a floor below in a room with a rotting balcony and a sixty-foot drop into the courtyard if I got it wrong.

Sound in the sky, the sound of the Tupolev.

The french doors were open, one of them hanging on a single hinge, and I stepped through the gap with my shoes clear of the littered glass and went to the end of the balcony and ignored the risk that he might notice movement in one of the broken window-panes down there as I had done, ignored it because I was moving as quickly as I could and there was no question as to whether the sixty-foot drop should be allowed to affect my thinking, only the question of working out the angle and the distance and the force needed to take me over the buckled railing and through five feet of space and then the drop.

A thin, loudening scream from the jets of the Tupolev.

Surprise was the only thing in my favour and it would have to be enough and I dragged on the railing to test its strength and thought it was sound enough and swung over it and felt the air-rush of the drop against my face and hit the balcony below on all fours and used the railing supports for leverage and pitched into the room.

He had the flat, featureless face that I'd studied so many times in the photographs, the eyes rather far apart and the nose running almost straight to the brow. The mouth was open a little at this particular moment and his expression wasn't one of surprise but of non-understanding, as if his known version of reality had slipped like a time-warp and left him suddenly a stranger in his own world, and untutored to meet the demands on him.

His hands were occupied and he couldn't reach for a gun or even defend himself as he could have done if they'd been free, and in any case I wasn't interested in attacking him because the urgent need was to deflect the missile and I managed it but his finger must have been on the launch-button because there was a squeezing sound and the thing jerked and the air in the room felt suddenly solidified with the intense volume of sound as the warhead burst against the wall across the corner of the building and the building shook, holding for a moment and then collapsing with the slow inexorability of an avalanche.

I suppose he was stunned, because he was physically slow to react and I chopped once and dropped him into the void and saw him whirling among the vortex of shattered concrete and timber and plaster lit by the flamelight of the explosion, and later I found him in the courtyard when I went down there, moving like a drunk amid the smoking rubble. His head was buried under the debris but he had one hand flung out, a finger pointing in my direction, as if he were blaming me for something.

27

TELLY

"I couldn't see much detail," I said. "There wasn't time. But it looked like a Stinger Mark IV. It was obviously hand-held and obviously a heat-seeker. He wouldn't have missed."

Cone gave me a glance and switched off the recorder. "That'll be enough for today. I don't want to tire you."

"I'm still thirsty, that's all."

He went over to the telephone and asked them to send some more tea up. I'd slept most of the day, not exactly sleep, you couldn't call it that, just a whole string of nightmares, running through falling buildings, planes blowing up, his white face and his arms tied to the chair, after-shock, I suppose, working itself out.

I got off the bed and went across to the window. The Wall rose against the night, an expanse of floodlit concrete, impregnable. One would have said, impregnable.

"You shouldn't be walking on that ankle," Cone said.

When the tea came he looked at his watch and turned on the television and played with the local channels.

. . . *What he called a natural corollary to the summit conference in the United States. Mr Gorbachev made a point of stressing that his visit to East Berlin carries no special political significance, but is simply to enable the General-Secretary to discuss with President Honecker the issues raised between himself and President Reagan.*

"I fear he doth protest too much," I said.

"Right. Blown his cover."

Cone looked at his watch again and switched channels until he got the scene in the park. Cat Baxter, her mass of blond hair framing her small kittenish face, her silver sweater and skirt shimmering under the fierce intensity of the spotlights, waving as the crowd gave her an ovation. Waving but glancing at the sky repeatedly, the dazzling smile fixed, frozen.

"Going crazy about her," Cone said. "Does her kind of stuff do anything for you?"

"I quite like it. I've got some of her tapes in the car."

We watched for a bit and then the phone rang and Cone went across to it and listened briefly and thanked them and rang off and came over to where I was standing.

"Bombers are airborne," he said.